Silver M

HAVE
OF 61
OF
EROTIC DOMINATION

If you like one you will probably like the rest

A NEW TITLE EVERY MONTH

Silver Moon Readers Service
c/o DS Sales Ltd.
PO Box 1100 London N21 2WQ

Distributed to the trade throughout North America by
LPC Group, 1436 West Randolph Street, Chicago, IL 60607

If you like one of our books you will probably
like them all!

Write for our free 20 page booklet of extracts from early books
- surely the most erotic feebie yet - and, if you wish to be on
our confidential mailing list, from forthcoming monthly titles
as they are published:-

Silver Moon Reader Services

c/o DS Sales Ltd.
PO Box 1100 London N21 2WQ
http://www.limitededition.co.uk

or leave details on our 24hr UK answerphone
0181 245 0985
International acces code then +44 181 245 0985

New authors welcome
Please send submissions to
PO Box 5663
Nottingham
NG3 6PJ

www.silvermoon.co.uk
www.silvermoonbooks.com

Bush Slave II, Lisa in Torment first published 2000,copyright Lia Anderssen
The right of Lia Anderssen to be identified as the author of this book has been asserted in accordance with Section
77 and 78 of the Copyrights and Patents Act 1988

BUSH SLAVE II
Lisa in Torment
by
Lia Anderssen

Our apologies to RACHEL HURST for the mis-
spelling of her name on the cover of "Little One"

This is fiction - In real life always practise safe sex!

Dedicated to Frank Evans, a man with great ideas.

Chapter 1

The interior of the long, low limousine was cool, the efficient airconditioning keeping at bay the sultry heat of the African night. The expensive-looking car purred smoothly through the streets, the driver doing his best to dodge the numerous potholes. Every now and again the black livery would be illuminated by one of the few street lights that still functioned in the neglected streets, and occasionally a pedestrian would appear, his or her dark skin illuminated by the powerful headlights of the vehicle. Each one of these walkers would shrink back immediately into the darkness at the sight of the vehicle, bowing deferentially as it passed.

The windows of the car were tinted a dark grey, so that, even with the soft lighting inside, it was almost impossible to distinguish its occupants. Anyone seeing them, though, would have almost certainly raised an eyebrow.

There were three of them, two men and a young girl. The men sat opposite one another in the spacious cabin, leaning back in their leather seats. One was white, a thin-faced individual with cruel lips and deep-set eyes. The African opposite him was grossly fat, the buttons of his shirt straining to hold it together as he lolled back in his seat, sweat trickling down his face.

It was the third occupant of the vehicle, though, that was most likely to hold the attention of anyone seeing her. Small and slim, the lovely young white girl knelt on the floor between the men. In contrast to their lounge suits, the petite beauty wore only a thin, ragged T-shirt that came just as far as her waist, leaving the lower half of her body completely nude. The T-shirt itself was barely adequate to

5

contain her beautifully shaped breasts. These were perfectly rounded, and they pressed against the threadbare material, the erect nipples clearly outlined.

As the vehicle bumped along, the two men spoke in low tones to one another. The girl, however was otherwise occupied, and she seemed to pay scant attention to what was being said. This was hardly surprising, since her attention was concentrated on the massive black rod that jutted from the fat man's open fly. As the car bumped along she sucked hard at it, her long, dark hair spilling into his lap as she worked her head back and forth, allowing his penis to slip in and out of her mouth, her pretty, kissable lips pursed about its girth. Seemingly oblivious to her surroundings she fellated him energetically, one hand caressing his balls whilst the other gripped his shaft, masturbating him with firm strokes.

The man grunted his pleasure as the pretty twenty-year-old sucked him. His companion sat back in his seat, casting his eyes over the girl's behind, the otherwise perfect white flesh of which bore an unusual mark, the shape of a leaping lion about an inch across. This was no tattoo or birthmark, though. Close inspection would reveal that it was a brand, burned into the tight, firm skin of her behind, a permanent indicator of her previous experiences.

But the unusual nature of the young girl's private parts did not end there. Crouching as she was, with her legs spread apart, an object could be clearly seen gleaming between her thighs. It was a ring, a thick, shiny brass ring, and it was attached to her through her pierced sex lips, the ring itself closed so that no join could be seen, making it as permanent a feature as the brand on her behind.

The beautiful young white girl was aware of nothing, however, but the thick black cock in her mouth. She moved

6

her face back and forth with apparent enthusiasm, coating the shaft with a sheen of gleaming saliva, her tongue darting over the man's bulbous glans as she concentrated on bringing him pleasure. She looked neither right nor left, her fingers manipulating his heavy testicles as she sensed the tension in him increase.

All at once the man came, filling her mouth with hot, sticky semen, her pretty mouth struggling to contain the onslaught of fluid that gushed into her as she gulped his seed down, fearful of staining his suit by allowing even a drop to escape. For a few seconds it seemed that her efforts would be in vain as spurt after spurt of his sperm spat from him. Then the tide of spunk began to decrease and she seemed to regain control, swallowing hard as she continued to suck at him.

At last the flow ceased altogether, and she was able to let his rod slip from her lips. She licked it carefully, running her tongue up the length of the shaft, removing all vestiges of his orgasm. Only when he was completely clean did she begin tucking his now deflating organ back into his trousers and zipping them shut. Then she settled back in a kneeling position, sitting down on her ankles, her lovely green eyes cast to the floor.

"You see she is well-trained Mr Mbogu," said the white man.

The fat man smiled. "You were right about that, Bulcher. She certainly knows her place."

"But that's the whole point. She doesn't have a place."

"So what do you want me to do about it?"

"Very simple. You are the Minister for the Interior in Negorvia. That makes you an important man in the government here. You could help me get her registered."

"I've already explained that such action is most un-

7

usual," said Mbogu, stretching back in his seat and placing his large, booted foot on the girl's lap.

"I don't see why," replied Bulcher. "After all, the law in this country permits slavery as long as the slave is properly registered."

"And marked."

Bulcher inclined his head. "As you say, properly registered and marked."

The large man shook his head. "Those laws were passed because we are at war with Kombu, in the north. It permits us to enslave any captured Kombians and put them to work for our own war effort, or to sell them to other countries as labourers. It was never meant for the likes of this girl."

"Oh, come on Mr Mbogu," scoffed Bulcher. "Everyone knows the law's purpose is to side-step the Geneva Convention rules on prisoners of war."

Mbogu's brow darkened. "You must understand you are in Africa now, Bulcher. We do not always have time for the laws of Europe here. Both the Negorvians and the Kombians have been enslaving their captives since long before the white colonialists came on the scene. We are merely following a tradition."

"Of course, Sir. All I'm suggesting is that you follow the tradition in this case."

Mbogu eyed the beautiful youngster kneeling silently before him, his eyes taking in the pale creaminess of her breasts, visible through a large tear in the material of her T-shirt. His gaze dropped down to the thin patch of dark hair that covered her pubis.

"It is a nice idea," he concurred. "But she's not actually a prisoner of war."

"Does the law insist that she should be?"

"No. Not strictly. But all the others registered as slaves are."

"The law is the law," insisted Bulcher. "If it makes no discrimination, then surely neither should you."

"What about international opinion?" asked Mbogu. "You realise that we run the risk of losing our foreign aid?"

"Surely, sir, your government has circumvented such opinion before?" said Bulcher quietly. "After all, your country is rich with oil. Such things help. Look at the Middle East."

"Yes, but this case is different. Let's not forget that the girl is British."

A cold smile crossed Bulcher's face. "She doesn't need to remain British," he murmured. "She could become a nationalised citizen."

Mbogu raised his eyebrows. "What?" he exclaimed. "Make her Negorvian?"

"Possibly," replied Bulcher. "But why not a Kombian?

"Are you serious? Make her a Kombian?"

"Certainly. After all, there's no record of how she entered the country."

"Even so, there is no evidence that she came in from Kombu."

"Surely a man in your position could arrange such evidence?"

Mbogu eyed Bulcher. "Hmm," he said thoughtfully. "It's an idea. But why should I?"

"Because I can sell you the weapons secrets from the Bellco corporation. Secrets that will allow you to construct the weapons you need to defeat the Kombians. You know that."

"You're right. We need that information," concurred Mbogu. "But what's you're motive? Why are you so keen to have this slut enslaved?"

Bulcher lowered his eyes. "The reasons are personal. They are not important."

"All right. But do you really have the secrets?"

"You've seen the data I've already given you, Mr Mbogu."

"Yes I have. And I must admit that it seems genuine."

"Then the price of the girl's official registration as a slave seems a small one." Bulcher leaned forward in his seat. "Allow that, and I shall enter negotiations about the secrets."

"So if I agree to send her for registration, you'll name a price?"

"I assure you Minister that I shall make my offer during dinner if you give me your word. After all, she'd be just another slave as far as the law defines it."

Mbogu inclined his head. "You are right, I suppose." Once again he allowed his eyes to stray over the submissive young girl's form. "It seems a shame to mark that body, though," he said.. "And the mark of a slave must be on view at all times, you know. That's what the law says."

"I know," replied Bulcher, a sudden gleam appearing in his eyes. "And I have an idea about that. I shall tell you about it at the same time as we discuss the secrets. I think my idea might amuse you."

Mbogu chuckled. "I'm sure it will. You are a very interesting man, Bulcher, and one whom I believe I can do business with."

"Then you agree?"

"I agree to discuss it with you. We are nearing the restaurant now, though. What should we do with this whore?"

"I thought we might lock her in the car, Mr Mbogu."

"No. She has no place in here."

10

For the first time, the beautiful youngster raised her head and gazed at the Minister, her eyes wide at his dismissive words. But there was no comfort in his expression.

"We shall put her out and collect her later," said Mbogu.

Bulcher's eyes narrowed. "Wait a minute..."

Mbogu raised a hand. "You want to make a deal, don't you?"

"Yes but..."

"Then she gets out here. You trust me, don't you Bulcher?"

Bulcher looked at him. "Of course."

"Good." Mbogu tapped on the window that separated them from the driver's compartment. "Stop here!" he ordered.

The limousine glided to a halt and the driver ran round to the rear door and opened it.

"Our passenger is disembarking here," said Mbogu. "We will collect her later."

"Yes sir."

The driver turned to the girl, who was staring at Mbogu with wide eyes.

"Get out, you."

She opened her mouth as if to say something, then clearly thought better of it. Slowly, she rose from her kneeling position and climbed through the door. The driver eyed her up and down, taking in the creamy whiteness of her bare behind. Then he closed the door.

As the car pulled away from the kerb, Bulcher turned to Mbogu.

"Was it wise to abandon her there?" he asked. "After all, this is a pretty rough part of the city."

"Don't worry," replied the big African. "My people

11

control this area. She will not escape or be abducted. I have patrols of vigilantes who will ensure that she doesn't go far. Meanwhile, they will enjoy having a near-naked white girl to amuse them."

A grim smile spread across Bulcher's features.

"In that case, let's go to dinner," he said.

Chapter 2

Lisa stood on the side of the road and watched in total dismay as the long, black vehicle disappeared round the corner. She couldn't believe that they had abandoned her, her crotch and backside bare, the small T-shirt she wore barely adequate to hide the swelling of her breasts. Even by the standards of her way of life, it was an extraordinary turn of events.

Just a few months before, Lisa Carling had been a computer programmer with the Bellco Corporation, one of the world's largest manufacturers of weapons. Then she had inadvertently assisted one of the company's directors, Conrad Lang, in stealing some company secrets and selling them to Bulcher. As a result, the company had put her on trial. She had protested her innocence, pointing out that Lang had been the guilty one, and she simply obeying orders, but her pleas had fallen on deaf ears.

Nothing could have prepared her for what happened next. To prevent her telling her story, the corporation had to get her out of the way. So they had abducted her, stripped her of her belongings and her clothes and sold her naked to an African slave trader. Things had got worse for the lovely youngster, though. On her way to be sold on she had been captured by Okama, leader of a rebel band. Like many of his people, he despised the whites who had oppressed his

12

nation for so long under colonial rule. He had had Lisa whipped, and then had put her to work as a whore for the amusement of his rough band of men. Okama had subsequently sold her to the chief of a tribe of hunters, who had used her as their naked prey, hunting her down through the bush and whipping and fucking her when they caught her. These people it was that had branded her backside and inserted the brass ring in her sex lips.

Then, about six weeks earlier, her life had changed once more. Bulcher and Lang had had to escape from the law themselves, and had taken up residence in Negorvia. There they had tracked her down, and had had her delivered to Bulcher's house. Since then it had been a life of frequent whippings meted out by Bulcher's servant Akran, and of being used as a sex slave by men whom Bulcher gave her to.

Until tonight, that was.

She had been surprised when Bulcher had visited her in her cell in the scruffy yard behind his house. She had been even more surprised when he had given her the T-shirt. It was the first garment of any kind that she had worn since leaving England. She had hoped to be allowed something to wear underneath as well, but her hopes were in vain. Instead she had been led out to Mbogu's limousine and made to kneel on the floor, then to fellate the obese politician.

And now, here she was, alone on this dark street in one of the scruffiest parts of the city. Even clothed and in company she would have been afraid to stray here. Alone, with her sex and backside bare, the situation was an appalling one, and she gazed about herself anxiously, searching desperately for some form of cover.

The street had once been tarmac, but this had long since

13

deteriorated into a series of deep potholes, so that it resembled nothing more than the surface of the moon. The houses on either side were shabby and unfriendly, the shop fronts boarded or closed off by heavy bars. There was a single street lamp burning, about fifty yards away, and she watched as a pair of skinny dogs paused to urinate on its base. Further down still she could discern the lights of a street bar, the sound of voices carrying faintly through the warm night air. Lisa couldn't imagine a more alien or unfriendly face.

From behind her she heard the sound of a car's motor, and for a second her hopes rose. Perhaps it had just been a trick on Bulcher's part. Perhaps they had simply driven round the block and were coming back for her. But the loud rattle of the engine told her that it was no limousine that was approaching, but an old taxi, so typical of those that drove through the streets of the city.

She could see the car's lights reflecting on one of the buildings now, and she knew it must soon turn the corner and come into sight of her. She glanced about herself, wildly seeking somewhere to hide. All she could see was a narrow gap between two buildings and she hurried toward it as the vehicle came closer. The gap was about two feet wide, but as she went to conceal herself in it, she realised that it was filled with builders' rubble, so that there was only a niche about eighteen inches deep into which she could squeeze. Still, there was nothing for it now, so she pressed her body backwards into the small opening praying that it would hide her.

Even as she did so, the taxi rattled into sight, its single working headlight probing the gloom. Lisa pushed her body back as far as she was able and held her breath as it approached.

14

The vehicle passed by without slowing, and Lisa breathed a sigh of relief as the darkness descended once more. It had been a close call, and had emphasised how vulnerable she was.

She peered out. Once again the street was quiet. But before she could consider her next move, she heard voices coming from her left, the opposite direction from that of the bar. Her heart almost skipped a beat as she realised that she was not alone on the street. Once again she pressed herself back into the niche, her heart thumping.

The voices came closer. There were at least two of them, both men, and they sounded drunk. Lisa waited motionless as they approached.

All at once they came into her line of sight. There were indeed two of them, and they were very much the worse for drink, clinging to one another and staggering as they made their way along. Lisa pressed herself back, hoping against hope that they would be too drunk to notice her.

She might have got away with it, but for the dog.

It had obviously been disturbed by the advent of the two men, and had run out into the road to investigate, only to receive a kick in its ribs for its trouble. Then it had spotted Lisa.

Immediately it ran across to her and began to bark loudly. Lisa tried to shush it, but her efforts made it bark all the louder. Instinctively she pressed herself further back into the recess, but by now the two drunks were looking in her direction and were making their way over to where she stood.

Lisa clutched her hands to her crotch as the pair approached. When they saw that it was a beautiful young white woman they stopped short, their jaws dropping in amazement. They were both in their late forties, scruffily dressed and carrying bottles from which they took occasional swigs. They clutched one another as they stood, sniggering at the sight of the half-naked youngster before them.

For a few seconds they stood back, then one of them lurched forward and grabbed for Lisa's breasts. She was unable to back off any further and he mauled at her, the stench of liquor on his breath almost overpowering her as he pressed his body against hers. He reached a hand down between her legs, trying to force her hands aside and feel for her sex, his fingers groping at her slit. For a moment she tried to fight him off. Then, with an almost instinctive movement, Lisa brought her knee up sharply into his groin.

At once he gave a cry, doubling up and clutching his balls. Lisa took her opportunity to push him aside, and he staggered backwards into his companion, still groaning. At this point the dog intervened again, snarling and snapping at the ankles of the two drunks.

To Lisa's relief, they began to retreat, heading off down the road as fast as they were able, pursued by the yapping dog. She stood and watched as they lurched away, clutching at one another for support and kicking out at the animal.

Lisa leaned back against the wall as the hammering in her chest subsided. This was an awful place, and her position was one of almost complete exposure. She sank back into her hiding place and contemplated her position.

She was at a loss what to do next. She wanted to get away and to hide, but had no idea where to go, and she knew she daren't walk the streets with her crotch and backside bare. Then there was Bulcher. He was certain to return for her, and she feared what he would do if he couldn't find her. She had no illusions that he would track her down easily. A white face in this town was unusual enough, but a young girl clad only a T-shirt would be totally conspicuous. Her only hope was to remain where she was, and to hope that nobody else would see her.

She glanced down at herself, wondering at the sight she must make. The T-shirt was tight across her breasts, the thin material torn in half a dozen places offering tantalising glimpses of the ripe swellings beneath. Her pubic hair was short and sparse. The tribe who had held her captive had regularly applied some kind of depilating cream to her mound, and only recently had the hair begun to grow back down there. Lisa had had mixed feelings about this. On the one hand, there was a strange kind of indecency about being shaved. Somehow she felt that it made a statement about her availability, conveying the message to any man who saw her that her cunt was there for the taking. On the other hand, the dark patch of hair seemed to draw attention to her sex, and the fact that the lips of her vagina remained bare meant that her slit was totally visible to anyone who saw her.

Now, as she stood in her hiding-place. She found her fingers straying down between her legs, stroking at the spiky little hairs, then delving further. She gave a small intake of breath as she found her clitoris. She was amazed to find that it was wet. She could scarcely believe that her situation could be in any way arousing, and yet she knew that the prospect of being seen in her current state was something her perverse nature found oddly exciting. Since her abduction, she had come to realise that there was a latent masochism within her that made her crave rough treatment and humiliation, but to be turned on now seemed totally perverse.

Yet even as these thoughts went through her mind, she

found herself rubbing her clitoris, sending sparks of pleasure through her lovely young body as she played with herself. Since falling into Bulcher's clutches she had been forbidden to masturbate and often went for days on end without being allowed an orgasm. Bulcher had quickly recognised her wantonness and his sadistic nature had made him keen to arouse her, then deny her the final pleasure she craved. Thus he would get Akran, his virile young manservant, to fuck her, but withdraw before she could come, forcing her to finish him off with her mouth. Then he would make the servant tie her with her back to the wall, her hands held high above her head, and would laugh aloud at her obvious discomfort, pointing to the wetness that trickled from her and ridiculing the way her sex lips would convulse as she fought down her desires.

The memory of the young black man, whom Bulcher had given her to so many times, brought a new surge of arousal to the youngster, and she delved her fingers into her vagina, beginning a regular movement in and out as she masturbated herself. For a second she forgot her desperate plight and the dangers that surrounded her, bending her knees and leaning back against the wall, thrusting her sex down onto her hand as shudders of lustful delight shook her body.

All at once she heard shouting, and she froze, her fingers still embedded in the heat and dampness of her sex. The voices were coming from far down the street, and she peered out from the recess. In the distance she could still discern the lights of the bar, and it was from there that the voices seemed to be coming. Lisa screwed up her eyes as she tried to make out what was happening. Then her heart sank.

The distant figures she could see were the two drunks,

18

and they were talking to somebody, shouting and pointing back in her direction. They were clearly telling someone of the young beauty they had encountered, wearing nothing below the waist. The question was, would they be believed? After all, the pair of them were in a pretty inebriated state. Perhaps the people at the bar would simply put it down to their condition. Lisa remained where she was listening and watching intently, hoping against hope that nothing would happen.

Then she saw the four figures detach themselves from the drunks and begin running in her direction.

Lisa hesitated for only a moment, then she too was running, suddenly gripped by panic as she realised how close she was to capture. As she did so, a shout went up behind her, and she knew she had been spotted.

She ran as fast as she was able, her bare feet slapping against the rough, broken pavement slabs. She knew in her heart that there was no escaping the men. They wore shoes and were able to run much faster, whereas she was obliged to pick her way between the stones and broken glass that littered her path.

She spotted an alley off to her left and headed down it. At the end was a streetlight that was, miraculously, still burning and she headed toward it. Then she gave a cry of dismay.

The alley was a dead end!

She ran on to the end, staring up at the bare, concrete wall, looking for a place to scale it, all the time aware of the footsteps behind her coming closer and closer.

There was a wooden box beside the streetlight and she dragged it to the wall, climbing up on it and stretching upwards. Her fingers just reached the top of the wall and she began trying to haul herself up, every muscle in her body straining as she struggled to scale it. She got her chin up to the level of the top and began to swing her leg up the side. Then she felt her ankle grasped by strong fingers.

She tried to kick out, but another hand closed about her other ankle, then they were pulling hard. Lisa had no choice but to let go of the wall.

She dropped down onto the box, then toppled to the ground. At the same time they released her ankles and she rolled over onto her back.

She looked up, and found herself staring into four grinning faces.

Chapter 3

Lisa rose slowly to her feet, her hands clutched to her crotch as she felt the intense gaze of the four young men. They were no more than seventeen years old, she estimated. All were dressed alike, in tattered white shirts and blue jeans stained with long wear. She recognised the uniform as that of the street vigilantes who wandered all over the city, administering their own forms of justice to anyone not toeing the party line.

The city was a place of anarchy, as Lisa well knew from what she had overheard from the conversations of visitors to Bulcher's house. Each of the local politicians had control of a different area and paid gangs of young thugs to patrol it and to exact protection money from the local bars and businesses. The official police force was no more than a sham, ridden with corruption and willing to turn a blind eye to anything as long as they received their cut. The problem for the young English girl was, in whose pay were these young men? Lisa knew she was deep in trouble, and her only hope was to try and make them think that she, too had influence.

"Please don't touch me," she said, backing against the wall. "I was brought here by Mr Mbogu."

At the sound of the politician's name, the young men hesitated, and she knew she had struck a chord. It had been a calculated guess. After all, she knew that politicians seldom strayed out of their own territory, and in the conspicuous limousine Mbogu would make an obvious target for his enemies.

One of the young men stepped forward. He was the tallest of the four, with long, sinewy arms, his eyes dark and calculating.

"Prove it," he said.

"M-Mr Mbogu dropped me off from his car about ten minutes ago," she stammered. "You must have seen his car go by."

The youth's eyes narrowed. Then he pulled a mobile phone from his pocket and began to tap in a number. Lisa wondered where he could have got hold of such an expensive item. It was almost certainly stolen, and it was unlikely that the bill was being paid by this scruffy young man.

Lisa stood, shivering slightly despite the heat, whilst the vigilante spoke into the instrument. She pressed her hands against her bare crotch, wishing that she was more decently dressed, only too aware of the sight she must make, clad only in the thin, torn T-shirt.

The man spoke for no more than a minute before pocketing the instrument once more.

"So, you came with Mr Mbogu?"

"Yes."

He smiled. "I was just speaking with the minister's

driver. He says that you are to be collected later. Meanwhile, you will stay with us."

"But I..."

"Silence!" Despite his youth, there was a real air of authority about the young man, one that broached no argument.

"Now," he went on, his voice softer. "You have two choices. You come willingly, or we tie you and take you ourselves."

Lisa stared at the four grinning faces. They frightened her, but she knew it was pointless to resist them. They were young, powerful men whilst she was a lone girl.

"What do you want me to do?" she asked quietly.

"Put your hands on the back of your head and spread your legs."

The command was a familiar one to Lisa, but even so she was reluctant to obey. She was accustomed to being forced to reveal her charms, but in a much less public setting. To have to uncover her crotch here in the street before these dark strangers filled her with dread.

"Do it!"

Lisa stayed as she was for a second longer, then her shoulders slumped in defeat. Slowly the youngster moved her legs apart. Then, her face glowing scarlet, she removed her hands from her crotch and placed them on the back of her head, allowing them to feast their eyes on her bare sex and on the brass ring that pierced her nether lips.

"That is better." The man moved closer to her until his face was only inches from hers, and she could feel his breath on her cheek. He felt for the ring, tugging at it and watching the expression on her face.

"Nice jewellery," he remarked.

Lisa didn't reply.

22

"I am called Kimuni," the young man went on. "And these are my men. You will call me Sir, do you understand?"

"Yes Sir."

"Good. What is your name?"

"Lisa, Sir."

"Well Lisa, for tonight you will be my girlfriend."

"What?"

"You heard me. Do I not suit you as a boyfriend?"

Lisa eyed him. He was about six feet tall, with the gangliness of a youth still not quite in control of the man's body he now had. He had the tight curls, wide nose and large lips so characteristic of the people of this country, and there was an arrogance about him that she disliked. There was no way she would normally have chosen him as a companion. But this was not a normal situation. She was alone in a dark alley with him and his three companions, her crotch and backside bare.

"Well?"

"Of course you do, Sir," she stammered.

"Good, then kiss me."

Lisa stared into his eyes. Then, tentatively, she kissed him on the cheek.

"No. A lover's kiss."

Lisa took a deep breath. Then she leaned forward and placed her lips on his. At once his mouth opened and his tongue snaked into hers. Despite herself, a shiver of excitement went through the young beauty as he pressed his body against hers. To Lisa, the man was totally unattractive, his breath smelling of tobacco, his skin of stale sweat. Yet the sensation of having his male body so close to hers, and of his tongue licking at her own, aroused passions she did not understand and she felt an unwanted wetness permeate her sex as he kissed her.

He pulled away suddenly, grinning down triumphantly at his lovely young captive.

"That is better," he said. "Later, maybe I will allow you to kiss my colleagues. For now, though, we must be going back to the bar. I feel thirsty after that chase.

Lisa stared at him. "Couldn't I just stay here?" she asked.

"Of course not. You are my girlfriend. You must come with me."

"But I've hardly any clothes on. I can't walk in the streets like this. Couldn't I get a skirt? Or at least some panties?"

His face darkened.

"We agreed not to use force on you," he said. "But only if you obey. Now you will behave exactly as if you were my girl. Understand?"

Lisa sighed. "Yes Sir."

"That's better."

He placed an arm about her waist, letting his hand rest on her bare hip. He looked at her for a second, and she lowered her eyes. Then she placed an arm about him.

"Good," he said. "Now come along, Lisa."

Lisa knew that they must make a strange sight as they stepped out of the alley and began heading back the way they had come. The three other men strutted along in front whilst Lisa and Kimuni followed, their arms about one another. In any normal circumstances they would have looked like a courting couple, but the contrast in the colour of their skin, along with the girl's lack of clothing below the waist made them a very odd pair.

Lisa walked in silence, glancing from left to right, fearful that at any moment someone would appear and would see her. Kimuni, though, seemed quite unbothered, his step jaunty as he ran his fingers over the soft globes of Lisa's backside.

All at once, Lisa heard the sound of a car's engine and saw the glow of a pair of headlights coming down the road. She was almost under one of the few working streetlamps and she began to draw back, afraid of who might be driving the car and of what they would think. But Kimuni pulled her along, heedless of her reluctance.

The car was closer now, and all at once Lisa found herself bathed in the full beam of the headlights as it rounded a bend just ahead of them. Then, to her utter dismay, the car began to slow, coming to a halt just in front of her.

"What's going on? Are you all right?"

The voice was a woman's, the refined tones betraying her as English. Lisa's heart sank. What on earth was an Englishwoman doing here, in these dark streets? Somehow, the thought of being seen by her compatriot was a hundred times worse than if it was a local woman. Lisa didn't fully understand why, but among these strange, dark people, coping with the humiliation of her treatment was just about possible. But an Englishwoman was her peer, and at once the full horror of her situation came home to her as she stood there in the middle of the road, her crotch bare, a scruffy youth as her companion.

"I said are you all right?"

"We're fine," said Kimuni, pulling Lisa closer to him. "Remember, you're my girlfriend," he hissed into her ear. "So do as you're told."

"Not you. I was talking to the girl," said the voice again. "What's he doing to you?"

Lisa said nothing.

"You! Girl! Come over here." The voice was full of

25

authority, but still Lisa held back. Then she felt Kimuni urge her forward.

"Come on, Lisa," he said. "The lady wishes to speak to us."

His arm still about her waist, he pressed her forward until she was standing under the streetlamp beside the driver's window. For the first time Lisa saw the car's driver. It was indeed a white woman, about twenty-five years old. She had long, blonde hair that hung to her shoulders. Her face was attractive, with high cheekbones and large eyes. Her body was slim, with full breasts. She wore a long, elegant gown that contrasted sharply with Lisa's own state of undress. Lisa stared enviously at the woman, so well-dressed and secure in the cocoon of her car. There was an air of haughtiness about her as she eyed Lisa.

"What on earth are you doing?" asked the woman. "Where are your clothes?"

"This is my girlfriend, Lisa," said Kimuni, grinning broadly. "She's very sexy, don't you think?"

The woman glared at him. "I told you I was speaking to her. Now what the hell does this yob mean by calling you his girlfriend?"

"It... It's true," said Lisa quietly, her face glowing red. "He's my boyfriend."

"But where's your skirt and knickers? Did he take them?"

"I... I wasn't wearing any."

"What?"

"That's right," said Kimuni. "She walks about the streets like that. She likes it. It means she can fuck whenever she wants to."

"What?" said the woman again.

"Lisa loves to fuck. That's why she goes around like

26

that. She's my girlfriend, but I let my friends fuck her if they want to. So she doesn't bother to cover her cunt. There's no point. We might want to take her at any time. Besides, she likes to show off this pretty decoration." He indicated the ring.

Lisa listened to the words in silence. She wanted to tell the woman that he was lying, and that she wanted desperately to cover herself and to wear decent clothes. But she dare not. Instead she just stood there, her eyes cast down, her face scarlet.

"I don't believe it," snorted the woman. "No English girl would behave like that. You are English aren't you?"

"Yes."

"Then tell me what's going on."

"Yes, tell her," said Kimuni. He stared into her eyes, and Lisa saw the menace in his.

"I-I don't wear anything down below when I'm out with my boyfriend," she said. "In case he wants to fuck me. Or one of his friends."

Kimuni grinned triumphantly at the woman. "You see?" he said. "It turns her on going about like that. It makes her wet. Spread your legs, Lisa."

Lisa glanced at him, a pleading expression on her face. Surely he had humiliated her enough in front of this elegant woman? But his face was stony. Reluctantly she closed her eyes and spread her legs.

"Oh!"

She couldn't suppress the cry as she felt Kimuni's finger slip between her thighs and penetrate her crudely. Despite her shame she gave a gasp of excitement as he twisted it inside her, his coarse digit suddenly stimulating the perverse lust that was never far from the surface in the wanton youngster. She hoped the woman would not see the effect that he was having on her, but she guessed the expression on her face would betray her.

Kimuni held up his finger and the sheen of wetness that covered it was obvious to all.

"You see?" he said. "She's hot for any man. Wearing underwear would be a waste of time. It would be off all the time. Lick my finger clean, Lisa."

Lisa glanced at the woman, whose expression was a picture of disgust and disbelief as she stared at the hapless girl. Then she opened her mouth and took Kimuni's finger in, sucking and licking her juices from it.

"Good girl," said Kimuni. "Now you must excuse us. We're going to the bar up there for a drink, after which we're going to fuck Lisa. You can come and watch if you like."

The woman shook her head. "You're surely not going into that scruffy bar dressed like that?" she said to Lisa.

Kimuni looked at Lisa. "You know, the lady's right, Lisa," he said. "You shouldn't go into the bar dressed like that."

Lisa stared at him. What was his game this time, she wondered. She didn't have to wait long to find out.

"The men in the bar won't just want to see your cunt," he said. "Take off the T-shirt so that they can see your tits as well."

The woman's jaw dropped. "What the hell do you mean?" she asked. "You can't make her take her top off as well."

"Of course not. I can't make her do anything. She's my girlfriend. She'll take it off because she wants to. Come on, Lisa, you want the men to see your tits as well, don't you?"

"I..."

"Don't you?"

Lisa hung her head. "Yes," she said quietly. "Yes I do want them to see."

"Well then."

Reluctantly the hapless youngster reached for the hem of her T-shirt. She cast a final despairing glance at Kimuni, but he was stony-faced. Slowly she pulled it up, over her head and off. Kimuni held out a hand and she gave him the shirt. He tossed it into the gutter.

"That is better," he said.

Lisa glanced down at her breasts. They stood out, pale and firm, the shape and size of ripe oranges, the nipples brown and stiff. She couldn't meet the other woman's eye as she stood there, totally naked in the middle of this street, accompanied by this motley crowd of scruffy young strangers, all of whom she knew intended to fuck her before the evening was out.

The woman shook her head. "What a total slut," she said. "Who are you, and where do you live?"

"My name is Lisa. I live at Mr Bulcher's house."

"Bulcher eh? That reprobate. And you spend your evenings wandering about starkers with the natives?"

"I... I go where Mr Bulcher sends me."

"And where your boyfriend takes you?"

"Yes."

"Of course she does," said Kimuni. And with that he pulled Lisa's face to his and kissed her lips once more, whilst his coarse, dark fingers roved over the creamy flesh of her breasts, squeezing and caressing them in full view of those watching. The kiss was a long one, and once again, despite her dislike of the streetwise teenager, Lisa felt her body respond to the sheer physicality of his caresses in a manner that was as exciting as it was unwelcome to the

29

naked girl. By the time he released her she was panting slightly, her nipples hard as bullets, the lips of her sex twitching as she fought to contain the wetness within her.

The woman ran her eyes up and down Lisa's body, her face creased in a frown of disdain.

"Disgusting little whore," she said. "I shall be calling on Mr Bulcher to find out more about you."

Then she slammed the car into gear and set off down the road, leaving Lisa and her four captors staring after her.

Chapter 4

For Lisa, it was a relief to see the woman drive away. The way she had spoken and acted toward the youngster had demonstrated nothing but contempt, and Lisa could understand why. Many of the expatriates who lived in this country, especially the Britons, had a strong, often baseless, dislike for the locals. Indeed they scarcely mixed with the Africans at all, restricting their social intercourse to only those most senior people, such as Mbogu, and even then often under sufferance. The idea of mixed-race relationships was anathema to such people, so the mere thought of a white girl having a black boyfriend was considered a scandal. For a girl to have behaved as Lisa had that evening, flaunting her nude body in front of the local people and admitting to her desire to publicly give herself to any one of the teenagers who were accompanying her, went so far beyond the pale as to be quite unthinkable. Lisa wondered what was going through the woman's mind as she disappeared round the corner, leaving her alone and naked in the middle of the street with her four companions.

Her relief was short-lived however, as the reality of her situation came back to her and she looked round at the four youths, all of whose eyes were fixed on the prominent swelling of her bare breasts. She was still standing with her back to the lamppost, so that its light illuminated her pale young body perfectly. Not for the first time she felt an urge to cover herself with her hands, but she knew that would only anger Kimuni and his men, so she simply stood, her hands by her sides, waiting to see what would happen next.

To her dismay she realised that the car had attracted some attention, and a small crowd had gathered to watch, the men pointing and grinning whilst the women tut-tutted, scowling at her.

Kimuni put his arm about her once more. "You see how fortunate you are to have our protection," he said. "These are unscrupulous men who would not hesitate to abduct you and enslave you but for our presence. Aren't you glad to have such a strong boyfriend?"

"Yes Sir."

"Certainly you are. Now come along, all this chatter has made me thirsty."

Lisa hung back. "Where are you taking me?"

"To the bar of course."

Lisa stared down at the discarded T-shirt in the gutter. "Couldn't I just put that back on?" she pleaded.

Kimuni shook his head. "You have beautiful breasts, so you should show them," he said. "After all, men will want to fuck you all the more when they see your breasts, and you love to be fucked, don't you?"

Lisa said nothing.

They moved on up the street, with some of the onlookers following them. Ahead Lisa could see the lights of the bar, and her heartbeat increased as they came closer.

They passed a shop. It was empty of goods but, amaz-

31

ingly, the glass of the window was intact. Lisa gazed at her reflection as they went by, seeing the prominent globes of her breasts, the nipples high and protruding, the firm flesh bouncing deliciously as she walked along. Her eyes dropped to her flat belly and to the smooth, creaminess of her thighs, the dark stubble over her pubic mound drawing her eyes down to the thickness of her sex lips and the prominent slit of her vagina, where her cunt-ring gleamed. She thought of the bar's customers seeing her exposed like this, and an odd shiver of excitement ran through her lovely young body. Lisa was deeply ashamed of her nakedness and the apparently casual way they made her flaunt herself but, along with the shame, there was another emotion deep inside her.

Since her capture, Lisa had been at a loss to understand the behaviour of her body when she was mistreated. Somewhere, deep down in her psyche, lurked a perverseness that was only too quick to rise to the surface when the circumstances were right. In the cruelty of her treatment, Lisa had discovered desires she would never have thought possible. Desires that gave her a thrill, sometimes to the point of orgasm when she was whipped. Desires that made her juices flow whenever she was naked, no matter what the circumstances. Desires that made her nipples and clitoris so sensitive that even the smallest touch would make them swell to hardness. Lisa had no idea how many men had fucked her since she had lost her freedom, but she knew that almost every one had made her come, and that even now the desire for an orgasm was dominating her thoughts as she was led naked through these hostile streets.

The bar, when they reached it, was a typical city bar. Above the door, a flashing neon sign announced the name of a popular beer, and through the entrance came the sound

32

of loud African pop music, with its twanging guitars and male voices singing in harmony. Outside was a jumble of tables and chairs, the table tops strewn with empty beer bottles. The occupants of these tables all looked on with interest as the naked white girl approached, her arm about the waist of her young companion. Lisa felt the blood rush to her face as she heard the comments being passed, but she dare not try to cover herself as Kimuni took her into the saloon.

In the hot, smoky interior, the noise of conversation died as the four entered the bar. Lisa tried not to catch the eyes of the other customers as a gale of laughter greeted her entrance. Kimuni led her up to the bar, where a number of men sat on rickety stools, most of them obviously the worse for drink and all of them with their wide eyes fixed on Lisa's bare body. Kimuni shouted an order to the barman and almost at once five bottles of beer appeared on the counter in front of them. He handed one to Lisa, then made an elaborate gesture of toasting her, clinking his own bottle against hers and those of his companions before taking a long draught. Lisa placed the bottle to her lips and sipped at it, but Kimuni shook his head.

"Take a long swig," he said. "It's good."

Lisa raised the bottle to her lips once more, but this time, as she tipped it, Kimuni took hold of it and held it inverted, so that the girl was forced to gulp it down, a trickle escaping from the corner of her mouth and running down her neck, through the deep valley between her breasts and on over her belly to her crotch. Lisa did her best to swallow down the warm fluid, aware that she was being watched from all corners of the room as she did so.

At last Kimuni lowered the bottle, allowing Lisa to take a breath. She shivered at the bitterness of the fluid, pass-

33

ing the back of her hand across her mouth, wishing she had some kind of cloth to dry off the stream that dripped from her crotch.

"You like beer?" asked Kimuni.

"I can't drink it that fast, Sir," she replied.

"But you must finish it. Then you can use the bottle for relief."

Lisa looked at him. "Relief?"

"You are turned on, aren't you? All these men looking at you gives you a thrill, doesn't it?"

"I..."

"Of course. Look at your breasts. The nipples are standing out hard. When a woman's nipples do that she is either cold, or she is aroused. It is not cold in here, is it?"

"No, Sir. But..."

"Then you must be horny."

Lisa dropped her eyes, staring down at he firm young breasts. It was true that her nipples were hard, standing out from her breasts in a way that couldn't fail to catch the eye, and she knew that it wasn't the cold that was causing it. Kimuni was right, she was horny as hell. The suppressed exhibitionism in her was beginning to dominate her emotions as she stared about the bar at the other patrons. It was like a nightmare, she thought, one in which all about her were normally dressed whilst she was totally nude and making no attempt to hide her charms. Behind the bar was a full-length mirror, and she glanced at her reflection, scarcely able to credit that she could be standing in so public a place with not a stitch of clothing.

Her mind went back to the last time she had been in a bar. It had been shortly after her kidnapping by the rebel Okama and his band. Then they had made her wait on table naked, an experience she had found totally humiliat-

34

ing. But that had just been a small, rural establishment. This was a typical city bar, with all the ruffians and rogues one associated with such a place. She knew that, without Kimuni by her side, being gang-banged was the least of her worries here. Yet still, her situation aroused her, the thought of the cocks that were hardening in the men's pants as they looked at her body sending small shivers of perverse excitement through her young body as she contemplated her situation.

"Finish the beer, then sit on the bar stool," said Kimuni, his lips so close to her ear that she could feel the heat of his breath.

Lisa picked up the bottle. It was made of brown glass, and had a long, slender neck. As she closed her lips about the end, she was only too aware of the eyes upon her. She tipped it, swallowing down the last of the fluid. Then she turned to Kimuni, her heart beating hard as she began to realise what was coming.

"On the stool."

The bar stool was made of wood, and it had seen better days. The joints were loose, so that it was none too steady, and the plastic seat was well-worn, it's smooth surface feeling cool against Lisa's bare behind as she climbed onto it. She sat facing Kimuni. Her knees clamped together, hunched forward slightly in an effort to hide the prominence of her pale breasts.

"Open your legs and lean back," the young black man ordered.

Lisa gazed pleadingly at him, but his eyes were cold. Slowly she moved her thighs apart and leaned back against the bar, placing herself in a posture of submission, looking for all the world as if she were offering herself to him.

"Now I want to see you come."

"Sir?"

"Use the bottle. And don't fake. I want to hear the sound you make when you have an orgasm. Pick up the bottle."

She gazed into his eyes. "Couldn't we go somewhere more private?" she pleaded. "You could do what you want with me there."

He grinned. "Do you think I don't know that I can do what I want with you? But I want everyone to see. Use the bottle here, in the bar."

Lisa looked once more into his eyes, but there was no mercy there. Slowly she reached out a shaking hand and picked up the bottle from the counter. She glanced down at her body. Her legs were spread wide, so that all those in the saloon could see the pink gash of her sex, and perceive the wetness within. A sudden thrill ran through her as she stroked her fingers down the hard, smooth neck of the bottle and contemplated how it would feel within her. With a shudder, she remembered how she had brought herself off with a bottle once before, at the rebel camp when they had held her captive. Somehow it seemed much worse to do it here, though, in the bright lights of this seedy establishment.

"Do it," said Kimuni.

Lisa moved the neck of the bottle down to her crotch, and a murmur went up from those watching as she ran it over the soft lips of her sex, the glass feeling cold and hard as she used it to tease her clitoris. Her cunt-ring clinked against it, and she winced at the sound, knowing it drew even more attention to what she was doing. She looked about her. Everyone in the bar was staring in her direction, those at the back of the room standing, not wishing to miss the extraordinary show that the young white girl was about

36

to put on. She wondered momentarily what the woman in the car would think if she could see her now, shamefully flaunting her beautiful body before these people. Then she caught Kimuni's eye, and she knew she must do what he demanded.

She began to press against her open vagina. For a second her flesh resisted, then the neck of the bottle slipped into her. She gave a low moan as she pushed it all the way inside, her cunt muscles contracting about it as it filled her deliciously. She twisted it round, and at once a new shock of pleasure ran through her. She stopped, her cheeks glowing, afraid of the way her body was reacting and of what those watching would think.

"Go on, Lisa," urged Kimuni.

She turned the bottle once more, biting her lip as the most exquisite sensations filled her. Then she could restrain herself no more, and she began moving the bottle back and forth inside her.

To Lisa the sensation was exquisite, a gush of wetness suddenly flooding her sex as she masturbated herself with the bottle, some of the fluid leaking from her and running over her fingers. This was not lost on those watching, and she saw the men nudge one another and point at her crotch as she moved the bottle in and out of it.

Somehow their amusement was beginning to arouse new perverse passions within her. It seemed that the more she masturbated, the more turned on she became, gripping the bottle in her fist and ramming it into her, using the same movements that a man might when wanking. As her passions began to overcome her, she lifted her backside from the stool, pressing her hips forward, her moans turning to cries. She was lost in her pleasure now, uncaring about the sight she made, the small naked white girl in this scruffy bar bringing herself off for the enjoyment of the customers.

She came with a shout, her breasts bouncing up and down, her fingers running with love juice as she worked the bottle back and forth inside her. The muscles in her thighs were taut as she raised her hips and stretched her legs as wide as she was able, offering those watching a perfect view of the way her sex lips convulsed with each wave of pleasure that shook her.

She came down slowly, lowering her bottom onto the plastic of the bar stool that was now wet with her juices and sweat. Her motions became less violent as the pleasure ebbed away, leaving shame to take its place as she contemplated the enormity of what she had done. Slowly she eased the bottle from inside her and placed it on the bar, where her juices dribbled from it onto the formica surface. Then she closed her eyes, too embarrassed to meet those of the other customers.

Kimuni leapt to his feet, grinning broadly. "You see how sexy my girlfriend is," he said to those watching. "She walks the streets naked simply to give pleasure to me and my men. Now she is hot to have a cock in her, isn't that so, little white beauty?"

Lisa looked at him, then down at her body, noting the way her nipples stood proud from her young breasts and the wet streaks that shone on her thighs.

"I'll do whatever you want," she said quietly.

"Get under the table and suck my friend's cock."

At the sound of the words a peal of laughter went up from the rest of the bar's patrons. But Lisa knew Kimuni wasn't joking. He was staring at her with an intensity that brought a knot to her stomach. It was clear to the lovely youngster that only total obedience would satisfy him.

38

She rose slowly to her feet, and walked across to where Kimuni and his companions were seated. Kimuni rose too, taking her hand and indicating one of the young men. He was a tall youth with broken teeth and a scar across his cheek.

"As my girlfriend I give you permission to kiss Joe," said Kimuni.

Lisa eyed the man. He was ugly, and the way he leered at her bare breasts repulsed her. But she dare not disobey Kimuni, so she leaned forward and kissed him on his thick lips. At once he took hold of her, one arm wrapping about her neck and pulling her down, whilst the other took advantage of the way her breasts dangled before him, grabbing hold of one and squeezing it tight as his tongue probed into her mouth.

All at once Lisa felt her arousal return, the sensation of having his tongue intertwined with hers whilst he caressed her breasts suddenly rekindling those desires that were never far from the surface in the wanton beauty. She couldn't understand why the degrading and humiliating treatment these people meted out to her turned her on so much, but even now, as she shared an intimate embrace with this rough stranger, she could feel her nipples stiffen and the warmth in her crotch increasing.

The kiss went on for some time, the shouts and whistles of the bar's customers echoing about the room as they watched the young beauty embrace the vigilante. Then he pulled away and, his arm still about Lisa's neck, he dragged her down to her knees, and pushed her under the table.

Lisa knew what was required of her, and she knew too that there was no question of her demurring. She was expected to suck him to orgasm and, whether she liked it or not, she had to obey. She moved round between the man's

39

legs. The floor of the bar was dirty and strewn with cigarette ends and spilt beer, but she ignored that, reaching for the man's fly.

Even as she pulled down the zip she could feel his hardness through the material. When she reached inside she found he wore no underpants, and she eased his stiff cock out so that it stood proud in front of her face, thick and black, the circumcised end shining. She ran her hand up and down the shaft a couple of times, making him grunt with pleasure. Then she opened her mouth and, for the second time that evening, tasted a man's arousal.

His cock tasted salty and had a musky aroma, and she began to suck at it hard, her head moving back and forth as she fellated him. Around her she could hear chairs scraping back and she knew the other customers were moving closer to watch as she pleasured the man. On the wall of the bar was an old mirror. Its surface was streaked with grease, but it still gave a true reflection and she found herself slightly shocked as she saw her image, the small, dark-haired white girl crouched naked on the floor of the bar, her lips closed about the man's shaft, her breasts shaking deliciously as she plunged her head down against his groin.

He came quickly, filling her mouth with his hot spunk as he groaned aloud, thrusting his hips up at her. Lisa gulped down his seed, slurping noisily, swallowing every drop, continuing to suck until the spurts ceased. Only then did she lift her head and gaze up at Kimuni, who was still standing beside the table.

This time he did not speak, simply grabbing her by the arm and pulling her to her feet, then shoving her back over the table.

Kimuni fucked her without ceremony, pulling out his long cock and plunging it between her thighs, bringing a

40

scream from the young beauty as she felt him penetrate her. She looked about at the sea of eyes that watched as he violated her. All were looking on hungrily and she knew that, given the slightest opportunity, they too would fuck her without a thought for her consent.

As he thrust hard into her, she contemplated her lot. Other young English girls of her age had lovers who took them in the comfort of a bedroom with the curtains closed and the lights dimmed. Lisa, though, was obliged to lie in a pool of spilt beer in the middle of a brightly-lit bar whilst a man she neither knew nor had any affection for fucked her before an audience of laughing, cheering men.

And yet still she couldn't control the desires that rose within her as he took her, and the cries that escaped her lips were cries of genuine arousal as she thrust her hips up at him, revelling in the roughness of his treatment of her, her backside slapping down on the surface of the table as he thrust his cock hard into her vagina.

When he came she came too, her shouts ringing round the room as she accepted his spunk deep inside her. He grinned down at her as she thrashed about on the table, her sex muscles tightening about his stiff member as if trying to suck his sperm from him, her lovely, firm breasts bouncing up and down with every jab of his strong hips.

He went on screwing her until he was spent, then he withdrew and another of his companions took his place between Lisa's thighs. Lisa glanced about at the watching men, wondering what they must make of the beautiful young European who allowed herself to be gang-banged naked in so public a place. Then another cock was forcing its way into her vagina and all else was forgotten as a new surge of lust ran through her ravaged body.

41

Chapter 5

The clanging sound of her cell door being unlocked, roused Lisa from her slumbers. She had been dreaming of an English garden, where she had been strolling amongst the flowers with her handsome young lover. Now reality came back to her with a jolt as she blinked up into the morning sunlight that streamed through the tiny barred window set high in the wall of the room. Her eyes began to adjust to the glare, and she realised that a figure was standing in the doorway. She recognised him at once as Bulcher's servant Akran, who was often charged with looking after the young captive.

As usual, Lisa felt her cheeks glow red as the large, muscular man gazed down at her naked body spreadeagled before him, her wrists and ankles shackled to the corners of her bunk by shining chains. She wondered if he would fuck her, as he sometimes did on such mornings. She knew she would be powerless to prevent him if he wanted to take her. However, he began instead to undo her restraints. As he set about releasing her, Lisa's thoughts went back to the events of the previous night.

She had been more than an hour in the bar with Kimuni and his companions, during which time each had fucked her twice, on the floor and on the table, whilst the rest of the bar's patrons looked on. When they had satisfied themselves the young men had dragged her out and tied her to a post outside the bar, her arms trapped high above her and had left her there in the glare of the bar's lights whilst they carried on drinking. The hapless girl had found herself at the mercy of passers-by, who took the opportunity to feel up the little white beauty, squeezing her breasts and fingering her sex, laughing aloud at the way her body reacted to their touch.

42

Lisa had begged them to leave her alone as she hung in this shameful position, but they had simply laughed at her, commenting on the stiffness of her nipples and the way her cunt muscles contracted about their fingers as they groped her body. They laughed even more when they made her come, imitating the way she cried aloud with lust, her control lost as many hands caressed her naked flesh.

It was there that Bulcher and Mbogu found her. The chauffeur was despatched to release her from her bondage whilst Kimuni conversed briefly with his political master. Then she was bundled into the car, where she was once more obliged to suck Mbogu's stiff rod during the journey back to Bulcher's house. On arrival she had been placed in Akran's care and, after a shower, had been chained into her cell.

Now Akran hauled her to her feet and shoved her out into the open air. Her cell was situated in a courtyard at the back of the house amongst the servants' quarters, and the men and women sitting outside their small apartments nudged one anther and grinned at the sight of the young-ster being marched across the yard, her hands behind her head so that her pale, firm breasts were projected forward. Lisa looked neither left nor right as she made her way to-ward the back door of the house, the gleaming ring through her sex lips chafing as it always did against her clitoris.

Akran led her through the kitchen and into a large, bare room with a desk at one end. Lisa was familiar with the room. It was where she had first encountered Bulcher af-ter she had been bought here from the clutches of the primi-tive tribe that had used her for hunting practice in the bush. Her stomach filled with butterflies as the servant made her take up her submissive stance, hands behind her head, legs spread, in the centre of the room. Being summoned to this

43

room was a bad omen, and usually meant that she faced punishment for some minor misdemeanour. She eyed the bench, with its leather straps, that stood at the side of the room, and the rack of canes behind it. She couldn't recall having done anything wrong, but Bulcher was an unpredictable man, so she took little comfort from that.

The wait seemed an interminable one. The African heat was oppressive and the fan was switched off, so that the heavily-built servant's face was shiny with sweat. Lisa herself felt the heat less, partly because she was naked, partly because long hours in the interminable stuffiness of her cell in the middle of the day had inured her to it. Still she was feeling very uncomfortable when the door finally opened and Bulcher came in.

He strode across to the desk and sat down, then eyed his young captive.

"Mr Mbogu was impressed with you last night," he said. "It seems that sucking these people's cocks is something you do well."

Lisa said nothing.

"I presume you heard our conversation in the car?"

"I couldn't help but hear, Master," said Lisa quietly.

"Then you'll know that this country has a tradition of enslaving men from neighbouring Kombu, where they've been fighting a war for years. The slaves must be registered at a government camp and marked to show their status."

"I had heard of such things, Master."

"Good. You see, That is where I'm sending you."

"Me, Master?" Lisa couldn't suppress a gasp.

"That is correct. You are to become an officially registered slave."

"But Master I..."

44

"What?"

"That mean's I'll never be free again, doesn't it?"

He smiled. "Surely you never expected that you would? This is your life now, little slut. The one you were born for. Your destiny is to bring pleasure to men. You understand?"

Lisa hung her head. "Yes Master," she said meekly.

"So. Do you have any objection to registration?"

"I... No Master."

"Good. They will be here for you in an hour. Akran will see to you. Now you may go."

Lisa turned to leave, then paused.

"Master?" she said, timidly.

"What is it?"

"The mark. What form does it take?"

"It is a tattoo. A small letter 'S' placed where it is always visible. The law insists that all slaves be marked in that way, and that the mark is visible at all times."

"I see, thank you Master."

Lisa's mind was preoccupied as she was led out. She was to be marked yet again. Already she had the thick brass ring through the lips of her sex and a brand of a leaping lion burned into her buttock. Both of these marks, she knew, were extremely erotic and had the effect of enhancing her appearance when naked. She wondered how men would react to a third.

Akran took her to a storeroom where he rummaged in a cupboard and pulled out a piece of grey cloth, which he threw to her.

"Put that on."

Lisa examined it. It was a dress. She could scarcely believe her eyes. She had not worn a dress for months. In fact the T-shirt she had had on the night before was the first garment she had been permitted to wear since her enslavement.

She struggled into it. It was a tight fit, the material clinging to her and emphasising the curves of her body. Half the buttons were missing at the front, so that her breasts were barely covered, the neckline plunging almost to her waist. The skirt was short, so that she knew her cunt ring would flash into view if she didn't take care as she walked. But at least it was some form of clothing, allowing her a degree of modesty she had been denied for many months.

Akran led her from the storeroom back into the main house, then out into the courtyard once more. There, an old pick-up truck was waiting. Akran lowered the tailgate, then indicated to her that she was to climb aboard She did so, and he climbed on behind her. He produced a pair of handcuffs and, dragging her forward, secured her wrists to a ring set into the back of the driver's cab, so that she was standing, facing forward over the top of the cab. Then he jumped down. He shut the tailgate with a bang before climbing into the driver's seat. There was the screech of the starter motor turning the engine over a few times, then it rattled into life and they were off.

It was all Lisa could do to remain upright as the van lurched through the streets. She felt very conspicuous standing where she was clad in the quite inadequate dress. It was normal in the city for Europeans to travel by car, and the sight of the young white girl on the back of the battered old truck was one that turned a number of heads.

The journey took about fifteen minutes. They drove through a part of the city that Lisa had never visited before, the buildings mainly shanty dwellings, the ragged people sitting outside them staring at her as she passed. At last the vehicle slowed and they pulled left and stopped outside a pair of tall iron gates. Beside them was a notice

46

bearing the words 'Ministry Of The Interior'. The gates were guarded by armed men, who spoke a few words to Akran before opening them and allowing the van inside. He drove across a wide parking lot and drew the vehicle to a halt.

Akran climbed up onto the van and released Lisa's cuffs, pulling her arms behind her and re-attaching them to her wrists. Then he gave her a shove and she jumped down to the ground. She looked about her. They were standing outside an austere looking building that she guessed was a relic from the colonial age. The door was guarded by two men with machine guns, and the pair regarded the young white girl with some interest. Akran took her arm and, saying a few words to the men, led her inside.

The interior of the building was in a dilapidated state, the wooden block floors covered in dust, the gloss paint on the walls faded and peeling. Akran took her to a window in the wall and rang a bell. They waited a few minutes, then the window opened and a face appeared. More words were exchanged, then a door opened beside the window, and Akran shoved Lisa through. She glanced back at him, suddenly realising that he was leaving her. Then the door slammed and she was alone with the man at the window.

"This way," he said.

He took the youngster's arm and led her to a heavy door at the back of the room. He banged on it and shouted a few words. At once there came the sound of the door being unlocked, and it creaked open. The man behind it wore a grey uniform and carried a large cane in his hand. He beckoned her to go inside. Lisa blinked in the darkness. She was in a long corridor with barred cells on either side. As he led her down, she saw men come to the bars, shouting and laughing at the sight of a white girl in such a

47

place. Lisa did not look at them, walking down between the cells until she reached an empty one. Here the man made her stop. He unlocked the door, then released her wrists and shoved her inside.

Lisa turned to gaze out through the bars as he slammed and locked the door. Her mind was a daze. She had no idea where she was, or who the other men could be. The place was like a prison, yet there had been no indication that it was when they had driven in. She could only guess that the men were also due to be registered as slaves. A shiver ran through her at the thought of what was to come. She was only thankful that she was clothed. She daren't think what it would be like if these rough men saw her naked.

For the next two hours, Lisa was left alone in her cell, listening to the shouts and laughter of her fellow prisoners. She sat quietly in the corner, not wanting to contemplate what awaited her. Occasionally she would imagine that the men were shouting to her, but since she didn't understand a word of their language she was unable to respond.

At last the door at the end of the corridor swung open again, and a group of men with guns appeared. They began emptying the cells, placing cuffs on each of the men and chaining them together in groups of six or eight. When they came to Lisa's cell, she too was brought out and her hands secured behind her, then chained to the man at the back of a group.

They were led back out into the courtyard, where four lorries stood. The backs of the trucks were converted into cages, and three of them were already full. Lisa's group was led to the fourth, where they hauled themselves up into the cages. There were already men inside, lined up on one side of the truck and Lisa's group was led down the other, where each one had his cuffs undone and attached to rings set into the wall of the cage. Lisa was the last one, and she stood, her eyes cast down to the floor as her hands were fixed behind her. She was acutely aware of the gaze of   the

en, where she had been strol She was only too mindful of the inadequacy of the dress to hide her charms, and she knew that the man beside her could see ample portions of her breast through the open front of it.

There was a good deal of shouting, then the gates to the compound were swung open and the convoy of lorries lurched forward. Soon they were out on the open highway, leaving the city far behind them.

Chapter 6
It was getting dark by the time the trucks finally slowed and pulled off the highway. They ran for some time along a rough track, then stopped outside a large compound. It reminded Lisa of a wartime prisoner of war camp. The buildings were long wooden single-storey affairs with tin roofs and the whole area was surrounded by tall barbed wire fences with high towers from which she could see guns protruding. The gates were unlocked and the trucks rumbled through. Then the cages were opened and the prisoners released one by one.

Lisa's cuffs were undone, then refastened behind her, and she was obliged to jump to the ground. The men were being herded into rows and she was taken across and made to stand with them. The trucks were driven away, and Lisa realised they were on some kind of parade ground. She felt very small and vulnerable surrounded by these large, rough men, and she knew that the comments they were making were addressed at her. She stood quietly, her eyes cast down, whilst the guards marched along the ranks, wielding long thin canes to beat the men into line.

All at once a bell rang, and the men fell silent. An officer appeared and mounted a small dais at the centre of the parade ground. He began to speak. Lisa could understand nothing of what he was saying, but she guessed from the murmurs of discontent about her that the speech was not going down well. The men with canes went into action again, lashing out at the grumblers, so that silence fell once more.

The officer spoke for a further five minutes, then stepped down. He made as if to walk away, then, to Lisa's dismay, his eyes fell on her and he paused. He called over one of the men with canes and said a few words to him, then turned and strode into one of the huts.

Someone barked an order and the prisoners all turned to the right, with Lisa taking their cue and doing the same. They started to march off. Then, to the youngster's consternation, the man who had been speaking to the senior officer shouted something at her. She pretended not to hear him.

Whack!

Lisa gave a cry of pain as a cane descended onto her thigh, delivering a stinging blow and leaving an angry red stripe across her pale flesh. She realised with a shock that another of the guards was right beside her. He indicated his colleague, then shoved her roughly out of the line in his direction.

Realising that resistance was of no use, Lisa scuttled across to where the man who had called her was standing.

He shouted more words at her and she shook her head.

"I don't understand."

"You come with me. See Colonel."

He set off at a fast pace toward the hut into which the officer had vanished, with Lisa close behind him. As she walked she threw a glance over her shoulder at the rest of the prisoners, who were marching silently toward another of the blocks. She almost wished she was going with them. Being singled out like this made her very nervous indeed.

The man led her up a short flight of steps and into the building. It stood on strong concrete legs, and the wooden floorboards rang with a hollow sound beneath the guard's heavy boots. They walked down a long corridor with doors on either side. At the end was another, larger door with the words 'Officer In Command' written on it. The guard knocked on it, then opened it and shoved Lisa inside, following close behind her.

The office was no better appointed than anywhere else Lisa had encountered since leaving Bulcher's house. It had a single threadbare rug on the floor and was furnished with an old table and a chair from which the stuffing was beginning to leak. The Colonel himself was standing by a cracked and dirty window, holding a swagger stick in his hand. He turned as Lisa was brought in. His age was difficult to gauge, probably in his late forties and, like so many successful men in this country, he had a large belly. His skin was an ebony colour, and his face glistened with sweat.

He walked over to where Lisa was standing, in the centre of the floor. She stood, perfectly still, her heart thumping as he walked round her. She was aware of how inadequately her dress covered her breasts, but with her arms trapped behind her there was nothing she could do.

"Why were you paying no attention during my speech?"

"Sir?"

"My speech. I spoke for five minutes and you listened to not a word."

"I listened, Sir."

"Then tell me what I said."

"I... I don't know, Sir."

Bang! He brought his stick down hard on the table top, making Lisa start with the suddenness of the noise.

"Then you weren't listening!"

"I don't understand the language, Sir."

"Why not? I spoke in Kombian."

"I don't speak that language Sir."

He went back to his desk and ruffled through some papers.

"Your name is Lisa Corling?"

"Carling Sir."

"It says Corling here."

"My name is Carling."

Bang! Once again his stick hammered down onto the table.

"Are you saying I am wrong?"

"Only that the person who wrote that document made a mistake, Sir."

Lisa was becoming more and more apprehensive as the interview continued. She had encountered men like the Colonel before. Men who still held a grudge about the colonial past of their country and who wanted to find some-one to blame. She had once been held captive by a gang of rebels for many months, and had been regarded by them as a symbol of white oppression. Some had even wanted to kill her, but instead she had been held as a sex slave, forced to whore for them every night. Now she saw in the Colo-

52

nel the same unreasoning prejudice, and she knew that, no matter what she said, he intended to take out some of his hatred on his helpless young captive.

The Colonel turned away from her and slumped into his chair.

"You know why you are here?"

"For registration, Sir."

"Registration, that is right. To be registered as the Kombian slut that you are, and to be given the mark that will forever brand you as a slave and as inferior to my people."

Lisa said nothing, but the words sent a chill through her.

"Tonight you will be medically examined," he went on. "Then tomorrow you will be registered and marked. After that you will be marched back to the city. Slaves are not important enough to be given transport."

"Yes Sir."

"Now, for refusing to pay attention to my speech, you will receive six strokes of the cane."

"But I..." Lisa's voice trailed away. She knew that arguing with this man would only make things worse. Instead she stood quietly, contemplating the injustice of this awful country, where what few rights she still had were soon to be stripped away.

The Colonel barked an order to the guard, who sprang forward and released the cuffs that held the youngster's hands behind her..

"Take off your dress."

Lisa eyed him for a second, then reluctantly reached down for the hem of her dress. She pulled it off in a single movement, then dropped it to the floor. On the wall opposite was an old mirror, clearly situated to allow the commanding officer to check his uniform before leaving the office. Now it reflected the pale body of the young English girl, her firm breasts jutting proudly forward, the nipples already hardening under the gaze of the two men. Lisa glanced down at her crotch. The hairs there were sparse, so that the lips of her sex were on open view. Her face reddened as she stood, her legs apart, her hands hanging at her side.

The Colonel rose to his feet again, crossing to her. He reached out and took hold of her breast, squeezing it roughly, then pinching the nipple so hard that tears filled Lisa's eyes. He grinned.

"What is the matter? Don't you like to be touched by a black man?"

Lisa remained silent.

The Colonel barked an order, and Lisa felt her arms grasped. Then the guard pushed her forward so that she sprawled over the table, the hard wooden surface pressing her young breasts flat. The edge of the table was rubbing against her pubis as he pulled her arms forward and made her grasp the far side of it. He kicked her ankles, forcing her to spread her legs.

Lisa lay quite still, trying to erase from her mind the sight she must make, her pale body stretched across the table, her legs spread wide, revealing her most private parts to the two men. Then she felt the cane tapping against her behind, and she braced herself for what was to come.

Swish! Whack!

The thin cane bit into the soft flesh of her behind, sending a searing pain through her young body so that she had to grit her teeth to avoid screaming aloud.

Swish! Whack!

Down it came again, catching the underside of her firm

buttocks and laying a second stripe across her pale flesh.

Swish! Whack!

The third stroke was high on her cheeks, the flexible cane bending round and smacking into her thigh. Still the youngster made no sound, though a sheen of sweat had broken out on her smooth skin and the tears were coursing down her cheeks.

Swish! Whack!

Lisa gripped the table edge as tightly as she was able, trying to blank out the agonising pain that the beating was bringing her. In the mirror she could see her small, naked frame spread out across the table and the vivid red stripes that decorated her behind. She braced herself as the guard drew back his arm once more.

Swish! Whack!

He wielded the cane with unerring accuracy, laying yet another excruciating weal across her backside, the pain like the stinging of a thousand wasps. It was all Lisa could do to avoid the temptation to cover herself with her hands, but she knew that to do so would simply worsen her plight.

Swish! Whack!

The final stroke was delivered with all the man's force, slicing into her tender flesh and finally eliciting a cry of anguish from the unfortunate youngster as the pain became too much to bear. Then it was over, and the room fell silent apart from the sobbing of the anguished Lisa.

The Colonel barked an order, and her guard clicked his heels and threw him a sharp salute. Then Lisa heard the office door open and close. She went to straighten herself, but a hand came down on her back, holding her in position.

"Do not move," he hissed.

Lisa remained where she was, her body still shaking as

55

the tears continued to come. Then she heard the sound of
a zip being pulled down and, almost immediately afterwards, felt something hard pressing against her bottom.

It probed down between her legs and rubbed against
her slit. All at once she gave a gasp as she realised that it
was the Colonel's rampant cock that she could feel, and
that he was about to fuck her.

Lisa's initial reaction was shock and disgust at what
was about to happen, Then she felt him rub up against her
clitoris, and she recognised with a shock that her cunt was
wet.

It was the beating, she knew, that had aroused her. For
some reason that Lisa had never been able to fathom, the
infliction of pain on her young body always had the effect
of making her aroused. Now, as she felt the man press his
cock insistently against the entrance to her vagina, she knew
she would be unable to resist, and a low moan escaped her
lips as he pushed himself into her.

He fucked her without care or feeling, ramming her
hips against the table as he took her, his long, thick cock
bringing delicious sensations to the wanton youngster as
she found herself responding to him with an enthusiasm
that she was unable to control. Despite the pain that burned
in her backside, Lisa was extraordinarily turned on and,
the more he pumped his stiff member into her, the more
aroused she became.

It was a hard, emotionless fuck. Clearly the officer's
only desire was to fulfil a physical need, and it wasn't long
before she felt him spurting his spunk deep inside her.
Almost at once, she came too, crying aloud as she felt his
seed fill her. She was beyond caring about her modesty
now, completely abandoned to her pleasure, her backside
thrusting back at him as he shot his load within her.

He withdrew as swiftly as he had entered her, tucking his cock back into his pants, leaving her still slumped across the desk, gasping for breath. He took hold of her arm, dragging her roughly to her feet. Lisa staggered as he pulled her across to the door and flung her out into the corridor, where a group of young soldiers were conversing. For a moment she stood, staring in confusion at the men, grasping her arms to her body to try to hide her modesty. Then the Colonel threw her dress out after her and she grabbed at it. She struggled into it amid the laughter of the soldiers, her face scarlet as she felt the Colonel's spunk dribble down her thighs. Then the guard grabbed her and, snapping the cuffs onto her wrists, led her out of the building, the men's jeers ringing in her ears.

Chapter 7

Lisa stood in the silent queue outside the surgery, feeling quite out of place amongst the burly men who were her fellow inmates at the camp. She had barely had time for a wash in cold water and to gulp down a bowl of thin broth before she and the others had been herded out onto the parade ground once more. There they had stood whilst groups of half-a-dozen at a time had been called out and taken to the hut that apparently served as a hospital for the camp. Lisa was among the last six to be summoned.

The guards had taken them into a room and ordered them to strip to their underwear. Lisa's protests that she wore none had fallen on deaf ears, and she had been made to discard her dress whilst the men remained in shorts. Now she stood, an arm wrapped across her breasts, a hand covering her pubis whilst the men made no attempt to hide their interest in the naked young beauty. She knew that, but for the presence of the guards, she would have been at the mercy of these men, Even with the guards there she felt none too safe, and she pressed herself back against the wall in a vain attempt to hide as much of her naked body as she could.

They were called in one by one, and at last it was Lisa's turn. When she entered the surgery she was amazed to find that the doctor was a European. He wore a white coat, and was seated behind a desk when she entered. He glanced up from the papers he was reading and took off his glasses.

"Number eight zero three?" he said.

"I don't know, Sir."

He strummed his fingers impatiently, then took another look at her papers.

"Lisa Corling?"

"Carling, actually, Sir."

"From now on it's eight zero three, understand?"

"Yes Sir."

Lisa was so taken aback by the presence of a white man, indeed an Englishman from the way he spoke, that she barely registered the indignity of his taking her name from her.

"Lie on the couch."

There was a hospital trolley parked against the wall with a sheet covering it. Lisa lifted herself onto it, still trying to cover herself with her hands. The doctor rose to his feet and walked across.

"Put your hands by your sides," he said. "I'm not going to hurt you."

He began his examination, running his hands over her body, checking her heartbeat and her pulse, as well as her blood pressure.

"When did you last have sex?"

"Sir?"

"You heard me."

"About two hours ago, with the Colonel."

He sniffed. "That figures. From now on you'll have to expect a lot more of that. Have you any contraception?"

"I don't think I'm able to conceive."

"Let's take a look. Spread your legs."

Her face glowing, Lisa obeyed, and the doctor began an intimate examination. Lisa had to grit her teeth as he probed her vagina to avoid betraying her reaction to being touched so intimately. At last he raised his head.

"You're right," he said. "You can't get pregnant. In your position that's kind of a mixed blessing."

"Sir?"

"There are some men who would want to breed from you. That option is clearly not open. However the alternative is that you be made into a sex slave, a whore for whoever buys you. Mind you, from the way you were reacting to my fingers, it's my guess that you're cut out for just such a job."

Lisa said nothing, but her red face betrayed her reaction. She had been told when still at school that she couldn't conceive, and it was something of a relief to have it confirmed, though the way she had been used since her capture had already told her that there was no likelihood of her ever bearing children.

All at once there was a crash of something breaking. It had come from a cupboard opposite, and the doctor swung round.

"What on earth..."

He went across and pulled open the door. Inside was a

figure, cowering back into the darkness. The doctor pulled him out into the open. It was a youth, about sixteen years old, Lisa guessed. He was staring at her naked body, and she could see the way his crotch was bulging.

Smack! The doctor brought his hand down hard across the boy's face, making him cry out in pain.

"Sneaky little sod, coming in here for a peek at the white woman!" he shouted. "You'll get all the chances you need after tomorrow, you little brat. Now get the hell out of my surgery."

He cuffed the boy twice more before ejecting him, slamming the door behind him. Then he turned back to Lisa.

"All right, eight zero three, I've finished with you now. You seem fit enough."

Lisa sat up and lowered herself from the trolley.

"Sir?"

"What is it?"

"What did you mean just then by saying he'd get all the chances he needs after tomorrow."

"Nothing. Just that whoever's having you marked seems to have a sense of humour."

"I don't understand."

"You will. Now get out of here."

Lisa made for the door, then paused.

"Sir?"

"What is it now?"

"You're English."

"So what?"

"Couldn't you help me?"

He walked across and stretched out a hand, stroking her cheek.

"Do you think I'd be here myself if I could help it?" he asked. "I can't do this anywhere else."

60

"You mean you're not a real doctor?"

"I'm qualified all right. A little altercation with the British Medical Council ended my career in England though. Then I got caught with certain illegal substances at the airport here, and they gave me a choice, work here for three years or spend the time in prison. That's why I'm doing this."

Lisa dropped her eyes. "I'm sorry."

"Don't be sorry for me. I get out of this filthy hole once the three years are up. You've got a life sentence."

"I see."

He suddenly became brusque again.

"You'll get by, eight zero three," he said. "Just keep playing the slut and letting them use that pretty little body of yours. From what I can see, you enjoy it. Now fuck off out of here, I've got work to do."

He turned back to his desk, leaving Lisa to let herself out of his room.

Chapter 8

Lisa felt very nervous as she stood, gazing out through the bars of her cell at the other cells in the block. The one beside her was empty, the inmates having been taken out about twenty minutes before. She had no idea what time it was, but she guessed that it must be late afternoon.

Her cell was the last one, set on its own in the corner of the block. The rest were in the centre, two rows that backed onto one another with a corridor on either side. Each one contained four men, and they had been being taken out, one cell at a time, since dawn. As one group returned, another was marched away. Each returning prisoner sported a fresh tattoo on his arm, a simple letter S, about half an inch in height, etched into the flesh of his forearm. The Kombians had lighter skin than the locals, so that it showed quite clearly. Where the men had been wearing long-sleeved shirts, the sleeve had been cut away to ensure that the mark was on view, and Lisa was reminded of the rule that, once marked, slaves were to keep the tattoo visible at all times. She was still wearing the tattered dress that Akran had given her, and she stared at her bare arms, wondering how the tattoo would look on her pale skin.

Lisa had spent a troubled night, the noise of the other prisoners keeping her awake until late. Her cell had only a simple mattress on the floor and, whilst she was used to discomfort, the strangeness of her surroundings conspired to keep her from falling asleep until the early hours, when her fatigue had finally got the better of her.

They had been awoken at dawn with mugs of weak tea and bowls of maize porridge. Then the procession to the marking area had begun.

All of a sudden there was a clang, and the door at the end of the corridor swung open. Lisa watched as the men were led in, the marks clearly visible on their arms. The cell door was opened and the four ushered inside. Then the guards turned to Lisa.

They unlocked the cell, and one of them stepped inside. He produced a pair of handcuffs and secured the girl's wrists behind her. Then he pushed her forward through the door, and the men led her out of the block, the whistles and calls of the other prisoners ringing in her ears.

Once outside, they led her across to a solitary hut in the middle of the compound. The leading guard opened the door and pushed her inside.

The room was sparsely furnished, with a single desk

facing the door, behind which was a couch like that in the doctor's surgery. A man sat behind the desk with a sheaf of papers in front of him. The only other occupants of the room were the doctor, and a man in an apron, who held an implement in his hand that Lisa guessed was a tattooist's needle. Her escort led her to the desk, then ordered her to stop. He removed her cuffs.

The man sitting at the desk was in his forties. He wore civilian clothes, and had a weary air about him. He looked up at her through thick spectacles.

"Number eight zero three," he said.

"Yes Sir."

"Forefinger of right hand."

At first, Lisa didn't understand what he meant, then he indicated an ink pad on the desk before him, and she realised he wanted her fingerprint. She held out her finger to him and he rolled it over the pad, then across a sheet of paper, leaving a blue imprint. Then he beckoned her to go past him to where the doctor and the tattooist waited.

Lisa avoided the eyes of the doctor, holding out her arm to the other man, but he shook his head.

"I'm afraid they have other plans for you," he said. "Remove the dress please."

Lisa stared round at the men in the room. There were three guards, the clerk and the tattooist.

"Must I do it in front of them?" she asked.

"Yes. Now hurry up, it's been a long day."

Her face glowing, Lisa pulled the dress over her head. The doctor took it from her and she stood, trying in vain to cover herself with her hands, whilst the guards looked on, grinning at her discomfort.

"Get up on the couch."

There was no expression in the doctor's voice as he

63

gave the order. Lisa turned her back on the trolley and pulled herself up into a sitting position. Then she lay down on her back, her hands still hugged to her body.

All at once she felt her arms grabbed by the tattooist and pulled up to the top of the couch. At each corner were attached leather straps and these were fastened about her wrists, holding them firm. Then her ankles were similarly secured. By the time they had finished she was spreadeagled and helpless, staring fearfully about at the men in the room.

"Raise your backside," ordered the doctor, producing a pillow from under the trolley. Lisa hesitated for a second, then did as he asked, arching her back and pressing her pubis up. He slid the pillow under her bottom, leaving her hips thrust forward. Lisa was at a loss to understand why she was being restrained in this way. Perhaps they intended to gang-bang her. If they did, she mused, there was nothing she could do to prevent them, and the thought sent a thrill through her as she contemplated her vulnerability.

The next thing to happen took her completely by surprise, however. The tattooist picked up a china pot from the shelf next to the trolley and began stirring the contents with a thick brush. Then he removed the brush from the mug and began applying a thick, soapy foam to Lisa's pubis. Only then did she realise what was happening.

She was being shaved!

She gave a cry of protest, tugging at her bonds, but there was nothing she could do. The man went on applying the foam down the length of her slit, rubbing it into the short hairs. Then he produces a long, shining razor and began running it up and down a leather strop.

He leaned forward over Lisa, placing a hand on the brass ring that penetrated her sex lips, and began to scrape at her bush. Lisa gazed down between her breasts, watching him work. With each stroke, the razor pushed a heap of foam and dark hairs before it, leaving behind a pale, smooth tract of skin. She had been shaved once before, by the cruel tribe who had attached the ring to her, but since then the hair had grown back. Now she was to be bare down there again, and her heart sank as she contemplated how sluttish a shaved crotch would look.

He worked his way over her mound and down between her legs, denuding her of every wisp of pubic hair. When he had finished he produced a jar of cream and began working it into her flesh. The slight burning sensation and distinctive smell told her that it was a depilation cream, designed to kill the roots of her pubic hair, thus ensuring that she would be hairless down there for many months.

He left the cream on for five minutes, before wiping it off. Then he turned to the doctor, who examined Lisa's crotch closely, and nodded. He picked up the needle.

At first Lisa couldn't see how he was going to make the mark on her. After all, her arms were drawn up in an awkward position. He would have to undo one of her wrists in order to do it properly. Then he pulled a small pen from his pocket and, leaning over her once more, drew a letter S on her pubis, just above and slightly to the right of her open crotch.

"No!" she cried. "Not down there! Please not down there!"

"Be quiet, eight zero three," said the doctor.

"But why are you marking me there? All the others were marked on their arms."

"It was a special instruction. Remember what the law states."

Lisa stared at him for a second, then her jaw dropped as

the import of what he was saying sank in. By law, she knew that the mark of her slavery must be on display at all times. If they marked her there, it meant never being able to wear anything below the waist again, whether it be skirt, trousers or panties. Wherever she went her vagina would be seen by all. And it would be shaved too, a clear indication of her promiscuity. It was the cruellest of jokes, and one which would mean permanent shame for the lovely youngster.

"No," she cried again. But already the tattooist's instrument was buzzing and, as he bent over her, she felt the first sharp prick of the needle penetrating her flesh.

Chapter 9

Lisa was led back toward the cell block, scarcely able to take in what they had done to her. She glanced down at her naked body, her mind in a whirl. There, on her shaved pubis, just above where the brass ring gleamed, was her mark, the tattoo that told all and sundry of her status as a slave. And she was forbidden to cover it. That small, black letter S was to be visible at all times. It was the law! She thought of the other slaves, with the mark on their forearms. It was easy for them to keep it visible, but for her it would be a never-ending nightmare.

The guards took her into the block and down the stone cells, throwing open the heavily barred door. Lisa hugged her hands to her private parts, her face scarlet as the rest of the slaves watched her being led past. Until now she had, at least, been able to cover her body with the dress. Now, though, they could see that she was nude, a small, naked white girl amongst the rough black men whose fate she now shared. The men laughed and whistled at the sight she made, reaching through the bars for her as she passed.

The guards came to the end of the passage and Lisa waited for them to unlock the door of her solitary cell and imprison her once again. Instead they went to the door of another cage, which already had four men in it. Lisa watched in horror as they swung the door open, then beckoned for her to enter.

"No! That's my cell," she protested, pointing to the empty one at the end.

The leader of the guards simply laughed. "In here now," he said. "With other slaves."

"No," she said again. "They'll..."

"What will they do?"

Lisa blushed "You know what," she said quietly.

"You go in cell now!"

"But you must know what will happen to me."

The guard guffawed. "You slave now, eight zero three. I no care. You dirty slut. Fuck anyone you told. Now go in cell."

Taking her by the arms, he thrust her inside, closing the door behind her. Then the guards were gone, tramping back up the passage and slamming the door to the cell block.

Lisa stood in the middle of the cell, her hands clutched to her breasts and sex, eyeing her cellmates. They were standing all around her grinning broadly, and she knew at once that they had been expecting her to be placed with them. She wondered what had gone on between them and the guards whilst she had been being tattooed.

"Show us your mark," said the man facing her. His English was broken, but there was an authority in his voice that sent a shiver through the youngster. She backed away.

"Show it to us, little English slut."

This time the voice had come from behind her, and she turned to see the second of her cellmates eyeing her.

"Please leave me alone," she said.

"Show it to us." This time there was no mistaking the menace in his voice.

Lisa looked round at them, then at the men in the adjoining cells, all of whom were watching. She glanced down at herself, wishing that they had at least left her some concession to her modesty. To be naked amongst these fully-clothed ruffians was awful.

All at once the full import of her situation came to her. She was about to be gang-banged by these men. She, Lisa Carling, shy young computer programmer from London was standing naked, her pubis shaved, in a dirty African prison cell amongst a gang of black ruffians. And, whether she liked it or not, she was about to be laid out on the floor of the squalid cell and fucked by four of these rough strangers, whose names she would never know, whilst others watched her degradation. It was scarcely imaginable, but it was true.

Yet, along with the fear and dread she felt, there was a stronger feeling. One that made her blush with shame. Without warning, the idea of being taken by these men was exciting the perverse slut inside her, an alter-ego that her ordeals since being enslaved so often had brought to the fore. It was a feeling that brought a flow of wetness to her sex and made her nipples suddenly harden into brown knobs. To Lisa's surprise she realised that she had a totally perverse desire to let all the male slaves see her body without clothes. Somehow, a kind of natural defence mechanism had turned itself on, bringing on a strong sense of arousal in the young beauty. For some incomprehensible reason she found herself wanting to flaunt her nudity, and to allow the men to feast their eyes on her breasts and cunt that she had been trying so desperately to cover. In a strange way, her body was telling her that her safety lay in submitting to these men's desires.

Slowly, her eyes still cast down, Lisa lowered her left arm, revealing her lovely young breasts to the watching men. Her face glowed as they whistled and shouted at the sight of her protruding teats, yet she found herself pressing her shoulders back, feeling the nipples harden still more as she did so under the hungry eyes of those watching. She glanced round at the men, her stomach churning. Then, with a sigh, she uncovered her sex, opening her legs and thrusting her hips forward. She stood, red-faced and naked, her hands hanging by her side, sensing the men's cocks hardening in their pants as they recognised that the naked youngster was surrendering herself to them.

"That is better," said the man in front of her. "You are ready to be fucked?"

"I..." Lisa was unable to admit to the base desires within her.

"You know what is about to happen?"

"Yes."

"Then lie on the floor, little slave, and show us what is ours to take."

Lisa stared at the man for a moment as his words sank in. She knew that she was acting like a cheap whore, giving herself to these rough black slaves to do with as they wanted. But she knew too that the alternative was to be raped. Forced to be fucked by these strong men. Better to give herself willingly. To bow to the inevitable, even if it meant revealing her lascivious nature to them, and admitting to her desires.

Slowly, to the cheers and whistles of the men watching, Lisa lowered herself to the filthy floor of the cell. The concrete was hard and uncomfortable, but she had no doubt that it was there that she would be taken. She hesitated momentarily. All the men were watching her, and she knew what they wanted to see. Taking a deep breath, the naked, wanton slave closed her eyes. Then, slowly, she spread her legs, the knowledge that they would all clearly see the wetness inside her vagina sending a shudder of pure desire through her small frame. Once her thighs were wide apart, and she was offering them the most intimate view she was able, she gazed down between the valley of her breasts and swallowed hard.

"You can fuck me now," she said quietly ".Just take me and do what you want with me. But please be as gentle with me as you can."

She watched as the powerful black man reached for his belt, undoing it in a single movement. As his pants dropped to his ankles she got her first view of his cock, a great rampant pole that jutted from his groin, the swollen end twitching slightly. He ran his fingers along the length of his shaft, grinning down at the beautiful youngster stretched out before him, submissively awaiting her inevitable ravishment at his hands. Lisa looked round at the other three, all of whom were gathered round her. The cells had gone quiet now, all eyes on the pale, naked girl.

The man dropped to his knees between her legs, his gaze fixed on the gash of her sex. As he leant forward over her, Lisa found herself raising her hips, suddenly anxious to feel his great rod inside her.

He penetrated her in a single movement, a thrust that brought a gasp of passion from her as his long, thick cock

70

entered her, plunging into her wet vagina and burying itself deep within her. If Lisa had intended to disguise her passions, she knew now that her plan would fail as she cried out with pure pleasure, bringing a cheer from those watching as they saw her lasciviousness.

He began fucking her at once, thrusting into her with such force that her entire body was shaken, her breasts bouncing back and forth, much to the delight of those watching. He reached up and grasped hold of her breast, his fingers closing over the hard nipple and tweaking it, bringing a whimper of pain from the youngster. It was an extraordinary onslaught, bringing Lisa an unimaginable pleasure. The muscles of her sex flexed of their own accord, caressing his massive member. He shouted something to those watching and, from the way they cheered she guessed he was telling his companions of the way her body was responding to him.

Not for the first time, Lisa wondered at the perverse way her body reacted to what he was doing. Any normal girl would have been overcome with the pain and degradation of her treatment, yet she was alive with desire, her hips thrusting up to him, her backside slapping down against the dirty, unyielding concrete of the cell's floor. She gazed into his eyes and saw the amusement in them as he realised that she was responding with such desire to his treatment. Then his eyes seemed to glaze and his body suddenly stiffened.

All at once her cunt was filled with his seed as he ejaculated, the hot fluid shooting to the very entrance of her uterus. The sensation was too much for Lisa and she climaxed with a scream of pleasure that echoed about the cell block. Another cheer resounded from the men as they realised she had come. The man went on thrusting into her

71

until he was spent, and she was left moaning and writhing on the floor as he withdrew and rose to his feet.

Lisa's respite was very short indeed, though. Already another of her cell-mates had dropped his pants and she cried aloud as she felt a second thick cock violate her most private place. Once again it was the roughest of fuckings, the man pinning her arms above her head with one massive hand whilst he took her, his other hand mauling her firm breasts. Lisa stared round at the other slaves, all of whose faces were pressed to the bars of their cells as they watched the young white beauty give herself totally to their companions, her naked body spread before them, her hips thrusting up against those of her ravisher. A sudden surge of lust ran through her as she thought of the sight she must make, fucking like some common whore with these scruffy, unkempt men, her own shameful reaction obvious to all.

The man came suddenly, the force of his ejaculation if anything even stronger than Lisa's previous lover, and once again triggering an extraordinary orgasm in the lustful youngster. Then he was off her and the third of her cellmates was ramming his rampant penis into her.

By the time the fourth man had finished with her, Lisa was panting with exhaustion, her sex lips still convulsing with her orgasm, forcing gobs of sticky white fluid out onto her thighs as she lay back on the floor, her chest heaving, her breasts reddened by the continued kneading of the men.

She raised herself up onto her elbows, her firm breasts quivering as she looked about her. It had been an ordeal, albeit one that had rewarded her with four delicious orgasms, but now they would let her rest, wouldn't they? It was a surprise and a shock, therefore, when she felt her arms being grabbed as the men hauled her to her feet. She looked up at them questioningly. Surely they didn't want her again already? But they weren't trying to fuck her. Instead they were carrying her toward the bars that separated their cell from the one next door. Then, with a shock, she realised that her ordeal was far from over. The cells were separated by vertical bars set about five inches apart, and already the men in the next-door cell were reaching through for the helpless young English girl.

They thrust her hard against the bars, so that her breasts projected through. At once there were hands all over her body, squeezing her breasts and groping between her legs, penetrating her sex and making her gasp as they frigged her. More hands grabbed hold of her arms and she felt leather wrapped about her wrists. They were winding their belts around them and attaching them high up to the bars. Below her legs were being pulled apart and more belts were used to immobilise them. She was quite helpless now, her naked body stretched wide and held tight against the bars. She tugged at her bonds, but in vain. Already the man in front of her had dropped his pants and was closing in on her.

She tried to pull away from the bars. Then came a loud thwack and a surge of pain as one of the men in her own cell brought his belt down across the pert globes of her backside, laying a thick red stripe across her bare cheeks. Knowing it was hopeless she surrendered, pressing her pubis against the cage and allowing the man in the next-door cell to thrust his cock into her vagina and begin to fuck her.

He took her with the same enthusiasm and lack of passion as had her new cellmates. Once he had come inside her he stood aside. Lisa braced herself to be penetrated for a sixth time, but instead the man climbed onto a horizontal

73

bar that ran across just above her waist, and she found herself facing his twitching erection. She hesitated, unwilling to submit, but another stinging stroke across her behind with the belt told her she had no choice. Glancing up at the man's face she nodded, then opened her mouth, allowing him to press his swollen knob between her lips. Then she began to suck as he jabbed his hips forward, her tongue licking at his shining glans.

When he came, his spunk was copious, filling her mouth and dribbling from her lips down onto her breasts as she struggled to gulp it down. Moments later he had gone, and she was being fucked again, her helpless body banging against the bars.

When the men in the next-door cell had all had her, Lisa was unstrapped and moved to the other side, where her bondage was re-applied. At once more cocks were thrust into the mouth and vagina of the powerless girl, whilst the men in her own cell continued to thrash her bare backside with their belts when she showed any sign of flagging. Lisa's mind was in turmoil as the men took turns to enjoy her exquisite charms, orgasm after orgasm coursing through her as her body responded to the men's treatment. Only when all had had her and she had lost count of her own climaxes was she allowed to rest, stretched out on the floor of the cell, her spunk-spattered body gasping for breath.

He rest was short-lived, however, as the door to the block clanged open and voices began shouting. Lisa raised her head and glanced about her. The men in the cell had all moved to the back and were standing with their hands clasped behind their heads and their legs apart. With a shock the girl realised that the guards had come back.

As she struggled to her feet they unlocked the cell and, taking hold of her arms, dragged her out. Lisa stumbled between them, trying to keep her feet as they pulled her along. They took her into their guard room, slamming the door behind them. Out the back was a bathroom where a bath stood filled with cold water. They threw her into this, then stood watching as she tried to clean the dirt and semen from her. No sooner had she finished than they dragged her soaking wet form from the water and back into the guard room, where they thrust her up against the wall. She immediately adopted the same stance as the other slaves had done. There were four guards, all burly men in khaki uniform, with stripes of rank on their arms. They stood round her, their eyes fixed hungrily on her firm breasts and the bare slit of her sex. Lisa said nothing as she stood, staring in front of her, the water dripping from her smooth, pale flesh.

The tallest of the four, a man with three stripes, spoke in a harsh voice.

"I see the other scum have made use of you," he said.

Lisa remained silent, her eyes cast down.

"Go and stand at that table!" He indicated a heavy table that stood in the centre of the room. Warily Lisa made her way to it.

"Stand close."

She moved as close as she was able, so that the hard edge of the wood was against her bare pubis.

"Bend over and spread your legs."

Lisa's heart was beating hard as she obeyed the command. Was she due for another beating? The wood felt rough and hard against her bare breasts as she prostrated herself and moved her legs apart, displaying her most intimate parts and also the livid traces of her beating.

A hand moved down between her buttocks and paused over her anus, probing it in a way that brought a sharp intake of breath from the youngster.

"I see those scum left this hole alone, as they were ordered," grunted the man. "Now it is our turn to enjoy our privileges."

All at once Lisa felt something wet and cool strike her buttocks. It was the man's saliva. He began to rub it into the tight star of muscles that were her anus, and she realised what was to happen. She closed her eyes, unwilling to meet those of her other three captors as she heard the senior warden unzip his trousers.

Something hard and hot began to probe at Lisa's nether hole, then press insistently against it. Lisa gritted her teeth, gradually relaxing the muscles of her sphincter as the man pressed harder. It was not the first time the youngster had been buggered, but there was always an initial pain as her rear hole was opened up by whoever was taking her.

She gave a cry as he penetrated her, his solid pole sliding deeper and deeper into her rectum with every jab of his hips. He pressed himself in until she could feel his pubic hairs against the soft, tender flesh of her behind. Then he began to move, thrusting himself into her and banging her body against the hard, unyielding table.

Lisa's sex was pressed against the edge of the wood, and the rough surface began to chafe her clitoris, sending shocks of excitement through her as the man continued his onslaught. Somehow the thrill of the table top rubbing against her love bud, combined with the extraordinary sensation of having her rectum stretched by a rampant cock were conspiring to turn Lisa on yet again, and she began to grunt with passion as the onslaught continued.

When she felt her backside fill with hot spunk, Lisa too let go, crying aloud as yet another orgasm engulfed her. Then the guard was withdrawing and the second man was undoing his pants.

The four of them took it in turns to bugger her, ramming their thick cocks into her backside, the friction of her clitoris against the table edge bringing yet more orgasms to the lustful youngster as her ordeal seemed to go on and on.

At last, though, the guards too were sated, and they grabbed their beautiful young captive and dragged her out of the room.

By the time they dumped her back in her own cell, Lisa was totally exhausted, flopping down on the floor dirty and dishevelled. Despite the shouting of the other slaves she fell at once into a deep sleep.

Chapter 10

The cell was oddly silent when Lisa woke. She blinked her eyes, staring about her as if in a daze. For a second she couldn't remember where she was. Then she looked down at her nude body and saw the tattoo in that most intimate place, and the awful truth hit her. She was now officially a slave, and unable ever to wear anything to cover her below the waist for as long as her enslavement lasted.

She stared across at the other cells. They were empty. Her fellow slaves must have been taken out in the early morning, leaving her alone. So deeply had she slept that she had heard nothing.

All at once she became aware that something had woken her. Somewhere a sound had aroused her from her slumbers, though she had no idea what it had been. Then, with a start, she realised that she was not alone. Slowly she turned her head and caught sight of a pair of bare feet right beside her. She glanced up at the figure standing over her, and gave a little gasp of recognition.

It was the young boy who the doctor had struck so hard when he had caught him spying on her medical examination. He was standing, his hands on his hips, staring down at her prostrate body. With the doctor present he had been cowed and apologetic. Now there was an air of quiet arrogance about him as he stood over her, a thin cane held in his hand. Though little more than a boy, there was an air about him that Lisa found intimidating and, despite her superior age, she felt his power as he prodded at her with the cane.

"You get up, English slut," he ordered.

Slowly Lisa rose to her feet. Her limbs ached from her treatment the night before, and her backside still stung from the blows that the men had rained on her. She stretched herself, blushing at the way the boy studied her body. She glanced down at it, noting the streaks of semen that ran down her legs from her sex and backside. The boy grinned at her discomfort.

"You have one sexy night," he said. "How many men fuck you?"

"I don't know," she said quietly.

"You stand proper."

Lisa placed her hands behind her head and opened her legs, aware that the stance drew attention to the gleaming ring that still pierced her down there. The young man reached down and fingered it, rubbing it back and forth against her clitoris and watching as she struggled to control her reaction.

"My job to clean cells," he said. "You must help me."

"Me?"

78

"Sure. Look all this spunk."

He pointed to a pool of semen on the floor. Lisa knew that it must have leaked from her during the night. Then he pointed across at the cell in which she had been placed the night before, and she saw similar wet patches, notably where she had been tied to the cell bars.

"You clean up spunk, slut."

She sighed. "Yes Sir. Where is there a cloth?"

"No cloth. Use tongue."

"What?"

"You lick up."

"But I..."

Whack!

The cane came down hard across her thighs, making her gasp with pain and leaving a thin stripe that ran round to her backside.

"You lick, now!"

Lisa gazed at the boy. He was holding the stick threateningly, and she knew he wouldn't hesitate to deliver another blow if she disobeyed. She looked down at the floor. Then, slowly, she dropped down to her knees.

"Legs wide," ordered the young cleaner.

Lisa spread her knees as wide apart as she was able. She knew this granted the boy a perfect view of her anus and sex, and her face glowed as she lowered her face toward the pool of white liquid. She protruded her tongue and lapped at it. As she did so her nipples grazed against the ground, sending an unexpected thrill through her. The taste of the spunk reminded her of fellating the slave through the bars the night before, and a sudden shiver of excitement shook her as she slurped down the fluid, swallowing hard.

She licked up the last of the pool, then moved across to

a second one beside it. Once again she prostrated herself. As she lapped at the sperm she felt the boy run the cane up the tight skin of her bottom. Then she gave a start as he pressed it against her anus and, twisting it slightly, penetrated her rear hole.

"Lick," he ordered, twisting the cane again and sending an extraordinary sensation through the naked young slave.

Lisa licked the floor clean of the spunk, then looked up quizzically at her tormentor.

"The other cell," he ordered.

She rose slowly to her feet, the cane still embedded in her rectum. She placed her hands behind her head, thrusting her bare breasts forward as she knew she must. Then she walked awkwardly out of her cell and across to the one where she had been the subject of that extraordinary gangbang the previous night. The grinning boy used the cane to guide his hapless captive across to the middle, then she was on her knees once more, thrusting her backside up at the stick that penetrated her so intimately, her solid nipples again brushing against the rough surface. She began once again to use her tongue to clean the men's sperm from the floor.

Lisa moved about the cell, licking up the spunk from the floor and bars of the cell with the boy behind her, urging her on with the cane, making sure that every drop was swallowed by the beautiful young captive.

She lapped up the last pool of sperm and swallowed it, then she looked up at her young warder. He laughed.

"You like to eat spunk, I think, little English slave. Now you taste a black man's cock. You like to suck cock too, I think."

Lisa said nothing, simply giving a little groan of relief as he slid his stick from her rectum.

80

"Stand up!"

She obeyed, rising slowly to her feet, noting how her knees were stained with the dirt from the floor. The youth was not tall, but still he seemed to tower over the young beauty as he reached out and fondled her firm breasts, making the nipples still harder as he squeezed them.

He took her arm. "Come."

He led her across to where a bench stood close to the wall. He straddled the bench, lowering himself onto his back.

"Kneel down."

Lisa obeyed, looking down at him as he stretched out, his hands tucked behind his head.

"Take out my cock, English slave."

Lisa reached out her hand. He wore a pair of dirty, tattered shorts, the fly being held closed by an assortment of odd buttons. She undid them one by one, feeling the way his strong young cock pressed against the material. As she unfastened the last button his rampant member sprang out, standing stiff and black from his groin. Lisa ran her fingers up its length, feeling it twitch as she did so.

"Suck me."

Lisa looked into his eyes, wondering how it was that she should be subservient to this scruffy youngster. Then she glanced down at her bare pubis and the tattoo that decorated it, and she knew how. Slowly she leaned forward and, opening her mouth, took him inside.

She began to suck him, making him grunt with arousal as she took him deep into her mouth, licking at the smooth flesh of his knob. She worked her head up and down, her breasts bouncing as she did so, the nipples standing out proud as they brushed against him. She glanced sideways at him, noting the expression of deep concentration on his

81

face as he thrust his hips up at her. She slipped a hand inside his shorts and began to caress his heavy balls, squeezing the tight sac as she sucked at him, bringing fresh groans from his lips.

All at once he pushed her face away, and she looked up at him, questioningly.

"Sit across me," he ordered. "Put my cock inside you."

The order brought a tight knot to the pit of Lisa's stomach. As usual she was at a loss to comprehend the way in which her body responded to such an outrageous demand. She should be disgusted at the prospect of letting this scruffy youngster invade her lovely body. Yet already she could feel a warm wetness invading her crotch as she stared at his glistening tool. Slowly she rose to her feet and, raising her left leg, straddled him, so that she was staring down at his prone form. Then she moved forward, so that her crotch was directly above his groin, and began to squat down.

She gave a little moan as she felt his stiff knob brush up against the soft flesh of her nether lips. She reached down and grasped hold of his shaft. Pressing it against the entrance to her vagina, she began to force herself down onto it. For a second her flesh resisted. Then, with a gasp, she felt him slip into her. His thick cock rubbed deliciously against the walls of her sex as she forced him ever deeper into her, going lower and lower until she was sitting astride him, his cock buried deep inside her.

He grinned at her, his hands still tucked behind his head as he allowed her to do the work. She required no order from him for what she did next, beginning to move her body up and down, letting his cock slide back and forth inside her, fucking him as hard as she was able.

As she did so, she felt her own arousal increase with every stroke. Despite her surroundings and her arrogant

82

young partner, Lisa was reacting as she always did to having a thick, throbbing cock inside her, and she began to moan aloud as she worked her body up and down, her firm young breasts bouncing with every stroke. The young man lay back, scarcely moving, but the expression on his face and the twitching of his stiff knob told her that he too was highly aroused, and that his orgasm was not far off.

All at once a movement caught Lisa's eye, and she looked up to see that someone had entered the room and was watching them. To her dismay she saw that it was the doctor, standing just a few yards away, watching as she rammed her body down against her partner's.

Lisa was instantly overcome with shame. Merely being caught in such a totally intimate act with the young cleaner was bad enough, but to be straddling him and actively fucking him whilst he lay beneath her was mortifying beyond belief.

At that moment, the young man gave a grunt, and she felt his semen spurting into her vagina. Unable to control herself, Lisa came too, a cry ringing from her lips as the exquisite pleasure of orgasm enveloped her. She thrust her pubis down against his, her hips gyrating lewdly as she gasped with arousal. Her face glowed scarlet as she contemplated the exhibition she was making of herself in front of the doctor.

It was a short time before Lisa was able to regain control of herself, and to cease her writhing as she sat there, impaled on the young man's cock. Only then did she raise her eyes to look at the doctor again, and was shocked to see that he was no longer alone. One of the guards had just walked in behind him and was standing, his mouth agape as he took in the scene that met his eyes.

He only stood for a moment, though, then he strode

forward.

Swish! Whack!

Lisa cried aloud as his cane descended across her bare breasts, leaving a thin, cruel line across the soft young flesh. Then he pushed her aside, sending her sprawling to the floor as he dragged the youth to his feet.

Swish! Whack!

Swish! Whack!

This time it was the boy's turn to cry out as the guard laid into him with his cane, landing blow after blow as he fled from the room, struggling to pull up his shorts with the guard close behind him.

The doctor moved forward to stand over Lisa. The youngster glanced down at her naked body, her nipples and breasts streaked with dirt, the red stripe that now decorated her succulent breasts darkening even as she watched. She rose slowly to her feet, feeling the youth's sperm trickle from her as she did so. The doctor shook his head.

"You're not supposed to fuck with the domestic staff," he said. "I reckon you've just earned yourself a few more stripes across your pretty behind."

"I... I thought..."

"You thought you could screw with whoever you fancy? Well now you're officially a slave you screw with who your master fancies, and as long as you're with these people, the guards are your masters."

"So that young man..."

"Is just a cleaner. The lowest form of life here. Still, you seemed to be enjoying it."

Lisa said nothing, her face red with shame.

"Now," went on the doctor. "You'd better get cleaned up. You're leaving for the city in ten minutes."

84

Chapter 11

When Lisa emerged from the cell block, the rest of the slaves were already assembled, standing quietly in lines, their wrists shackled in front of them and attached to long chains that strung them together in groups of about a dozen. A cheer went up as the naked youngster emerged into the sunlight, still showing the evidence of her seduction by the boy.

There was a metal tub filled with water beside the parade ground and they took her to this.

"You wash," ordered the guard.

Lisa stepped into the water. Like that in the guardroom the night before, it was cold, and she shivered as she bent down and picked up the large cake of soap that lay beside it. Then, much to the delight of the catcalling slaves, she was obliged to wash herself, cleaning the grime and sperm from her pretty young body.

When she had finished, she stepped, still wet, from the tub. At once her guard grabbed her and dragged her to the side of the parade ground, where a rail ran along about three feet above the ground. He ordered her to grasp this and bend forward, kicking her legs apart as she did so. Then he tapped her backside gently with the cane, and she knew she was about to be punished for the episode with the cleaner. She glanced back over her shoulder at her fellow slaves, all of whom were looking in her direction, their faces wreathed in grins.

Swish! Whack!
Swish! Whack!
Swish! Whack!

He laid three stripes in quick succession across Lisa's pert behind, each stinging blow bringing a cheer from those watching. The tears ran down Lisa's face, mingled with the water that still dripped from her as she was pulled to her feet once more. Then they dragged her across to the front of one of the lines of slaves.

The guard produced a pair of manacles and she held out her arms to him. Instead he made her turn, securing her wrists behind her. This puzzled Lisa, since the other slaves all had their wrists attached to the chain that joined them. Then the guard pulled out a narrower chain, like a dog's lead and slipped it around the joining chain. He beckoned to the young beauty to step forward and she did so, still not certain what was to happen. Then he reached for her cunt ring, and she understood.

He threaded the smaller chain through the ring, taking the opportunity to touch her up, his fingers probing at her vagina. Then he fastened the chain with a small, strong padlock and stood back.

Lisa had never felt so exposed, standing there at the front of a line of grinning black men, they all clad in shorts and shirts, she totally nude, her pale skin contrasting with that of the men who surrounded her. She looked down at the chain that attached her so intimately to them. It was just long enough to allow her to walk comfortably as long as she stayed close to her fellow prisoners. But she feared the way the chain would affect her when she walked. The ring chafed against her most sensitive place as it was. The chain would make the friction worse, and already she could feel her love bud swelling and the wetness beginning to form inside her.

The gates to the prison were swung open, and an order was shouted. The first of the lines of slaves moved forward, shuffling out of the compound whilst another moved up behind. Then it was Lisa's turn, the guard poking at her with his cane to make her step forward. As they marched through the gates Lisa threw a glance behind her at the compound. Somehow, even in there amongst the men, she had felt some degree of protection. Now, though, she was walking on the public highway totally naked, her firm breasts bouncing in full view as she walked along, her pretty backside showing the marks of her punishment to all and sundry.

There were six gangs of slaves, with a guard assigned to each. The guards all wielded their canes with enthusiasm, and Lisa was careful to keep up the pace demanded, not wanting her pale flesh marked again. At the guards' waists were large calibre pistols, and they made sure that the slaves could all see these weapons, so that no attempt to escape was made.

They walked on for more than two hours along dusty roads. Fortunately for Lisa the road was quiet, with hardly anybody on it, though those she did encounter stopped and stared at the vision of beauty that marched past them, joined in the most intimate manner possible to the queue of scruffy men behind her. Then the traffic began to increase, and she realised with a sinking feeling that they were approaching a town.

It was quite a large town, and as they reached the outskirts the people came out onto the streets to jeer at the slaves. At the sight of Lisa, their jeers turned to shouts of laughter, and the youngster's face glowed as she marched past them, her eyes cast down. As they moved further into the town the crowds thickened, and Lisa's shame deepened. In all the ordeals she had been through since her adventures had started, she had never been naked in so public a place as this. To be forced to walk completely nude down a busy street, her hands trapped behind her, her breasts sex and backside on open display was like her worst nightmare. Worse still was the way she was attached to the chain by the gleaming ring that pierced her sex, a ring that shone with wetness as the rubbing of the chain against her sex kept her in a state of continuous arousal.

The narrow street down which they were walking suddenly opened out into a large, busy market square, where traders sat on mats on the ground, selling their wares. All around were rows of vegetables, piles of eggs, bags of brightly-coloured spices and cages full of live chickens. The slaves were led to the centre of the square, where stood a number of sturdy posts. Each line of slaves had their chain locked to one of the posts, then three of the guards repaired to a small hotel on the edge of the square, leaving the other men on guard.

The crowds gathered round the slaves, laughing and jeering. Lisa, naturally, came in for particular attention. It was clear that none of the townsfolk had ever seen a white slave before, and the fact that she was a naked young woman was of particular interest. The guards kept the people from actually touching the prisoners, but they came as close as they were able. The men made rude and suggestive gestures at the youngster whilst many of the women spat at her, their spittle trickling down her breasts and stomach. For herself, Lisa kept her gaze fixed on the ground, though the continued attention of the onlookers was sparking an arousal within her that she was barely able to control, the thought of being seen naked by so many awakening the familiar exhibitionist tendencies within her.

They stood in the square for nearly an hour whilst the guards drank in the hotel. Then those who had been drinking emerged and allowed the other three to go and slake their thirst. One of the emerging guards made his way toward her, clearly affected by the alcohol he had imbibed. Lisa watched him approach with some trepidation, aware that his gaze was upon her.

He stopped in front of her, his eyes travelling up and down her body. Lisa did not recognise him as one of the men who had taken her in the backside the night before, but the expression on his face told her that he desired her. He moved close and placed an arm about her waist, making her shiver at his proximity.

The crowd had watched with some interest as he had approached the young beauty, and he soon noticed their attention, beginning to shout to them. Whilst, as usual, Lisa had no idea what was being said, she knew it was about her from the way he acted. He reached up for her breasts, indicating the bright red stripe that had been laid across them in the cell block. He bounced them up and down, pointing to her erect nipples, much to the delight of those watching. Lisa gritted her teeth whilst this went on, trying hard to fight down the excitement that his treatment was arousing within her. He toyed with her breasts, making the nipples harden even more, tweaking them between finger and thumb until Lisa gave a cry of pain.

He turned her and made her bend forward. Then she felt his fingers tracing the weals that decorated her backside and the crowd laughed aloud as he wielded his stick as if beating her again. Then he made her straighten and turn to face them once more.

"Open your legs, slave,"

The words were spoken quietly right beside her ear. Lisa looked out at the crowd, all of whom were staring at her, the women glaring, the men laughing. She felt the guard's boot kick against her ankles and, reluctantly moved her feet apart.

89

"Wider, or I thrash your arse again."

Lisa moved her feet again, this time spreading them wide, aware of how visible the gash of her sex was since her pubic hair had been removed.

"Push your hips. Let them see your cunt."

The words sent a shiver through her, but despite herself, she felt a sudden heat in her belly as she thought of what was being asked of her. As usual, she was unable to understand why it was that exhibiting her most private parts excited her so. She closed her eyes. Then, bending her knees, she pressed her hips forward, leaning back against the guard and displaying her open sex to all those watching. A gasp went up from the crowd, and Lisa's colour deepened as she thought of the exhibition she was making of herself. She, Lisa Carling, demure little English girl who, until only a few months ago was innocent and celibate, standing stark naked amongst this crowd of dark-skinned strangers and flaunting her cunt to them like some cheap whore. She glanced down at herself. Her nipples were like brown knobs now, her clitoris hard, a sheen of moisture coating her sex lips. She knew that all these things must be obvious to those watching, and that her arousal was as public as her nudity.

The guard began toying with her breasts once more. Then, even as the crowd was expressing its astonishment at her wantonness, she felt one of his hands slide down her ribs and across her belly, inching ever further toward he most private place. She knew she should stop him, protest against the liberties he was taking, but her excitement was overshadowing her shame now, and she felt the muscles in her sex convulse in anticipation, forcing a small bead of moisture onto her thigh.

When his finger found her clitoris she gave a little cry

of desire, a shudder running through her as he began to rub it. His hands were large and rough, and the sensation they gave her was exquisite, so that she found herself pressing her pubis forward even further, her body consumed with desire as his fingers probed her.

He thrust two fingers into her hot sex, making her cry aloud once more as he forced the lips apart, giving the crowd the most intimate view imaginable of her gaping love hole. Then he began to frig her, his thumb brushing against her clitoris as he pressed his fingers deep into her. Lisa was lost now, and she knew it. He had taken her beyond shame, and had rekindled those base instincts within her that transformed her into the lascivious slut that was her alter ego. It was almost as if she had a dual personality, on the one hand the demure and modest little English rose, on the other the insatiable wanton whose desires could be aroused by any man, and whose body she would give gladly to accommodate a stiff cock, no matter whose it was.

He began frigging her hard, his fingers making a squelching sound as they moved in and out of her sopping vagina. Lisa had her head resting on his shoulder, her body arched backwards, her hips thrust forward in a pose of total abandonment, her breath coming in short grunts as she ground her hips down against his hand.

She came with a cry, her juices leaking onto her thighs as her sex muscles contracted about his fingers. Her breasts shook deliciously as her orgasm overcame her, much to the approval of the men watching. He kept his fingers firmly embedded inside her, still mauling her breast as he held her body close to his, continuing to frig her as her body shook with passion.

She came down slowly, the excitement ebbing from her as the reality of what she had been doing slowly struck her.

She looked about at the sea of grinning faces in front of her, suddenly overcome with shame at her lasciviousness.

He withdrew his fingers, wiping them on her belly, making silvery streaks across her skin. Then he laughed aloud, slapping her backside hard with his hand before swaggering off, leaving the young slave red-faced and exhausted to face the jeering crowd.

Chapter 12

The journey back to the city took them two days. Two days of slogging along dusty roads whilst the crowds jeered, hurled missiles and spat at the unfortunate slaves. Lisa was, unsurprisingly, often the butt of their derision, the naked young English girl standing out amongst the strong black men who surrounded her. Men and women alike would walk alongside her, laughing and pointing as she tried to avoid their gazes.

They stopped for the night in a small town, not unlike the one where they had broken for lunch. The slaves were herded into the town square and shackled as before, after which they were fed bowls of thin stew. The men were then given blankets and settled down on the ground to sleep. Lisa, however, was unshackled and taken into the hostel where the guards were staying. Once again they split into groups of three, one group keeping watch whilst the others relaxed. Lisa was made to wait on those in the hostel, delivering their food and drink to the table. Afterwards she was taken upstairs to a small bedroom where she was tied spreadeagled to the bed with strong, coarse ropes. Once she was helpless the men took it in turns to fuck her, occasionally turning her onto her face so that they could gain access to her backside. Then the guard changed over, and she was forced to undergo the ordeal again with the second set. She had very little sleep that night, as the guards returned to her bed time and again, obliging her to satisfy their sexual desires with her mouth, vagina and anus.

The next day she was taken back to her group, her naked flesh streaked with semen, much to the amusement of her fellow slaves. Then she was forced to march on, the evidence of her ravishment leaking from her as she plodded along.

They reached the outskirts of the city in the early afternoon, but still faced more than an hour's tramp through the busy streets whilst the inhabitants turned out to mock them. For Lisa this was the worst part of the journey, as she made her way through the busy metropolis, her breasts and sex bared to all. Occasionally a car would slow and a white face would peer from the window, their eyes wide at the sight of the girl. Somehow, for Lisa, this was doubly shaming, and her face glowed red as her fellow countrymen saw her degradation.

They arrived back at the ministry building from which they had first set out as the shadows were beginning to lengthen. There Akran was waiting for her. He grinned broadly when he saw he tattoo.

"Mr Bulcher know where best place is to mark you," he said.

Lisa said nothing.

He took her out to the truck. This time there was no dress to cover her, she was simply shackled to the roof of the cabin, then driven out of the compound. She clung on tight to steady herself as Akran drove through the busy streets. All about her people were laughing and pointing at her and she longed to get back to the relative shelter offered by her cell.

They came to a halt at a busy crossroads, and once again Lisa was obliged to endure the mockery of those about her. Then a car on her left caught her eye. There was something oddly familiar about the smart saloon, and she found herself glancing in at the driver. As she did so, her heart sank.

It was the woman who had stopped and spoken to her when she had been with Kimuni and his friends the previous week. Now, once again, the woman's shocked gaze rested on her lovely naked body and the colour in her face deepened as she considered the sight she must make, standing up on the back of the truck and baring all. As she watched, the woman wound down her window and shouted something at Akran, who replied in a deferential manner. The woman had spoken in the local tongue, but Lisa had managed to make out Bulcher's name in Akran's reply. Now she stood, the woman's eyes burning into her as she prayed for the lights to change.

As they moved off at last, the woman's car remained alongside them for a time. Then, to Lisa's relief, it peeled off to the left and was lost to view.

On arrival back at the house, Lisa was given a tin bath of cold water to wash in, set out in the courtyard so that the other servants could watch as she removed the dirt of the journey from her flesh. She looked about her in vain for Bulcher, who she thought at least might come out to see how they had marked her. Somehow his failure to appear upset her. It was as if she had undergone the ordeal of registration in order to please him, and had been rewarded by indifference. Nevertheless she was pleased when, at last, she was taken back to her cell and allowed to sleep.

For the next three days, Lisa was left to her own devices, spending the time in the heat of her small cell, where the temperature became almost unbearable in the middle of the day. She was allowed out only to perform her ablutions and for the hour's strenuous exercise she was obliged to carry out every day in order to keep her body in trim. This consisted of press-ups, pull-ups, a cycling machine and a number of other apparatus. During these periods Akran kept a close eye on her, occasionally using a small cane to encourage her to work harder when he considered she wasn't trying hard enough.

It was on the fourth day that, on emerging from her afternoon shower, Lisa found herself being taken, not back to her cell, but into the main house. Akran led her into a dressing-room with a large mirror and watched as she brushed her hair. Lisa studied her naked form, noting with dismay that there was no sign of any hair growth about her pubis, and noting too how prominently the gleaming ring that pierced her outer sex lips drew attention to her slit. She ran the brush through her hair a few more times, then Akran led her out and in the direction of the front room.

Lisa was apprehensive as she padded along the corridor behind the servant. On the one hand she was glad to have a break in the monotony of her everyday existence, but she knew that any summons from Bulcher might lead to some new ordeal for her, and she feared what he might have in mind this time.

As she entered the spacious room, she saw that Bulcher was seated in an easy chair close to the window. Then she felt a knot form in her stomach as she realised that he was not alone. Sitting opposite him, with her back to Lisa, was a woman.

The girl's footsteps faltered for a second, then she felt Akran's cane poking her in the back and she knew she must go forward. As she came abreast of the two seated figures, her heart sank. It was the white woman who she had first encountered when she was with Kimuni, and whose car had been alongside the truck those few days earlier.

The woman turned, and Lisa felt the blood rising in her cheeks as she studied her lovely young form. She was elegantly clad in a white dress that hugged her figure beautifully, and Lisa noted with envy the expensive cut of her clothes. Her eyes were green, and held a look of contempt tinged with amusement as she studied the young unfortunate.

"This is Mrs Sadler," said Bulcher. "I believe you've met before."

"We certainly have," said the woman. "It's Lisa isn't it? Where's that boyfriend of yours?"

"Boyfriend Mistress?"

"That disgusting urchin who was feeling you up in the street the other night."

"He... He wasn't really my boyfriend, Mistress."

"But you said he was."

"Just for that night. "

"So, he was a one night stand. Did he screw you?"

Lisa dropped her gaze and said nothing.

"Answer Mrs Sadler when she speaks to you," barked Bulcher.

"Y-yes. Yes he did Mistress."

"And his friends/"

"Yes Mistress."

"All of them?"

"Yes Mistress."

"I see. You enjoyed that, did you?"

"I was only doing as I was told."

"So you didn't enjoy it?"

"I..."

"Did you come?"

"Yes Mistress."

Mrs Sadler turned to Bulcher. "She certainly is a little slut, isn't she? Just look at the way she's flaunting her breasts. And in front of a servant, too."

Bulcher inclined his head. "She is completely without shame."

"And now she's officially a slave?"

"As you see, she bears the mark. Show Mrs Sadler your mark, girl."

Reluctantly Lisa turned to face the woman, placing her feet apart. Mrs Sadler reached out and ran a finger over the smooth, bare flesh of Lisa's pubis and smiled.

"An ingenious place to put it, I must say. And that ring. She certainly likes to draw attention to herself down there."

"As you said, she's a slut."

"Good. Well, I think she'll do, if you can spare her."

"Certainly. I'm currently negotiating when she goes to auction, but I'll be happy to let you use her."

Lisa listened to the conversation with a mixture of dismay and curiosity. What did he mean by when she went to auction? What kind of an auction could he be referring to? Surely he couldn't mean what she thought he did? They didn't hold slave auctions any more, did they? And what did he mean by letting the woman use her? What could she want with her?

The questions were unanswered, though, and a tap on her buttocks from Akran's cane told her that the interview was at an end. As he led her out, she glanced anxiously over her shoulder at the couple, who were now deep in conversation again.

Chapter 13

They came for Lisa the following afternoon. Akran had taken her from her cell earlier and watched as she showered. Now she stood in the courtyard, her hands cuffed behind her, a lead attached to her cunt-ring, her heart thumping with anticipation.

The vehicle that collected her was a large, black saloon driven by a chauffeur. Akran pushed her into it, attaching her lead to a ring set in the floor. Then the door was closed and the vehicle purred away.

Lisa peered out the window as they drove through the city. They were going in quite the opposite direction from that followed by Akran when he was taking her for registration. As they left the bustle of the city streets behind them, she realised that they were entering a much smarter part of town, where the roads were wide and flanked on both sides by high walls. Every now and then there was a break in the walls and Lisa spied large houses behind strong iron gates. This was clearly an area occupied by expatriates and diplomats.

They drove on for some time before slowing and stopping outside one of the houses. A man in uniform pushed open the gates and they drove through. The house was huge, almost a mansion, the driveway running up to a covered area where a doorman waited. They did not stop there, however, the car following a road that ran round the back of the house, where they finally drew up.

A servant opened the car door, his eyes wide as he surveyed Lisa's naked form.

"Madam, can I help you?" he asked.

"Pardon?" Lisa was taken aback by his subservient manner.

"Your clothes Madam."

"I..." Lisa was too embarrassed to reply.

"You are naked, Madam. What happened? You want me to get you something to wear?"

The driver laughed. "This one not called Madam," he said. "Look at her mark."

He undid Lisa's lead from the car and pulled her from her seat, turning her to face the young servant.

"Look," he said, pointing to her crotch.

The servant's jaw dropped at the sight of the tattoo.

"This one slave girl," went on the driver. "The Mistress say you treat her like slave."

He gave Lisa's lead to the servant, then he closed the door and climbed back into his seat. Moments later, the car was gone.

The servant hesitated for a moment longer. Then, realising that the girl was making no protest, he tugged at her lead. She followed obediently as he led her away.

As she walked, Lisa stared about her. The house was set in a huge garden. On the lawn out the back a marquee had been erected and a number of men were busy setting out tables and chairs. At the sight of the nude youngster they stopped their work briefly and watched as she was led through the back door of the house.

Lisa found herself in a vast kitchen that was filled with people, all rushing this way and that, intent on what they were doing. Large tables were laid out with huge piles of food and, even as she watched, more was being pulled from the ovens by the army of workers who toiled away in the steaming heat of the room. It was clear to Lisa that some large function was being prepared for in the house, and that that was almost certainly the reason she was there. She glanced down at her body. She knew full well that she was forbidden to cover herself below the waist, and she shivered as she contemplated what might await her in the large, busy house.

She was taken through another door at the end of the kitchen and into a room that was surrounded on all sides by lockers. A desk stood in the corner, and a long queue stretched from it about the room. Behind the desk sat two women, and as each person in the queue passed they were handed a uniform, starched white for the men and traditional black maids' uniforms, with white aprons, for the women. All those queuing turned to stare as Lisa was brought in. Her escort took her to the back of the line, then released her cuffs and undid her lead.

"You wait here," he ordered. "Get uniform."

Then he was gone.

Lisa looked about at the men and women in the room. Every eye was fixed on her naked body. She longed to be able to cover herself but dare not, so she stood, eyes cast down, her face glowing, her hands hanging at her sides. For a short time all movement in the room ceased whilst the other people studied the young beauty. Then somebody barked an order and the distribution of the uniforms began anew.

The young English girl waited silently amongst the African servants, avoiding their eyes as best she could as the queue shuffled forward. When at last it came to her turn, the woman behind the desk placed a maid's outfit before her. Before she could pick it up, however, the other woman snatched it back, shaking her head. She reached under the table and pulled out a plastic shopping bag, which she handed to Lisa. Then she waved her on.

The queue of servants split immediately after collecting their uniforms, with the men going through one door and the women another. Lisa followed the women and found herself in a large, empty room, with benches set about the walls. Here the others were putting on their uniforms and chatting. As Lisa entered the chatting stopped, and a sea of hostile eyes was turned toward her. Lisa surveyed the women. They ranged in age from youngsters like herself to matronly women in their fifties. All were in various stages of undress, though their modesty was preserved by white underwear that made a stark contrast to the blackness of their skin. Some of the younger ones giggled at the sight of the naked white girl, whilst the older women shook their heads and tut-tutted.

Lisa opened her bag, placing the contents on the bench in front of her. It consisted of a small black top that mimicked the top of the maids' dresses, but that would cover her no lower than her navel. Even the apron was there, but this too was abbreviated so as not to fall below her waist. The only other things in the bag were a pair of sheer black hold-up stockings and a pair of shiny high-heeled shoes. Lisa stared at the outfit in dismay. She was not surprised at the brevity of the costume, after all she was forbidden by law to cover the S tattooed on her pubis, but the thought of having to go about with her buttocks and vagina bare was one that gave her a hollow feeling in the pit of her stomach.

She pulled on the top and fastened the buttons. It was very tight indeed, so that her breasts pressed against the thin material, threatening to burst it open. She pulled the stockings up her thighs, then slipped on the shoes. There was a mirror on the wall close to where she was standing and she paused to look at herself, a stifled moan of anxiety escaping her lips as she surveyed her body. It was as if the short top and the stockings drew attention to her nudity, the gleaming ring that so cruelly pierced her sex gleaming in the light. She turned to look at the black women, all neatly dressed in their uniforms, and her cheeks glowed with shame as she contemplated how she must appear to them.

A man shouted something, and the women began to file out of the room. Lisa followed as they made their way into yet another room. A man was standing on a stage calling out names, and Lisa realised that he was handing out job assignments. One by one the women went forward, received their orders and joined one of the groups that were forming in different parts of the room. In the end, Lisa was the only one left, and the man beckoned her forward. He was a heavily built African, wearing a smart suit and bow tie and he eyed her with contempt.

"You will work in the bar," he said, and indicated three young girls and an older woman standing in a group together. Lisa joined them, avoiding their gazes as she did so.

Immediately the older woman took charge.

"Follow," she said curtly, then set off out of the room with the three maids behind her.

They made their way out into the garden again and across the lawn to the marquee. Lisa wondered what the men setting out the chairs must think as they saw her walking past, her bottom and sex bare, amongst these smartly dressed girls.

The bar was at one end of the marquee, and the woman immediately set her charges the task of arranging the bottles and glasses. She spoke English, much to Lisa's relief. There was a lot to do, and for a short time Lisa was able to absorb herself in her work, though she was constantly aware of the whistles and catcalls of the workers as she moved back

102

and forth.

At one point Mrs Sadler appeared. She said nothing to Lisa, but spoke a few words to her supervisor, who nodded. When she had gone, the supervisor approached Lisa.

"You, slave," she said.

"Yes Madam?"

"You serve behind bar when visitors come. Understand?"

"Yes Madam."

Lisa contemplated this order. It would mean that, initially at least, her lack of clothing would not be immediately apparent to those entering the marquee. However, she recognised that, as soon as anyone approached the bar, they would see how she was dressed, and she guessed that she had been given the job precisely to increase her humiliation, as more and more people became aware of her unclothed state.

By the time the bar was fully set up the workmen had finished their tasks and were heading away. A band arrived and began tuning up on a stage on one side of the tent, whilst the tables were laid out with food. Then the work was complete and an air of quiet expectancy fell as they awaited the first guests.

To Lisa's surprise, they came in rickshaws, each couple sitting side by side whilst a strong young man pulled them along. Clearly they were leaving their cars outside the gates. There must have been a dozen of the large-wheeled traps, and soon they were arriving at regular intervals to be greeted by Mrs Sadler and a dark, handsome man who Lisa took to be her husband.

At first the guests took their drinks from the waiters who circulated amongst them, so that Lisa's modesty remained protected by the bar. However, she knew that she must stand out as the only white servant amongst all the Africans, and she noticed a number of heads turning in her direction as she passed the drinks over the bar to the waiters.

The first guest she served was a middle-aged man, who wandered up to her and asked for two drinks. As she turned to pour them she knew he would see her bare behind and, sure enough, when she placed them on the bar his eyes were wide and fixed on her crotch. For a second he remained standing exactly where he was, his mouth agape. Lisa said nothing, her face scarlet as he took in her bare pubis and the slit of her sex. Then he took his drinks and, still shaking his head, returned to the group he was with.

Lisa watched as he spoke to his companions, her embarrassment deepening as their heads turned in her direction. Then two more men were making their way toward her, and she knew that her temporary respite was over.

The pair arrived at the bar and leaned against it. One of the African maids came to serve them, but they waved her away and beckoned to Lisa. The youngster approached them slowly, her face glowing.

"So this is the little white slave," said the first of the pair.

"Yeah," replied his companion. "I'd heard there was some slut been mixing a bit too much with the locals, but I didn't know Pamela had hired her for the party. Turn around, darling and let's see your backside."

"Did you want any drinks, gentlemen?" asked Lisa quietly.

"In a minute. Now turn round and let us see that lovely arse of yours."

Reluctantly, Lisa turned her back on them, aware that they would see the lion-shaped brand that had been burned

104

into her rear cheeks all those months ago. The men whistled.

"She certainly knows how to decorate herself," said the first man. "What with that ring in her cunt and the rest, it's no wonder she wants to show it all off."

"Fucking slut," replied his partner. "Okay girlie, get us two whiskies and bring them across."

Lisa's heart sank as she heard the words. They were deliberately asking her to abandon the temporary sanctuary of the bar and to go out into the open where everybody would see how she was dressed. Once again it struck her how much more difficult it was to appear like this before other English men and women. Somehow, when confronted by the local people, she was able to perform as she did more easily. But these people were supposedly her peers, and to see her walk about naked below the waist would be completely beyond the pale to them. In a place like this, the old colonialist racist attitudes still survived amongst the remaining whites, and she knew that the idea of fraternising too closely with the locals was anathema to them. What she was doing, shamelessly displaying her most private charms and humiliating herself before the servants, went way beyond that.

She put two glasses onto a tray and made her way to the end of the bar. Then, taking a deep breath, she stepped out.

For the first few paces she was paid scant attention. Slowly but surely, though, eyes began to turn in her direction, men nudging one another and indicating her whilst the women looked on in disbelief. Lisa tried the best she could to ignore them, but all the time was aware of the gleaming ring that pierced her sex, and the way it chafed against her clitoris as she walked along through the crowd of smartly-dressed people.

105

The two men were standing with Mrs Sadler, and as she approached they turned to their hostess.

"You certainly know how to pick your staff, Pam," said one of them. "Where did you find this modest little thing?"

The woman laughed. "She's the little slut who was whoring for the rebels a few months ago," she said. "She's completely shameless, look at her."

"I've never seen anything like it," said a female guest, who wore an elegant black evening gown with pearls about her neck. "She can't be English, surely?"

"That's just it, she is," replied Mrs Sadler. "But she lets the locals do what they want with her. Do you know, when I first encountered her she was walking about the streets with a vigilante gang stark naked?"

"What, just in the street?"

"That's right. Some filthy urchin claimed she was his girlfriend and she was just standing there letting him kiss her and feel her up with everyone watching."

"You mean he was actually touching her?"

"Yes. Touching her everywhere. And she was loving it, you could tell. The girl's a total slut. I reckon that old pervert Bulcher did her a favour persuading Mbogu to have her enslaved."

"Probably the best thing for her kind," put in another woman. "After all, she could never be one of us, just look at her."

"The interesting bit is where they put the slave mark," went on Mrs Sadler. "Still, I don't suppose it bothers her. The girl's got no shame at all."

Whilst this talk was going on, Lisa had been obliged to wait patiently, still holding the tray of drinks. Normally, when people spoke about her she couldn't understand what they were saying. To hear herself talked about like this in

English was almost unbearable. Yet the way the men eyed her bare crotch was already having a very unwelcome effect on the beautiful youngster, and, despite her shame, she could already feel a wetness seeping into her vagina.

At last, the two men took their glasses, and she was able to turn away and head back to the bar. She hadn't gone more than a few steps, though, before she was stopped by another man who, his eyes travelling down her young body, ordered more drinks.

For the next hour or more Lisa was obliged to mingle with the guests, carrying her tray back and forth. The reactions varied from laughter, to sexual innuendoes and to disgust amongst the smartly-dressed crowd as the petite youngster hurried amongst them, feeling humiliated and shamed.

At last though, the food was served, and she was able to absorb herself in opening and pouring the wine, after which she was allowed to retire behind the bar for a short period.

Once the guests had eaten, an entertainment began in the house. A girl was singing, followed by a juggling act. Most of the guests went inside to watch, and for the first time Lisa found herself almost alone as she hurried about collecting glasses.

She was just stacking the last of them onto the shelves when she felt a hand on her shoulder. She turned to see about ten men standing at the bar. There was nobody else in sight apart from the other servants. One of the men was the one who had first ordered her to bring him a drink. It was he who spoke first.

"All alone little slave?"

Lisa didn't reply.

"Everyone else is watching the entertainment," he went on. "It's a bit boring though, so we thought we'd offer an

107

alternative. You're coming with us."

"I... I can't Sir," stammered Lisa, suddenly alarmed. "My supervisor..." she indicated the older woman, who was looking on suspiciously.

"We need this girl in the house," said the man. "You'll have to find another barmaid for the time being." As he spoke he pulled a banknote from his pocket and slipped it to the woman. She took it and nodded.

"Good. Come on, barmaid. Come with us."

Reluctantly Lisa stepped out from behind the bar and set off with them across the lawn. They took her round the side of the house. Through the windows she could hear the music playing, but they weren't taking her in that direction. Instead they led her in through a small door and down a flight of steps. The room they took her into was brightly lit and was clearly a storeroom, strewn about with boxes, with an old mattress lying to one side. There were two more party guests in the room, and three young black men, who Lisa took to be some of the workers who had been employed in setting up the marquee. They were all about eighteen or nineteen, with scruffy clothes, and they eyed the young beauty with some interest.

"They going to perform?" asked Lisa's escort.

"No problem," replied one of the men. "I paid them a few bob, but I reckon they'd do it for nothing."

"Good." He turned to Lisa. "Now, young lady, you're going to be the alternative entertainment."

Lisa stared at him, then at the three workers.

"No need to look so alarmed," said the man. "You're just going to be doing what you do best. Tom, stay by the door and keep watch. Some of the ladies might not appreciate the alternative cabaret."

The guests arranged themselves about the room, sit-

108

ting on tables and packing cases. Then Lisa was pushed forward to stand in the centre. She stared about at the faces watching her, then at the three young men. As she watched they rose to their feet and began to move toward her. She looked round, but there was nowhere to go. She stood, her stomach knotted, her heart pounding, as the young men began to circle her.

They stalked about her as if performing some kind of ritual dance. Lisa stood stock-still in the centre watching them. Then a hand reached out and ran across her backside, the palm pressed against her soft flesh.

Another hand stroked her belly, the fingers running across her pubis. Then yet another reached for her breasts, squeezing them through the thin material of her top. As they touched her, Lisa felt the stirrings of her own excitement deep inside. She glanced about at the men watching. She knew they were there to watch her perform with the servants, and the thought of what was to happen sent a shiver of anticipation through her. She was aware, too, of the contempt they felt for the fact that she gave herself to the local men. To them, with their colonialist and racist outlooks, to consort with the servants was unthinkable. And yet they would get their kicks from watching her do just that.

All at once she felt her arms grabbed from behind, as one of the young Africans took hold of her and pinned her elbows back. At the same time, one of his companions stepped forward and, taking hold of her top, pulled it apart, the buttons flying in all directions as he bared her firm young breasts. The men watching shouted their approval at the sight of Lisa's creamy flesh, her nipples brown and hard. The man grabbed at them at once, pinching her teats until she squealed with the pain. Then she was being forced

109

down to her knees.

The youth in front of her unzipped his fly and pulled out his cock. It rose from his pants, thick and hard, projecting like a great black pole in front of her face. He thrust it forward. Lisa glanced to left and right. The party guests were leaning forward, their eyes hungry as they waited for her to react. She knew only too well what was required of her, though she still hesitated, mortified by what was about to happen.

"Come on girl," one of the guests shouted. "You know what he wants." .

Lisa stared at the stiff rod that rose up in front of her. Then she opened her mouth and took him inside, tasting his arousal as he pressed his cock to the back of her throat. Almost instinctively she began to suck at him, taking hold of his thighs, her tongue licking at his glans as she fellated him. Then someone grabbed her wrist and she felt her hand close about another hefty erection. She glanced sideways as the man beside her moved her hand back and forth, urging her to masturbate him. Seconds later her other hand was placed on the third man's cock. Still sucking hard, she began to work both men's foreskins back and forth.

The young man on her right grabbed her head and pulled it off his companion's knob, pressing his own between her lips, and Lisa found herself sucking a fresh penis, whilst she tried her best to stroke the shiny one that had just vacated her mouth. All about her she could hear the laughter and shouts of encouragement from the party guests as they watched her give herself to the trio, her lovely breasts shaking as she worked her head back and forth.

They went on like that for some time, taking it in turns to force their cocks into the mouth of the kneeling girl whilst she did her best to keep the others satisfied. Then

110

one of the men watching gave an order, and Lisa heard the trio laugh.

All at once she felt her arms grabbed, and they dragged her to her feet. They stripped the tattered blouse from her, leaving her clad in only stockings and shoes. At the same time one of the three prostrated himself on the mattress, his great cock standing straight up from his body. His two companions dragged the naked beauty across to where he lay, positioning her just above his groin. Then their hands pressed on her shoulders, and Lisa knew what she must do.

She lowered herself onto his cock, spreading her legs as she did so. When the stiff pole brushed against the soft flesh of her nether lips she gave a little gasp, and the men laughed as they realised that she was becoming aroused. She reached down between her legs, taking hold of his shaft and guiding it toward the heat and wetness of her vagina, moaning softly as she felt herself penetrated by him. She continued to squat down, trying not to show the exquisite pleasure his rod was giving her as it forced his way deep into her sex.

At last he was all the way in, his young cock filling her deliciously, kindling those desires that were never far from the surface in the wanton youngster. She began to fuck him, moving her body up and down with smooth, rhythmic strokes, small cries of pleasure escaping from her lips as she did so.

All at once she felt hands on her shoulders, pushing her forward. She complied, prostrating herself across her partner, her pale breasts pressed against his strong black chest. Then she felt a gob of saliva strike her bottom and a pair of strong fingers begin to rub it into the tight hole of her anus, and she knew at once what was coming next.

It was not the first time Lisa's front and rear holes had been used to pleasure two men at once. She had experienced the bittersweet sensation of double penetration once before, when she was initiating three young warriors in a ceremony in the native village where she had been imprisoned for so long. Still she bit her lip as she felt a swollen knob forcing its way into her anus, the young man paying no attention to her cries of pain as he filled her rectum with his throbbing erection.

Tears coursed down Lisa's cheeks as he penetrated even deeper, until she could feel the short, wiry curls of his pubic hair against the globes of her bottom. Then both men began to move, fucking her hard front and back, their thick knobs ramming into the petite young beauty, shaking her back and forth with the force of their movements.

A hand grabbed hold of her hair and pulled her head round, bringing her face to face with the third man's twitching penis. Then it was between her lips and she was sucking hard at it as he thrust it into her face.

Lisa could hear the cries of her audience as the three men took her, urging them on as they battered her young body back and forth. She tried to match the rhythm of their strokes, but couldn't, so she simply relaxed, allowing them to thrust their cocks into her vagina, anus and mouth at their own pace, giving herself entirely to them, her pale, naked body sandwiched between the two muscular black youths whilst the third filled her mouth with his manhood.

The man on her back gave a grunt, and all at once her backside was filling with hot fluid as he ejaculated into her, his cock spurting his seed deep into her rectum. Almost at once the man in her vagina let go, his cock jumping as it emptied his sperm into her. The sensation of being doubly filled was too much for the lascivious young

112

girl and she gave a muffled cry as a mighty orgasm shook her small frame. Then her mouth was filling with creamy spunk as the third of her violators let go within her.

Lisa's orgasm overwhelmed her as the men continued to thrust their cocks into her, shaking her body back and forth like a marionette whilst the cheers of those watching rang in her ears. Her entire consciousness was filled by their stiff manhoods as they triple-fucked her without mercy. At last, though, they began to flag, the force of the thrusts diminishing. Then the man behind her withdrew from her backside and pulled her to her feet.

Lisa staggered slightly, still barely able to credit what she had just done, accommodating three lusty young Africans whilst a group of her own countrymen watched and cheered. Now, as she stood, she gazed down at herself, taking in her red and swollen breasts and feeling the cold semen as it trickled down her neck and escaped from her vagina and anus onto her smooth white thighs.

At that moment the man at the door gave an urgent shout.

"Someone's coming!"

Immediately the guests made for a door at the back of the storeroom, crowding through it hotly pursued by the three servants who were struggling to fasten their pants. Barely had the last one gone than a figure appeared in the doorway.

"What the hell have you been up to?" asked Mrs Sadler.

Chapter 14

Lisa stood in the centre of the cellar, her hands clasped behind her head, her legs spread whilst Mrs Sadler inspected her ravished young body. All the men had escaped, and she was on her own, standing naked and bedraggled before the woman, the spunk trickling down her smooth inner thighs.

Mrs Sadler was not alone. There was another woman with her, about twenty-five years old, slightly plump with hair dyed platinum blonde and a rather brassy look about her. Mrs Sadler had referred to her as Dot, and now she stood beside the woman, a grin on her face as she surveyed the unhappy youngster.

"Looks like she's had a pretty good shagging," she said. Her voice was loud, with a trace of a Cockney accent and she pulled at a cigarette, blowing clouds of blue smoke into Lisa's face.

"Little slut's been screwing with the servants," replied Mrs Sadler, curling her lip. "She's insatiable, this one. Can't seem to get enough of the locals."

"You reckon some of the men set her up? I know my Frank would have enjoyed it. He's always watching those porno videos of black studs. You should see the size of some of their cocks."

Mrs Sadler laughed. "Really, Dot, you're incorrigible."

Dot laughed too. "That's not the word my Frank uses. Who is she, anyhow?"

"She's a slut, like I said. She's English you know. Though apparently she changed her nationality to Kombian."

"Kombian?"

"That's right. Little fool. She should have known they'd

114

enslave her. Look where they put the mark."

She pointed to Lisa's bare crotch, where the workman's spunk was still oozing from her.

"She likes to decorate that sexy little body, doesn't she?"

"It's a pity the little tramp doesn't try decorating it with some clothes. Just look at her standing there, bold as brass with not a stitch on. A disgrace I'd call it."

"And you say she was originally English? You know there's something familiar about her. Where have I seen her before?"

"Probably parading through the streets in the nude. She does a lot of that."

"No, that's not it. What's your name girl?"

"Lisa, Mistress."

"Lisa eh? You ever lived in London?"

"Yes Mistress."

"Wait a minute. I know. You were in the hostel. We thrashed your arse and you got the hots. Had to bring you off with a dildo."

Lisa stared at the woman, her mouth open. Then she remembered. It had all happened years ago. She had been living in a hostel after leaving school. One night three of the older girls had accused her of spying on them, and had thrashed her behind. It had been the first inkling to her of her own masochistic tendencies. When they had seen that she was aroused, they had used a dildo to bring her off.

And one of the women had been called Dot. At the time she had thought her a prostitute. Possibly she had been. Now here she was, face to face with her once again.

"You really know her?" asked Mrs Sadler.

"Sure I do. She's a right little perve. Gets turned on when you whip her behind. You must really enjoy this slave lark, isn't that right darling?"

115

Lisa did not reply, but she knew that the expression on her face told the woman all she wanted to know.

"I still don't understand how you could have met," said Mrs Sadler.

"Lived in a hostel for a while when I was hard up," said Dot. "That was where I was living when I met Frank. He was working on a building there. Then he got his engineering diploma and landed the contract here. Who'd have thought we'd find little Miss Hoity-Toity fucking about over here? She used to be a right little prude, and now we see her true colours. It's a real turn-up for the books!"

At that point another figure was suddenly framed in the doorway. he was a man, of rather stocky build, wearing a striped suit and a wide, brightly-coloured tie.

"So here you are, Dot," he said. "They said you'd come..." he broke off, staring at Lisa. "What the hell..."

"Little slut's been fucking with the servants, Frank" explained Dot.

"Looks like they've given her a right good shagging."

Dot laughed. "It's all she's good for."

The man turned to Dot. "Listen love, Bill says there's a snooker hall in the village. Offered me a game. Want to come?"

Dot turned to Mrs Sadler. "We can't just leave Pam's party."

The woman smiled. "It's no problem. We'll be on the go for hours yet. It's a bit of a scruffy dump, though. It's really just for the locals."

"That's okay," said Frank. "I don't mind slumming it. Should be good fun."

"Why not take a couple of the rickshaws, then," said Mrs Sadler. You could..." she paused and a smile crossed her face. "You could use our little friend here as pony. I'm

116

sure she'd love to go into the village."

Lisa stared at the woman in alarm, then at Dot and Frank, both of whom were laughing.

"That's a great idea," said Dot. "Do you get a whip with one of those things?"

"It can be arranged." She turned to the naked youngster. "Go and get that spunk cleaned off you, you little tart. Then pick up a rickshaw and be out the front in five minutes. Hurry!"

Lisa scurried off. There was a bathroom off the kitchen and she went in there, blushing at the leering glances she got from the staff. She cleaned herself up as best she could then, still nude, hurried round to where she had seen the rickshaws being parked. A man was already waiting for her there, holding the shafts of one of the small carriages. He handed them to her.

"You hurry round front," he ordered. "Mistress waiting."

Lisa took hold of the shafts and began to pull. With its large wheels the vehicle felt remarkably light, and she set off around the house, towing it behind her. As she came in sight of the house, her footsteps faltered. With both hands occupied pulling the vehicle, she felt very exposed indeed, her pert breasts jutting forward uncovered and unprotected against anyone who might wish to touch them. She still wore the black hold-up stockings and high heels she had been issued earlier, and she was only too aware of the way they enhanced her nudity, drawing attention to her bare pubis and the prominent gash of her sex. Up ahead she saw another rickshaw already drawn up outside the house, being held by a powerful young black man. She felt very conspicuous as she made her way toward it.

Dot and Frank were standing on the steps, watching

117

her as she approached. In the other rickshaw another couple sat, and they too were clearly amused by the naked youngster's plight, craning round to watch as she brought the vehicle to a halt beside them.

Lisa held tightly to the shafts as her two passengers climbed aboard. It was all she could do to take the strain as the buxom Dot and her husband hauled themselves into their seats. Once they were settled, however, she discovered that the way the seat was balanced over the large wheels made it reasonably easy to support. She knew that moving it would be a different matter, though.

A small crowd of guests had gathered to watch, and there was much hilarity at the sight Lisa made. She tried to ignore the lewd remarks that were being passed all around her as she stood and awaited her orders.

"You go ahead," called Dot to the other couple. "We'll be right behind you."

The other rickshaw moved off. Then:

Whack!

Lisa gave a cry as the leather tip of a long whip cracked into the bare flesh of her behind.

"Come on, girl," said Dot. "Get a move on."

Lisa strained, and the rickshaw began to move forward. It was extremely heavy, and the muscles in her arms and legs were stretched taut as the vehicle gradually gained momentum, the wheels turning slowly at first, then gathering speed as they headed off down the driveway.

Whack!

The whip cut into her behind again, and Lisa pulled harder. The other vehicle was getting away from them now, Lisa's petite young frame being no match for that of the powerful man ahead, but she strained harder and managed to break into a trot as Dot brought the whip down across

118

her naked body yet again.

As they reached the gates to the building, a man pulled them open. Lisa felt extremely unhappy about leaving the house in her naked state, but she knew she could expect no mercy from these people. She glanced guiltily about her as they turned onto the road and began heading away from the house.

They trotted on for about ten minutes, with Lisa growing hotter and more exhausted with every step. Dot kept her moving by frequent use of the whip, however, and soon her pretty white backside was covered in angry red stripes where the lash had landed. As they progressed they left the smart buildings behind them, and shortly they veered off the road onto a track and Lisa saw the lights of a village ahead.

Once more the young beauty felt the urge to hang back, but the insistent pain in her bare behind told her that any reluctance on her part would incur the wrath of her passengers, so she trotted on. As they came closer she became aware of figures watching their progress by the roadside. Her face turned crimson as they shouted and laughed at the sight of the beautiful young white girl trotting past them, her bare breasts bouncing delightfully with every step.

Ahead, Lisa saw that the other rickshaw had drawn up at a low building, outside which a neon sign was flickering. As she came closer she realised that this was the snooker hall. The place was simply furnished, just a large, open room with white walls and harsh strip lighting, in which two snooker tables stood side-by-side. At each one a pair of men was playing, but they stopped to watch as the two rickshaws pulled up. At the sight of the naked young beauty, their faces creased into broad grins. Lisa's face

119

was red with embarrassment and exertion as she stood, waiting for her passengers to dismount.

"Damn," said Frank. "It looks as if both tables are being used."

"That's a pity," replied Dot. "Still, maybe we can persuade them to let us have the table whilst we divert them with something else."

"What do you mean?" asked her husband.

"I just thought we might brighten their evening a bit." She used the whip to poke Lisa in the back. "How do you feel about entertaining a few more studs, darling?"

"I-I don't understand, Mistress."

"You will. Come on, Frank, Bring our little pony inside."

Lisa placed the shafts of the cart on the ground. She was still exhausted from the effort of pulling the pair such a distance. When she realised she was being led into the glare of the lights, though, she tried to hang back, but Dot was having none of it.

"Get in there," she snarled. "Or I'll take the whip to you again."

The building was shabby, with a dusty stone floor that rang with the sound of Lisa's heels. The tables themselves were old, the green cloth worn black and shiny in some places. In the corner was a small bar, manned by a man of indeterminable age. Frank went to him and spoke a few words, and he eyed Lisa, laughing. He spoke to the players, who laughed too, then began removing their belts. Lisa watched nervously as they approached her.

"Don't worry, darling," said Dot. "They're not about to thrash you. Not if you behave, anyhow. Now get up on that bar stool.

There were three stools standing at the bar, and she

indicated the middle one. Lisa looked about her nervously, then, turning her back to the grinning barman she hoisted herself up and lowered her bottom onto the seat. The plastic felt cool and smooth against her stinging behind, and she bit her lip as the pain of the whip returned.

Almost at once two of the snooker players moved in on either side of her. Before she knew what was happening they had grabbed her arms and wrapped their belts about her wrists. There was a metal bar running along the edge of the bar top and they looped the strips of leather about this, pulling them tight so that they bit into her pale flesh. They secured the belts leaving Lisa without the use of her arms.

Almost at once she felt her legs grasped. The other players had pulled the two remaining bar stools close to the one on which she was sitting, and now they hauled her thighs apart, draping one stockinged leg over each, then using their belts to secure her ankles to the legs of the stools. Once they had finished, they stood back to admire their handiwork.

Lisa was quite helpless, her wrists and ankles held fast by the belts. She glanced down at her body in dismay, noting how her hips were thrust forward, her spread legs giving perfect access to her most intimate place. She turned in alarm to the two couples who had come with her, but they had already taken up the cues that the men had discarded and had started a game, the women playing together on the far table whilst the men were on the near one, all apparently oblivious to Lisa's plight.

A hand grasped her breast, and she craned back to see that the barman was reaching round her body and fondling her soft flesh, making the nipple pucker to hardness under his coarse fingers. Then another man took hold of her knee, his fingers running over the fine nylon of her stockings, making her shiver as he moved it higher. She turned to face him. It was one of the snooker players, the delight clear on his face as he eyed her naked and helpless body. Behind him his companions looked on, their eyes gleaming at the sight of the young beauty so deliciously presented to them.

The man's hand slipped further up her thigh, reaching her stocking tops and the bare, creamy flesh above them. Lisa drew in her breath sharply as she felt his touch, barely able to suppress a moan at the sensation of being fondled so intimately.

He found her sex, his finger slipping crudely into her vagina and twisting back and forth, bringing a gasp from the hapless captive. Once again the reaction of her body was totally at odds with the way she felt. To be trapped naked like this in a lowly snooker hall whilst these scruffy strangers mauled her body was the height of degradation and humiliation. And yet the sensation of the man's fingers as he rammed them into her vagina was totally stimulating and a gush of wetness flowed through her as he worked his hand back and forth.

Dot lowered her cue for a moment and stopped to watch Lisa being frigged. She nudged her companion, as the young beauty groaned aloud with arousal, her backside coming clear of her stool as she found herself pressing her hips forward against the fingers that invaded her so intimately. One of the men had unzipped his fly and pulled out his erection. Now he stood, fondling his glans as he watched the show.

"Looks like she's about to get what she wants," remarked Dot.

"Dirty little tart," remarked her companion, but she kept

her eyes pinned on the tableau as the man moved between Lisa's spread thighs.

He brushed the other man's hand away, then moved in closer. Lisa watched with apprehension, knowing that she was about to be publicly fucked, but helpless to prevent it. The man took hold of her thighs, and she felt the heat of his stiff knob as it brushed against her flesh. Then he took hold of it and guided it toward the centre of her desires.

He penetrated her with a single thrust, his cock sliding over the wetness of her sex walls as her cunt muscles contracted about it. Lisa gave a cry of passion as he pressed it in, suddenly alive with lustful desire. He rammed it all the way home, until his hips were pressed hard against hers and he was staring her right in the face. Then he started to fuck her in earnest, thrusting his stiff erection into her and making her cry aloud.

All at once, Lisa's shame was forgotten as she revelled in the rough screwing he was giving her. She stared about her at the other men, all of whom were watching her being taken, her breasts shaking with every stroke. She could barely believe that this was happening to her, trussed naked at the bar whilst a total stranger fucked her hard and his companions waited their turn to gang-bang her. Yet all she could do was moan louder, her sex positively convulsing as the excitement within her grew.

When he came, she was unable to hold back her own orgasm, screaming aloud as she felt his semen pumping into her. It was the second time in less than an hour that a cock had spunked inside her, yet the orgasm was more intense than ever, the muscles standing out on her inner thighs as she pressed her pubis up and forward, devouring his seed with her hot sex, oblivious to those witnessing her debauchery.

123

She had barely started to descend from her peak when he abruptly withdrew, a drop of come still hanging from the end of his organ. There was no respite for Lisa, though, as a second man moved into his place and began pressing his knob into her, oblivious to her cries for mercy. In no time he was inside her, and fucking her with gusto, bringing her to new peaks with his rough thrusting. Behind him the two other men were already undoing their flies, and Lisa knew that her ordeal was only just beginning.

Chapter 15

Lisa spent more than an hour strapped to the bar whilst the men took their pleasure in her. When all four of the snooker players had had her, they handed her over to the barman, who fucked her hard. Once he had shot his load into her, they unstrapped her and tied her face down over the stool, her breasts pressed against the bar. Then they took turns to slap her behind, first with their hands, then with another belt, turning her pretty backside red with their hard blows and making Lisa beg for mercy. All the time Dot continued to encourage them, counting the strokes as the unhappy girl cried out with pain. Whilst she was still tied down, three of them took her again, bringing yet more unwanted orgasms to the lascivious youngster. By the time her companions had finished their games of snooker, Lisa's vagina was running with sperm, her stockings stained with the seminal fluids of the five men.

A small crowd gathered to watch as the exhausted Lisa was led from the hall to where the servant waited with the rickshaws. She lifted the shafts wearily and waited whilst

Dot and her husband climbed in behind her. Then they were off again, with Lisa straining to keep up with the fit young man as they rumbled off into the night.

Halfway back to the house, Dot called a halt, and the four Europeans gathered round to watch the delighted rickshaw man fuck the white youngster on the side of the road. Then they were off again, Lisa straining to get the vehicle moving whilst all the time the semen ran from her vagina and down over her stocking tops.

Back at the house, the party was still going strong, and the guests stood and watched as Lisa hauled the rickshaw up the drive, the evidence of her ravishment on display to all.

Once Dot and Frank had dismounted, Lisa was allowed to shower and change her stockings. Then she was back on duty, serving drinks, her naked body a constant delight to the guests. On four occasions she was trapped in some corner of the house and pinned down whilst one or more of the male guests fucked her, so that, by the time the party ended and she was shown to her bed in the servants' quarters, she was quite exhausted.

She was woken in the middle of the night by Mrs Sadler's chief servant, a burly man who led her to his own room and took her in the backside. It was in his bed that Mrs Sadler found her next morning, her lips closed about his massive cock. The woman waited whilst she fellated the man to orgasm, then dragged her out and laid half a dozen whip strokes across her backside before handcuffing her to the back of an open truck and sending her back to Bulcher.

As soon as she arrived back, Lisa sensed that something was going on in Bulcher's household. Cars came and went, containing fat and important looking men. Two or three times a day she would be dragged from her cell by Akran and paraded up and down the courtyard, then made to stand whilst the most intimate examinations of her body were carried out. On two occasions she was taken inside and made to suck men to orgasm whilst Akran encouraged her with the use of his whip. All the time Bulcher kept his distance, though she knew he was watching what was happening with interest, and that Akran was reporting back to him at all times.

Then, one morning, she was woken early by Bulcher's servant and made to shower and wash her hair. She was given a light breakfast, then led into Bulcher's presence. He was sitting behind his desk and, as she took up her submissive stance in front of him, he pushed back his chair and rose to his feet.

"So, little slut," he said. "It is time for a new phase in your training. I must return to Europe, where I have a deal of business, but you, my dear, will remain here. You understand that you are a slave, now, with no rights whatsoever?"

"Yes Master."

"I have decided that, whilst I am away, you will be sold to a new master for a year. You will be entirely in his power for that time. At the end of the year I may choose to take you back, or I may sell you to someone else, possible permanently. Is that clear?"

"Y-yes Master."

"Good. It will amuse me to think that, whilst I'm enjoying the pleasures of London night-life, you will be chained naked in some dank cell waiting to find out who wishes to whip, fuck or bugger you next."

Lisa said nothing, stunned by what he was saying, the sheer hopelessness of her situation overwhelming her. His mention of the London night-life struck a deep chord in her. She could barely remember a time when she had been able to hide her breasts and sex from men's eyes, or had been allowed any say in what she did, or who was permitted to violate her pretty body. The thought of those days of freedom before her involvement with Bulcher brought a sudden pang of remorse to her.

The pain must have shown on her young face, because she saw Bulcher smile as he reached out and stroked her breast.

"You were born for slavery, little wanton slut," he murmured. "Let's hope your new master understands your proclivity for pain and rough sex. It's all you're good for."

Lisa said nothing, but she felt the blood rush to her cheeks as she recognised the truth of his words. She glanced down at her nude form, and thought of the number of men who had enjoyed her body since her enslavement, and the number of times she had come at their hands, orgasm after delicious orgasm coursing through her. Even now, the sensation of Bulcher's fingers on her firm breasts was causing her nipple to stiffen and bringing a warmth and wetness to her groin. And now she was to move on to new humiliations and degradations at the hands of cruel strangers. She shivered as Akran led her from the room, but she wasn't sure if it was fear or anticipation that prompted the reaction.

Chapter 16

It was nearly noon when Akran came to get Lisa from her cell. The day was, as always, extremely hot, and the confinement of her accommodation was almost unbearable.. As she stepped into the sunlight, she blinked, momentarily blinded by the glare. She had expected to see a vehicle waiting for her, but instead there were just three young men, all three grinning broadly when they saw her nudity.

Lisa eyed the trio shyly. They were no more than seventeen years old, probably members of one of Mbogu's vigilante groups, like Kimuni and his friends. She knew that only people with such power would be entrusted with her. It was most humiliating for the lovely twenty-year-old to be placed in the power of ones so young, and she guessed that this was precisely why Bulcher was doing it.

"This is Umangu," said Akran, indicating the middle one of the trio. "He will be taking you to the auction. You will obey him at all times. Do you understand?"

"Yes Master," replied the young beauty as she eyed her escorts.

Umangu moved close to her. He was a small, wiry boy with a penetrating stare. His eyes travelled up and down Lisa's body.

"This one will fetch a good price," he sneered. "Especially if she is as good a fuck as I've been told. Tell me, English bitch, do you like to fuck?"

Lisa said nothing, her eyes cast down.

Whack! The young man slapped her breast, making her give a cry of surprise and pain.

"Answer me. Do you like to fuck?"

"I... Yes Master," she mumbled, her face glowing.

He grinned. "Good. Now you must say goodbye to Mr

Akran, here."

Lisa looked at Akran. "Goodbye Master."

"No," barked Umangu. "You must kiss him goodbye. After all, you will not see him for a long time."

Lisa turned to Akran. To be leaving him gave her no sadness whatsoever, his cruelty having blighted her life for so long. But she had been given an order and, despite the brash youthfulness of the one giving it, her training had taught her that not to obey would be sheer folly. Reluctantly she moved closer to Bulcher's servant, offering her pretty mouth to his. He took hold of her, his hands mauling her bare breasts whilst his tongue snaked into her mouth, almost devouring her. Lisa responded with her own tongue, showing all the enthusiasm she could muster as she embraced the man she disliked so much.

When he finally broke away, she was gasping for breath. She steadied herself, then turned to Umangu.

"Now you must kiss his cock goodbye," said the grinning youth.

Lisa stared at him in dismay. At first she was quite unable to respond to the outrageous demand. Then he raised a hand as if to slap her once more, and she knew he was serious. She looked about her. There were about twenty people in the compound, all standing round watching. Beyond, in the house, she could see the figure of Bulcher standing at the window. She bit her lip, then turned back to Akran and dropped to her knees.

She reached for his fly, pulling down the zip. His cock was already hard, and it sprang out in front of her face, the end twitching slightly. He was so close that she could smell him, and a shiver ran through her small frame.

"Go on," ordered Umangu.

Lisa leaned forward. Then, taking hold of Akran's thick

129

shaft, she planted a kiss on the tip of his penis. She leaned back and looked up at her young master.

"Kiss again," he said. "Kiss until his cock responds by rewarding you with the milk of life."

Lisa knew exactly what he meant. In fact she had known all along what was really required of her. After all, she was little more than a whore to these men. Less than that, she reflected. A whore was paid. These people used her for nothing, as if it was their right to do so.

She turned back to Akran's thick erection. She hesitated for a second, then opened her mouth and took his great black pole inside, tasting his maleness as she did so. She began to suck, moving her head back and forth and bringing a groan of pleasure from the servant.

Lisa fellated him with an expertise gained of long experience as a sex slave. She sucked greedily at his knob, her breasts shaking as she moved her head back and forth. Akran reacted by grabbing hold of her locks and pressing his hips hard against her face, almost making her gag as he fucked her open mouth.

He came suddenly, filling her mouth with hot, bitter semen. Lisa swallowed it down as best she could, but his ejaculate was copious and she could feel it leaking from her mouth and dribbling down her chin. He seemed to go on coming forever, great gobs of his spunk coursing down her throat, almost choking her as it kept on flowing.

At last, though, he was spent, and she was able to sit back, eyeing his saliva-coated knob. She licked the last vestiges of his semen from the tip, then used her fingers to gather the trickles from her chin, swallowing them down. Once she was certain that she had devoured every drop, she sat back on her heels and gazed up at Umangu.

"That is better," he said. "On your knees is the fitting

place for a slut like you." He turned to Akran. "I will take her now. Give me her bonds."

Akran pulled a pair of handcuffs and a chain lead from his pocket. Umangu took them from him, then barked an order at the other two boys, who took hold of Lisa's arms and dragged her to her feet. They spun her round and locked her wrists behind her back with the cuffs. Then they clipped the lead onto her cunt-ring and handed the end to Umangu.

He tugged at it, clearly enjoying Lisa's discomfort as she felt her hips yanked forward.

"Come," he ordered. Then he set off out of the court-yard with the hapless young beauty scuttling after him.

The trio of young men swaggered up the street with their charge between them. Everywhere people turned and stared at the pretty white girl walking totally naked through the streets, her bare pubis and swelling breasts on open display. Lisa hated this total disregard for her own modesty. All about were men and women fully-clothed, as she should be. Instead she was forced to suffer the total humiliation of her nudity. Even her hands were trapped behind her, preventing her from covering herself in any way.

There was something else, though. Something that Lisa simply couldn't understand. It was how her body responded to the way she was treated. Even now, when being led to what might be a terrible and frightening destiny, she could feel the arousal inside her increasing with every minute. There was something about the way men looked at her that was totally exciting to the lascivious youngster. It was almost as if their eyes caressed her bare flesh, making her nipples harden to tight brown buds and bringing a wetness to her sex, a wetness that was exacerbated by the chafing of her cunt-ring against her clitoris as she walked. She wondered, not for the first time, at the perversity of her

131

nature as she padded quietly along behind her captors.

They walked for nearly an hour along busy streets, past shops and houses where ordinary people were going about their ordinary lives. Lisa yearned for an ordinary life herself as she was led along. To be able to wear clothes again and to walk freely about as these people were. Even such simple luxuries as to be able to pull on some underwear and a dress and go out with a friend to shop, or to a disco were distant memories to her. She was no more than an object now, to be paraded naked, her breasts sex and backside bare for all to see, and to be whipped or fucked by whoever wanted her. Yet even now, contemplation of her fate made her nipples harden and her sex convulse with desire as her body rebelled against her once more.

They walked on. Everywhere they went, the sight of the naked beauty brought incredulity and laughter from the passers-by. Occasionally they would encounter another white person, and Lisa's cheeks would glow as they stopped and stared at her, clearly astounded at the sight she made. Once again she was reminded of the contempt these people held for the Africans. A contempt that made her captors' treatment of her all the harsher as she became their scapegoat for their hatred of the former colonial oppressors.

The boys were obviously aware of the discomfort of their charge, shouting comments at the people, who laughed aloud at what were obviously lewd jokes at Lisa's expense. One of the boys had produced a thin cane from his belt, and he used this to drive Lisa on if she showed any sign of reluctance, bringing it down hard across her buttocks, much to the amusement of those watching.

The market, when they finally reached it, was quiet and empty. A guard opened a large metal gate and admitted Lisa and her escort, and they led her past rows of stalls. At

132

the end was an open area, with seats set around in tiers, in the centre of which was a large stone block about three feet high, with thick metal rings set into it. Along the wall at the back were more rings, with heavy chains hanging from them. Lisa realised at once that this was where the auction of the slaves would take place. She shivered as she stared at the block and wondered what was in store for her.

The three boys took her round the back of the sale area and through a door set into the thick stone walls. Inside was a dank corridor with uneven floor and a heavily barred gate at one end. Two more guards stood by this, and they looked up as Lisa was brought forward, clearly interested in the sight she presented. Umangu pulled some papers from his pocket and handed them over. The guards studied them, then nodded and one of them unlocked the gate.

Umangu turned to Lisa, running his hand over the soft swell of her breast.

"We will be back for you, little slut," he said quietly. "You will put on a good display of your talents on the auctioneer's block, we will see to that. Go now, and think about what is to come."

He unclipped the lead from her ring, allowing his fingers to stray to her clitoris. Lisa knew he could feel her wetness, and saw him smile as he ran a coarse digit over her swollen love bud. Then he straightened, turned and was gone, his two companions following him.

The guard pushed her through, and his companion locked the gate behind her. He led her down another dismal corridor. On either side were crude cells fronted by rows of thick bars. Inside she could see hunched figures, their eyes following her as she was led past. At last they stopped before an empty cell, and the guard turned a key in the lock and swung the door open.

Inside the room was bare, apart from a single mattress on the floor. The guard took her arm and, swinging her round, threw her down on her back. As Lisa gazed up at him, her arms still pinned behind her by the cuffs, she saw him reach for his fly, and she knew he was going to fuck her. He dropped to his knees, pushing her thighs apart, and a sudden thrill of lust ran through her young body, making the muscles in her sex contract and forcing a small bead of moisture onto her thigh.

As he rammed his stiff cock into her she raised her head and looked behind him. In the cells opposite her fellow slaves had come to the bars and were watching her ravishment. One of them had pulled his cock from his shorts and was masturbating as the guard began to thrust hard into her.

He fucked her dispassionately, taking her as he might an inflatable doll, his face just above hers as his hips pumped back and forth. For Lisa, the excitement of her prolonged exposure and the chafing of the ring had made her extraordinarily aroused, and she found herself revelling in his treatment of her, thrusting her hips upwards and gasping with lust as she let her passions overwhelm her.

He came suddenly, grunting as he filled her with his spunk. Lisa's own orgasm was a delicious one, her cries loud and shrill, betraying to all the perverse pleasure the guard was giving her.

He withdrew, climbing to his feet and fastening his trousers, barely giving a glance to the lovely white girl splayed naked across the mattress, his spunk already oozing from her twitching vagina. She watched him as he turned and strode out the cell, amid the cheers of her fellow prisoners. He left the door ajar, and she wondered for a moment why he had done so. Then she heard the footsteps of his companion approaching, and another shiver ran through her as she realised that, before they sold her, she was going to be gang-banged.

Chapter 17

Lisa lost track of time as she sat in the dismal cell awaiting the start of the auction. Once all of the guards had used her body, they had given her a bucket of cold water with which to wash herself, then had locked the door of the cell and left her to her own devices. The other slaves, too, soon stopped gazing at them, though she saw more than one of them masturbate over the sight of her nude body, their semen spurting out into the passageway as they came.

Lisa's cell had a small window set high in the wall that allowed a sliver of light in, and this told her that it was still daylight when they came for the first of the slaves. The men were cuffed and then led out down the passageway. When they reached the end, the guards opened the door into the market square, and Lisa's heart sank as she heard the hubbub of the crowd.

For more than an hour she watched silently whilst one after another the cells were opened and the inmates marched out. Then the guards stopped outside her cell, and a knot formed in her stomach as they turned the key.

As they took her down the corridor, she saw three figures waiting beyond the bars, small black figures whose faces spread into wide grins as she approached. Umangu stood in the middle, holding her lead, whilst the other two boys flanked him, one of them still carrying the cane. the guard unlocked the door then shoved her forward to where the three youngsters stood.

135

"Stop and spread your legs, slut," ordered Umangu.

Lisa obeyed, and watched as he fastened the lead to her cunt ring. She wished that she had anyone other that these three as her escorts. It was belittling and humiliating to be in the power of ones so young, and she realised, once again, that Bulcher had chosen them entirely for that reason. Now, as Umangu dragged her off down the corridor, she prayed that the ordeal would not last too long.

The boys opened the door that led to the market and at once Lisa was overwhelmed by the noise that struck her. The seats were all full now, and beyond she could see that the market stalls were doing a busy trade.

As she came into view, a cheer arose from the crowd. This was clearly what they had come to see. Whilst the sale of some of the male slaves from their neighbouring country might be entertaining to them, the sight of the slim, beautiful white girl paraded naked before them was a far more engaging prospect, and Lisa felt the blood rise to her cheeks as the three youngsters led her up onto the rostrum.

They stopped at the top and made the unfortunate youngster turn to face the onlookers. As she surveyed the throng, Lisa was dismayed to see pale faces in the crowd. There, in a specially roped off area at the front of the auditorium, sat Bulcher, with Mrs Sadler beside him and Dot and Frank beside them. All were laughing at her as the boys rapped her thighs with the cane, forcing her to part her legs. Lisa did her best to ignore her fellow country-men, staring straight ahead and trying to close the jeering of the crowd from her mind.

A man walked onto the dais next to her. He was holding a microphone in his hand and speaking into it. As usual, Lisa couldn't understand a word that was being spoken, but his gestures and the laughter from those watching told her that it was her to which he was referring. As he spoke, Umangu moved close to her and, in response to the other man's words, began drawing attention to parts of her anatomy. He grasped her breast, squeezing it in his hand, tweaking the nipple so that she gave a cry of pain, much to the amusement of those watching. He took hold of her cunt ring, tugging at it and stretching the lips of her sex apart. he delved a finger inside, making the girl gasp at his intimate probing and bringing a cheer from the audience as he held up the finger to indicate how wet she was..

Next Umangu made her turn and face away.

"Bend over, little slut," he ordered. "The buyers want to see your arse."

Obediently Lisa bent forward, spreading her legs apart. Then, at Umangu's bidding, she grasped hold of the cheeks of her backside and pulled them apart, giving those watching an unrestricted view of her sex and anus. Another cheer arose as she felt Umangu insert a finger into her backside.

Lisa had never known such shame. Of all the humiliations she had been forced to endure, this was by far the worst. Yet, even now, her perverse nature came to the fore, and she felt the juices flowing inside her as Umangu rotated his digit in her behind and she thought of all those behind her witnessing what was happening to her.

Umangu made her straighten up and face the audience once more. The man beside her was still talking, but she could tell that the auction had not yet begun. She wondered how much longer her ordeal would last. She was certain that there had been no such ritual when the men had been sold before her.

She heard a peal of laughter and, looking to her right, she saw that one of Umangu's companions was approaching , carrying a tray. At first she couldn't make out its

137

contents, then she felt a hollow feeling at the pit of her stomach as it became clear to her. The youngster was bearing a variety of phalluses out onto the dais. He moved to the centre of the stage, then held the tray in front of the young slave's face.

Lisa surveyed them with a sinking feeling. There must have been about twenty, of all different shapes and sizes. Some were long and smooth, with bullet-like heads. Others were exact replicas of penises, with every curve and detail precisely reproduced. Some had strange protrusions, clearly designed to stimulate, possibly even to hurt the one using them. The longest must have been all of ten inches, with a girth in proportion, the smallest not more than six inches, and some were no more than half an inch in diameter. Lisa ran her eyes over them with trepidation, as Umangu looked on with undisguised delight.

"You like cocks, slut?" he said. "Many cocks here. Which one you like?"

Lisa said nothing, but she felt her stomach tighten into a knot as she contemplated what they might have in mind for her next.

The young man with the tray had turned to the crowd, and was holding up the objects in turn. Each time he did so there was a cheer from those watching. Lisa could see Mrs Sadler and her group laughing, and she wondered for the umpteenth time at the cruel fate that had brought her here to stand naked and helpless before this baying crowd whilst her own compatriots looked on uncaring.

All at once she noticed Umangu's second companion had come onto the stage from the other side. He was carrying two bags, one in each hand, and he held them up to the crowd, bringing roars of laughter as he shook them in the air, much to the puzzlement of Lisa. The man in charge was speaking again, bringing new cheers from those watching, then the youngster was holding up the bags to her.

"Take one ball from each bag," said Umangu. "Then you will know how much pleasure you can expect."

Lisa eyed the bags suspiciously. Her mind went back to the time when she had been the captive of a rebel band. They had drawn lots every night to decide who was to fuck her. This reminded her of those days, though surely there couldn't be a number for each of the members of the audience?

Whack! Umangu brought the cane down hard across Lisa's bare buttocks, bringing a cry of pain and surprise from her and a fresh shout of laughter from the audience.

"Take the balls!" he ordered.

Slowly Lisa reached out her hands and dipped them into the bags. The balls were made of rough wood, and she fingered them nervously before drawing two out. She handed them to Umangu, who inspected them, then showed them to her. One bore the number five, whilst the other was marked seventeen. Umangu went to the tray and picked up one of the phalluses. It was about eight inches long and very thick, its length studded with protrusions. It was only then that Lisa noticed that the base was inscribed with the number five. So she had been right about the lottery, though this time it hadn't been a man she was choosing, but a dildo. She shuddered as Umangu held the object up to the cheering crowd.

"Turn and bend again, English slave girl," the youngster commanded.

Lisa looked at him. He was at least three years younger than her, not much more than a boy. Yet she had no choice than to obey this arrogant youth and to accept the humiliations he was subjecting her to. She glanced down at the

139

long, thick object he held in his hand, and a sudden shiver of excitement ran through her. She couldn't be aroused surely? Not by this awful scene? Yet she couldn't deny the unmistakable wetness that was seeping into her bare crotch at the thought of what was to come. Her cheeks crimson, she turned her back on the crowd and bent forward, her eyes closed. Then she spread her legs.

At the first touch of the phallus, her entire body shuddered, and she bit her lip to suppress a cry. Umangu was rubbing the end of the thing up and down the soft, creamy flesh of her inner thigh, the cool, hard wood making her shiver, despite the heat of the day. He moved it up between her legs and rubbed it back and forth along her slit, and she gasped as she felt it run over the now swollen bud of her clitoris. She knew she was wet down there, and that her lubrication was coating the end of the dildo. She knew too that those watching would see how aroused she was.

He moved the object so that it was positioned right at the entrance to her vagina. Then he began to press, twisting it as he did so. For a moment, her flesh resisted. Then she gasped aloud as it penetrated her. He pressed harder, forcing the hard, knobbly object deeper and deeper inside her until it filled her completely, stretching the walls of her sex with its hard, unyielding solidity.

For Lisa it was both an exquisite and a devastating experience. The lascivious young slave loved the way the phallus felt against the sensitivity of her sex. Had it been a lover in the privacy of her bedchamber using the toy on her she would have been in heaven. But she was here, on this barren dais, before an audience of strangers, her naked body displayed to all whilst the scruffy youth performed this most intimate act on her. Yet even here she couldn't suppress a moan of pure desire as he twisted the object inside

140

her, sending new shocks of pleasure coursing through her lovely young body.

Umangu took hold of her hand and guided it down to where the base of the object still protruded from her vagina.

"You hold," he ordered.

Lisa took hold of the phallus between her fingers. Already she could feel the wetness that had seeped onto it and she clenched her teeth as the desire to frig herself grew. So absorbed was she in the sensations that the phallus was engendering that she barely noticed that Umangu had turned back to the tray that his companion was still holding. It was with a terrible shock, therefore, that she realised that something else was being held up before those watching, something that brought renewed shrieks of laughter. Umangu lowered his arm, then held the thing in under Lisa's bowed head, and she gasped in surprise.

It was another dildo. This one was longer and thinner than the one inside her, but no less gnarled. Stamped on the base was the number seventeen. Then she understood. The first bag had contained the numbers of the ordinary dildoes. But the balls in the second bag represented these more slender objects, designed to penetrate an even more intimate part of her anatomy.

Even as the realisation came to her, Umangu snatched the dildo away and moved round behind her. Lisa bit her lip as she felt the cool, hard wood touch the dark star of her anus and begin to press. She cried aloud as it penetrated her, worming its way into her backside as he continued to press and twist it. Once again he slid it all the way inside until it was almost out of sight of the laughing onlookers.

Lisa's body was on fire with a combination of pain and desire. The sensation of the double penetration was exquisite. It felt almost as if the two long, hard objects might meet inside her, so thoroughly was she filled by them. She gripped the one inside her vagina hard, trying her best to resist the temptation to move it as the desires inside her overcame her.

Umangu took hold of her other hand and guided it to the object projecting from her rear. Lisa could only imagine the sight she made to those watching, bent over almost double, her legs spread wide, the two dark, ugly objects projecting from her, their hard shiny texture in complete contrast with the smooth softness of her skin.

"Turn round, slut," ordered Umangu.

Lisa straightened slowly, still gripping the two phalluses. Then she turned to face her audience, her legs still spread wide, her face glowing with shame as the shouts of those watching reached her ears. She dropped her eyes, staring down at her slim, beautiful body, her pert breasts standing proudly, the nipples hard and prominent, and yet another shiver of lust shook her young body.

Umangu smiled. "See," he said to those watching. "She is aroused. This slave will love to please you and to please herself at the same time. Come on slave, show us your arousal."

Lisa stared at him, and he lowered his gaze to her crotch. "Do it, slave," he ordered. "pleasure yourself."

Lisa remained still for a moment longer. Then, almost imperceptibly, her hands began to move. She gave a small cry of excitement at the sensation of the two dildoes working back and forth inside her. She moved them again, and her knees buckled slightly as a new pulse of desire ran through her, bringing a fresh surge of wetness that leaked onto her fingers.

She began to increase the force with which she was

pressing the two phalluses into her, beads of sweat forming on her brow as she fought to keep her emotions under control. Each time the hard, rough objects moved inside her the lust within her increased, and her hands began to pump all the harder.

The wanton youngster bit her lip to suppress the screams that were rising in her throat as she became lost in her lewd pleasure. She knew that her behaviour was shameful, and that she was the object of derision as she stood there, brazenly masturbating with the two dildos, but the sheer physical gratification that they were giving her overcame the vestiges of her modesty and she began to work them back and forth with renewed vigour.

Lisa was barely in control now, facing the crowd, her head thrown back, her lovely young breasts shaking up and down as she rammed the dildoes into her vagina and backside simultaneously. The wetness from her cunt coated her bare sex lips with a sheen of shiny moisture, and a tiny trickle ran down her inner thigh as she masturbated hard.

Her orgasm, when it came, was a long and loud one, her cries ringing out as she let herself go. Such was the force of her passion that her knees buckled under her and she dropped to a kneeling position, her legs spread wide, her hands still pumping back and forth at front and back.

It took some minutes before she finally came down, the actions of her hands slowing gradually as her passion ebbed from her. At last, though, she was at rest, the objects of her desire still projecting from her, her head bowed so that her long dark locks obscured her blushing face, a small bead of sweat running down her neck and through the valley between her breasts.

For a moment there was silence. Then the crowd erupted into a roar of noise. Lisa wanted to cover her ears. She wished the ground would open and envelop her, hide her from the shame of her actions. She peered up through raised eyelashes at the people in front of her, all laughing and cheering. Then she heard Umangu's voice above all of them.

"Let the auction begin!"

Chapter 18

Lisa blinked into the heat haze, then narrowed her eyes. There, in the shimmering mirage, she seemed to see something other than the desolate bush that was all about her. She kept her eyes fixed on the point ahead of her, and slowly the shape of the buildings began to become clear. There was no doubt about it, she was approaching some sort of town.

She glanced down at herself and, despite the heat, gave a shiver. She was wearing only a small, ragged top, her hard nipples perfectly outlined against the material. The top didn't even come down as far as her waist, below which she was, as usual, naked, her shiny cunt-ring and degrading slave mark on open view. On her feet were small leather sandals to protect them from the hard, stony ground on which she was walking. Out here, in the open bush land, she was, at least, free from prying eyes. But ahead, in the town, there would be people, and she knew they would come out to catch a sight of the shameless young Englishwoman being led through their streets.

It was three days now since the auction. The sale itself had gone frighteningly quickly, with bids coming in from all sides as she had stood on the dais, traces of her recent arousal still visible in the sheen of moisture that covered

144

her bare sex. She had had little idea of who was bidding, or how much, but she could judge by the audience reaction that it was a hard-fought sale. At last, though, the hammer had come down, and she knew she had a new owner.

Afterwards she had been hustled off the stage by Umangu and his companions, who had taken the opportunity to feel her up one last time in the shadowy corners behind the dais before handing her over to the guards again.

They had incarcerated her in a new cell on her own that night, and early the next morning a man had opened the door and ordered her out. She had been given the skimpy top, then they had handed her a jar of sweet-smelling ointment and ordered her to rub it onto her skin. She had guessed that this was some sort of sun block, as she knew her fair skin was greatly prized and her masters were careful to preserve it. She had massaged it into her bare flesh under the watchful eyes of her guards, then her hands had been manacled behind her and she had been pushed out onto the street.

The walk through the town had been an ordeal. All about the people laughed and jeered at the sight of the beautiful young white slave as she walked along, her eyes cast down, her private parts visible to all. It had been quite a relief when they had finally left the urban conurbation behind them and set out into the open countryside.

They had walked for two days, just Lisa and four gun-toting roughs who were her guards. They would stop every three hours or so for food or drink, then move on. Not a word was spoken to the young slave, and her orders were given by simple gestures. When night fell they chained her ankle to a stout tree and left her to sleep under the stars. Despite the fact that her backside and cunt were bare at all times, they made no attempt to molest her, much to her

145

surprise. She guessed that her new master must be a powerful man to keep his servants under such control, even
when unsupervised.

Now, as she saw the buildings ahead, she sensed that
she was nearing journey's end, and new fears began to as-
sail her. Somewhere ahead was her new master. What
would he be like? What would he demand of her? She was
no stranger to cruelty, and she knew that her body was
extraordinarily desirable, so she had few illusions as to what
would be demanded of her once she arrived.

As they came closer to the town, Lisa saw figures emerging from the buildings, peering out at the strange procession that was approaching. She felt her cheeks glowing at
the thought of her bare sex and the brand across the soft
cheeks of her bottom, but there was nothing she could do
to cover herself, so she marched on, trying not to catch the
eyes of the people as she and her companions walked up
the dusty road between the houses. Already she could hear
the laughter as people pointed at her, calling their friends
out of their houses to see the extraordinary sight of the
bare-arsed white girl being led chained through their midst.

It wasn't a large town, no more than two miles across,
she estimated. In the very centre was a house much larger
than the others, toward which they were heading. She
sensed at once that this was the home of her new master,
and her heart thumped as they came closer to it. It was
surrounded by a high fence topped with barbed wire, beyond which she could see half a dozen shiny sports cars
parked, though where anyone could find to drive them in
such a place as this, she couldn't think.

A guard stood at the entrance, carrying a rifle similar
to those of her escorts. As they approached he pushed the
gate open, his eyes fixed on Lisa's bare crotch. She walked

through, glad to be away from the jeering crowds in the street, though still filled with trepidation about what lay ahead of her.

The building was a large one, three stories tall, with an ornate frontage that spoke of the country's colonial heritage. She was led up the stone steps and through the double doors. Inside she found herself in a large entrance hall. The floor was bare stone, and the air was considerably cooler after the dry heat of the trail. The decor was more Arabic than African, with ornate carved tables and expensive looking tapestries hanging from the walls. A few months previously, Lisa might have been fascinated by its ornateness. Before her capture and descent into her present life of debauched servility, Lisa had taken an interest in such things and the demure youngster had spent many hours in museums and public libraries studying Arab artefacts. Now, though, she was allowed no time for her own pursuits, her entire life dedicated to satisfying the cruel whims of her masters.

She was led down a passageway and through a small door. Here the decorations were much less grand, and she guessed that she was in the servants' quarters. They took her down some stone steps and into a large, barely furnished room. There were two young black women there, no more than girls really, about sixteen years old, Lisa guessed. They were dressed in identical white skirts and tops. Both held their hands to their mouths and giggled at the sight of the barely clad white girl.

Lisa's guard removed the manacles from her wrists, and she rubbed the skin where she had been wearing them, glad to relieve the stiffness at last. The men spoke a few words to the girls, who giggled again. Then the guards turned and abruptly left, closing the door behind them.

147

Lisa stood, her legs apart, whilst the two girls walked around her, making remarks to one another that Lisa was unable to understand. They reached out and touched her skin, pinching her bottom and running their fingers over her brand and tattoo, making her shiver slightly as their soft, brown fingers stroked her pale flesh. All the time Lisa stayed perfectly still, saying nothing, her cheeks glowing red as she allowed herself to be inspected.

One of the girls tugged at her top, and made a gesture that told her she was to remove it. Reluctantly she grasped hold of the hem and dragged it up over her head, revealing her creamy, firm breasts, the brown nipples already stiffening as she reacted to baring them to this pair.

They felt her breasts, pinching her nipples and twisting them, laughing at the expression of pain on her face as they did so. Then, still laughing, they took her hands and dragged her out through a door into another room. In the centre of this room was a large stone bath filled with water, and it was toward this that they were taking her. They gestured that she was to climb into it, and she did so. The water was cold, but that was not unwelcome to the youngster after the heat of her trek. When one of the girls offered her a cloth and some soap she accepted them gratefully and began washing down her body, stooping and immersing the cloth, then rubbing it over her firm breasts, letting the water run down her body and carry away the grime of her long walk whilst the two girls looked on.

Once she was clean again she stepped from the bath. On a side table was an array of liquids in bottles and she was led across to this. She lifted the lids from some and sniffed at them. They were perfumes, some sweet, some musky. She chose one she liked and dabbed it behind her ears and between her breasts. As she did so she thought of sitting at her own dressing table in London, where she had made herself up every morning. That seemed a million miles from this awful place, and the Lisa of old was completely different from the young slave who now stood naked, waiting for her guards to manacle her hands behind her once more.

To Lisa's surprise, the girls then produced a cloak. It was a simple white garment that fastened at the neck, and they placed it round her, tying the draw cord above her breasts. It hung down almost to her ankles. With a start, Lisa realised that it covered her slave mark, and she glanced around herself nervously. It was a strange thing, she pondered, that, whereas any normal girl would be afraid to be seen naked, she was uncomfortable at being clothed. It said a lot for how her psyche had been changed by the circumstances of her slavery.

They took her from the room back into the main part of the house. As she walked the cloak opened in front of her, revealing the length of her legs, her cunt- ring occasionally flashing into view. Here and there they passed other servants who paused in their work to stare at the strange sight of the barely clad white girl as she was led past them, her gaze fixed on the ground. The girls led her down a series of corridors, then approached a large pair of double doors. On either side stood a tall, mahogany-black guard, dressed in fine uniform. They had on maroon jackets and trousers trimmed with gold, and each carried a curved shiny sword. As the trio came close they pushed open the doors.

Before Lisa was a long, green carpet that led to a large chair set above the floor on a platform. A man was seated in the chair. He was aged about fifty, rather overweight and dressed in flowing, expensive robes, a turban perched on his head. With a sinking feeling, Lisa realised that this

149

was her new master. On either side of the room were more guards lining the walls and around the platform were a number of finely dressed people. Lisa was reminded of a throne room from a film set in mediaeval times.

The girls shoved her forward, then retired back through the door as it closed behind her. Lisa felt very exposed and vulnerable as she made her way forward, stepping tentatively, aware that all eyes in the room were on her, and afraid that the cloak would open too far, revealing her naked body beneath. She was only too aware of the inadequacy of the cloak to cover her, and the colour rose in her cheeks as she made her way toward the throne.

She came to a halt at the foot of the steps that led up to where her master was sitting, placing her legs apart as she had been taught. She glanced shyly up at the man seated before her. His skin was paler than that of the locals, as was that of many of the people who surrounded him. Lisa stole a glance at them. There were both men and women, all of whom had an air of affluence about them. All were staring at her. Some were laughing, others, particularly the men, were eyeing her with interest, and she shivered slightly as she felt their eyes on her body.

A man stepped out from beside her. He wore a uniform not dissimilar from that of the guards, though his was decorated with a thick gold sash and the turban on his head sprouted brightly-coloured plumes that clearly depicted that he was of a higher rank than the others.

"This is the slave, Your Honour," he intoned in a deep voice. It was the first time Lisa had heard English spoken since she had been auctioned, and it took her by surprise.

The man on the throne nodded. "What is her name Askari?"

"Her name is Lisa, Your Honour."

He turned to the apprehensive youngster.

"Is it true what they say about you, Lisa?"

With a shock, Lisa realised that he was addressing her directly.

"I... I don't know what they say, Sir," she stammered.

"That you give your body freely to men. That you are a slut. That you love the feel of a man's cock inside you and the taste of his spunk. That you relish the bite of the whip on your flesh, and that your cunt runs with wetness whenever a man touches you there."

Lisa hung her head. "I have been forced to do many things, Sir. I am but a slave."

"Do you know who I am?"

"Are-are you my master, Sir?"

"I am Omar Sulkami. I own this town and the surrounding countryside. And, as you seem to have realised, I own you. I own your pretty breasts and your tight little cunt, and I will do with them as I wish."

The words sent an odd shiver through Lisa's young frame. She had never really thought of herself as being owned until now. She looked up at the man on the throne, sensing his power over her, and she shivered again.

"Yes, Master," she said quietly.

"I am going to have you stripped naked for the delectation of my guests," he said. "Do you object?"

This was the first time Lisa could remember that anyone had asked her permission before making use of her beautiful body. She knew, though, that there was only one answer he would accept.

"No Master," she said. "I don't object. Strip me if you wish."

"You don't object to being seen nude by my men?"

"I do not object if that is your wish, Master."

"But surely only a slut would strip naked in such company?"

Lisa looked away from him. "Perhaps that is true. Were I not a slave, then I might object."

"But you are a slave. My slave."

"Yes Master. So if your wish is to have me stripped, then that is my wish too, Master."

"So be it. Strip the slave naked, Askari. Let us see her most private places."

The man called Askari stepped forward and reached for the cord that fastened Lisa's cloak. She stood rigid whilst he undid it, her heart racing. He slipped the knot and let it fall to the ground, leaving her completely nude. A low murmur went up from those watching as they saw her cunt ring and the slave mark on her bare pubis. Lisa simply stared ahead of her, her face crimson. Even after all this time she still couldn't come to terms with being seen in the nude, and the brief respite of the cloak had simply served to remind her of the shame of her nakedness.

"Turn round."

Obediently Lisa turned, revealing to them the brand, in the shape of a leaping lion, that decorated the pale flesh of her pert behind, whilst the rest of the guards feasted their hungry eyes on her breasts and sex.

Sulkami made her turn to face him again, then ordered Askari to release her hands. He undid the cuffs, and Lisa let her arms drop to her sides.

"I'd like to see an example of what I paid for," said Sulkami. He turned his gaze away from her. "You! Come here!"

He addressed one of the guards, who stepped forward smartly to stand beside the young English girl. He was tall, well over six foot, with jet-black skin.

"This man is clearly aroused by the sight of your body," he said to Lisa. "Will you submit to him?"

Lisa blushed. "Yes, Master, if that is what you wish."

"Make him hard."

Lisa felt her stomach muscles tighten as she heard the order. Her natural instinct was to question it, but she dare not. Besides, her time spent in slavery told her exactly what he meant.

She turned to face the man beside her, then dropped to her knees and reached for the flies on his uniform trousers. She heard a grunt of approval from her master as she took up this submissive position, so she knew she was doing the right thing.

She undid the man's trousers and let them drop to his ankles. His cock hung down from his groin, thick and flaccid, his heavy balls dangling behind. She reached out a hand and closed it about his shaft, pulling back the foreskin and uncovering his glans. As she did so she felt his large, fleshy organ stir beneath her fingers.

She brought her other hand up from underneath and cupped his balls, caressing them gently. A small moan escaped his lips as she did so and his large black cock began to grow. She glanced sideways briefly at her master, whose eyes were fixed upon her. Then she raised the man's shaft to her lips and took him into her mouth.

Lisa's training at the hands of her previous owners had taught her how to arouse a man. By now, she had done it so many times that it should have been no more than an automatic series of movements. But, such was her lascivious nature, she couldn't suppress the emotions that the taste and feel of a man's cock always aroused within her. As she wormed her tongue under the guard's foreskin and tasted

153

his secretions, a tremor of excitement shook her, and she found herself sucking hard as his cock swelled to erection.

She continued to suck, her pretty breasts shaking as she worked her head up and down on his now erect organ. But she was mindful of the order she had been given and, once she was sure that his cock could stiffen no further she released it from her mouth and turned her head towards Sulkami, gazing questioningly up at him whilst her small hand continued to work the guard's foreskin back and forth.

Her master nodded. "You do indeed make a good slut, Lisa," he said. "You clearly enjoy the taste of a man's cock, even a lowly guard's."

At this a ripple of laughter ran about those watching and Lisa felt the heat in her cheeks increase.

"I fear, though, that this man has been too long without a woman," Sulkami went on. "Look at his face, little white whore."

Lisa glanced up at the guard. His features were contorted into an expression of concentration that she knew all too well. At that very moment she felt his organ twitch beneath her fingers and suddenly hot spunk was spurting from his penis onto her upturned face and breasts. By the time she managed to get him back into her mouth, three copious loads of semen had erupted from him over her naked form, yet there was still more to suck and swallow down as his orgasm continued.

Lisa kept him in her mouth until the spurts dwindled to a trickle, then to nothing. Once she was sure he was done she released his shining knob from between her lips and rose slowly to her feet, turning to face her master. The room had gone quiet now as the people stared at the young beauty, her face and breasts splattered with sperm that trickled down onto her belly and on toward her crotch.

Sulkami eyed her for a moment, then nodded.

"Good," he said. "I think you will be very suitable."

Chapter 19

The next few days saw an unexpected lull in the cruel behaviour to which Lisa had become accustomed since her abduction from London. She was given a small cell high up in the top of her master's house, with a barred window that overlooked the town. To her surprise, she was allowed to keep the cloak that she had been given on her arrival so that, for the first time she could remember, she was able to hide her breasts and sex from the eyes of those she encountered. As far as day-to-day life was concerned, she was given more privacy than she could remember since her enslavement. She received her meals in her cell and, twice a day, she was allowed out to walk around the courtyard in the centre of the building. During all this time, no sexual demands were made upon her.

All this was puzzling to the youngster. Her new master seemed to be taking no interest in her at all. Yet he had paid a great deal of money for her, so there must be a reason why he wanted her.

It was nearly a week after her arrival at Sulkami's residence that Lisa noticed that something was happening in the town outside. People were arriving from the countryside in droves, most on foot, but some in vehicles. Lisa sat at her window and watched them come in. Hawkers had set up food stalls in the streets to feed the newcomers and, before long, there was a carnival-like atmosphere out there. Then, as dusk fell, Lisa noticed that the crowds were drifting toward the only other large building in the town, a big arena-like structure about two stories high located about half a mike from where she was incarcerated.

The two maids arrived at Lisa's room just as it was getting dark. They had been virtually the only people Lisa had encountered since her meeting with Sulkami, delivering her food and escorting her when she left the cell. Now she saw that they were carrying a pair of cuffs, and they clicked these onto her wrists, fastening her hands behind her back. Then they took her from the room and down the narrow staircase that led into the main part of the house. Instead of escorting her along her accustomed route to the courtyard, however, they took her another route through the back of the building.

They led her through a door into what appeared to be a small, bare box-room. It was only when the sliding door descended, plunging her into darkness, that Lisa realised she was in the back of a van. Moments later she heard the sound of the engine starting up, and the vehicle lurched forward, almost throwing the youngster off balance.

It was a short journey, the van bouncing along through the streets. After no more than five minutes, it drew to a halt and reversed a short distance. When the door was lifted once again, Lisa found herself staring down a long, bare corridor.

Her escorts appeared from either side and led her out of the van and along the passage. The place was starkly lit, the walls and floor devoid of decoration. Every now and again they would pass a pair of Sulkami's guards, whose eyes would follow the young white girl as she hurried by.

As they progressed, Lisa became aware of a sound that at first she couldn't identify. It was like a rushing of wind or water, a wave of amorphous noise that seemed to fill

156

her head. Then she realised what it was. It was the sound of voices. Hundreds of voices, possibly thousands. It was the excited chatter of what must be a huge crowd, and it was not far ahead.

At once Lisa's stomach began to churn as she contemplated what could possibly lie in store for her. She had no doubt that they would put her on display again, and that some kind of ignominy would be heaped upon her. Yet there was nothing she could do about it, and she knew there was no point offering resistance.

She was surprised, therefore, to find herself being taken, not onto a stage, but into a small room, on the far side of which was a long, narrow window. It was positioned at eye level and was about a foot deep. Standing next to it, peering through, was Askari, and he turned as she was brought in. He barked an order to the maids, who undid Lisa's cuffs. Then the pair retired, leaving her alone with this intimidating man.

"Come here."

She crossed to where he was standing, walking carefully so as to preserve her modesty in the loose-fitting cloak. As she did so she took a good look at Askari. He was about forty years old, she estimated, tall and powerfully built. He was the same ebony colour as the rest of the guards, and clearly was not of the same racial origins as Sulkami. As she came up to him, he indicated the window and she peered through.

They were in a large building, almost certainly the one she had seen from her room. It was indeed an arena, with tier after tier of terraces set in a huge circle. The terraces were a sea of excited people, shouting and cheering, many drinking an amber liquid from bottles. Set in the middle of the terraces was a walled-off area. There sat Sulkami in all his splendour, surrounded by his court followers and guards. The centre of the arena was a pit, about fifteen feet deep and twenty-five feet across. There were two heavily-barred doors set opposite each other, and the floor of the area was completely empty.

Without warning there came a creaking of metal, and one of the gates began to rise. As it did so, a hush fell over the crowd and all eyes turned toward the entrance to the arena. The door ascended slowly, and, all at once, a huge, hairy hand appeared, grasping the thick metal. It began to shake the bars, rattling them with such force that Lisa feared that whoever or whatever had hold of them might tear the door from its frame. Then, as the entrance widened, a figure swung under it and into the arena, to a roar of approval from the crowd.

Lisa stared down into the arena in total shock. He was the biggest and ugliest man she had ever seen. He must have been more than seven foot tall, she estimated, with huge muscular shoulders. Although he was stooped forward, she could see that his upper body rippled with muscles, his neck alone being wider that the English girl's waist. His face was grotesque, like some gargoyle, with small, beady eyes and a broad, flat nose. His lips were thick, his mouth twisted into a snarl. Above all, though, Lisa was staggered by the sheer size of him, his biceps rippling as he waved his arms and bellowed at the crowd, who roared back at him.

The young girl watched in horror, scarcely believing that it was a man she was looking at. His brown body was covered with a thick layer of hair, and his deep-set eyes showed nothing but aggression as he stared round at the crowd, his teeth bared. He wore only a loin cloth, and the bulge beneath it told Lisa that his genitals were in proportion to the rest of him.

"Mountain man," said Askari. "Bred to fight."

She turned her questioning eyes toward him.

"They are a primitive tribe from the mountains to the south. The men fight incessantly, especially over women. Our Honourable master had him captured and brought here to fight in the arena. It takes six men to subdue him, and even then he must be tranquillised first."

"But what is he here for, Sir?"

"It is the local amusement. That one is Hako, our leader's fighter. A challenger has been brought in from outside."

Even as he spoke, another roar sounded from below and the second door began to rise. Hako swung round to face it and, as he did so, a second mountain man sprang into the ring. At once a shout went up from the crowd and the two monstrous men began to circle one another, snarling.

"They'll kill each other," said Lisa in alarm.

"That does sometimes happen," said Askari, "But it's rare. They'll simply fight until one is down and out."

As he spoke, the second man leapt forward and dealt Hako a blow with his fist that would have broken the neck of any other man. Hako reeled back for a moment, then he was on the offensive, his arms flailing as he threw himself at his foe.

It was the most violent thing that Lisa had ever witnessed, the two men crashing about the ring, the sickening thump of fist against flesh ringing about the arena whilst the crowd cheered them on enthusiastically. Lisa watched in quiet fascination, wincing at every blow.

The men went at it hard, their bodies thudding together. First one would be on top, then the other. There seemed to

159

be no rules whatsoever, with the two monstrous men punching kicking and head-butting each other whilst the onlookers screamed encouragement. Lisa could barely watch as the pair fought, covering her eyes as some of the blows fell.

For some time it was impossible to say who would win, each man seeming to give as good as he got. Slowly, though, the one called Hako began to get the upper hand, landing two blows for every one his opponent could muster, and Lisa sensed that the fight was drawing to a close. Soon the other man was staggering, and Hako was able to push him back against the bars. Blow after bow landed on his body, and his eyes began to glaze over.

When Hako dealt the final punch, sending his opponent crashing to the floor, the crowd went mad with delight, even Sulkami rising to his feet to applaud the fighter. This seemed to enrage the mountain man even more, and he began jumping up, trying to scale the walls and get at the jeering onlookers. Then one of the guards appeared at the ringside with a long blowpipe. He took aim and a small dart shot across and pierced Hako's neck. The massive man gave a roar of rage and rushed across to where the man was standing. He never got there, however. Halfway across the arena he staggered, then his eyes seemed to empty of all expression and he slumped to the floor.

Askari turned away from the view.

"Well, what do you think?"

"It's terribly violent, Sir. I thought Hako would kill him."

Askari sniffed. "That was no more than a sparring match," he said.

"I don't understand."

"In two weeks there will be a challenge for the area

160

championship. There is a lot of money at stake for your master. Much more than the price of a slave, even a white female."

Lisa stared at him, slightly confused by the remark. Why should he equate the price that Sulkami had paid for her with the amount he had invested in Hako's win? Unless she was involved somehow. But how? Even as these questions were filling her mind, someone walked into the room behind her. She turned to see a heavily-built man standing there. He was of the same race as Askari and the guards, his narrow eyes glowering out of a cruel looking face. He wore a cloth about his waist of a similar colour to the guards' uniforms, though it was old and faded. It was held up by a black belt, into which a leather horse whip was tucked. As he surveyed the youngster, Lisa found herself cowering away instinctively pulling her cloak across the front of her body.

Askari said a few words to the man, then turned back to the girl.

"This is N'dovi, Hako's trainer," he said. "Now it is time for you to start earning your keep."

Once again Lisa stared at him in confusion, but he seemed to have lost interest in her, turning to gaze out at the arena once more.

N'dovi grabbed Lisa's arm and made a gesture with his head toward the door. Lisa followed him out, her heart beating hard as she wondered what could possibly be in store for her now.

Chapter 20

Lisa stood in the dismal, dark cell, staring out through the bars into the passageway beyond. It had been almost an hour since N'dovi had brought her here from the room in which she had witnessed the fight. She had heard the noise of the crowd departing, still in high spirits over the result, but now the place was quiet, only the occasional banging of a metal door telling her she was not alone. She hugged her meagre cloak to her young body, wondering for the umpteenth time why she was there.

This cell was very different from the one she had been kept in at the big house. There she had had a proper bed and a window to stare out of. Here she had a sack stuffed with straw and nothing else. Except the cloak. That too puzzled her. Why had she been allowed to cover herself like this? After all, apart from anything else, it was against the law for her pubis to be hidden. Yet they had treated her with more consideration than anyone since her initial abduction. It was as if they were softening her up for something, and she suspected that she was about to find out what.

A clank of metal told her that the door at the end of the corridor was being opened. N'dovi came through, accompanied by two other men. Like N'dovi, they were clad only in cloths about their waists and, like him also, both carried whips in their belts. Their faces spread into wide grins as their eyes fell on the youngster and she shrank back in her cell. They undid the lock and held the door open, gesturing for her to come out. Lisa summoned up as much courage as she could and stepped out of the cell, grateful for the cloak to cover her nakedness from these men.

They took her through three more doors, each one sturdier than the last, then up to the entrance of a large cage. The bars on this were three times the thickness of the ones on her own cell, yet still she could see places where some mighty force had bent them. Then she saw Hako.

The huge mountain man was standing at the back of the cage. At first his stance seemed strange to the young girl, as if he was raising his arms in greeting. Then she saw that he was chained there, his great bear-like arms held outspread by thick chains and manacles attached to the wall. His ankles were similarly bound, so that he was quite unable to move. At the sight of N'dovi he gave a fearful roar, indicating that whatever they had used to tranquillise him had already worn off.

Even despite the way Hako was immobilised, Lisa felt a pang of alarm as the door to the cage was opened. N'dovi pushed her inside, and she stood, staring up into the face of the monstrous fighter, her heart hammering.

At the sight of Lisa, Hako had ceased to struggle, his expression turning to one of astonishment as he studied her.

N'dovi laughed. "Hako not see woman for many years," he said. "Hako like white woman."

Lisa watched Hako's face. His eyes were wide as he took in her small form, and she shrank back, only to bump into N'dovi, who was standing behind her. As she did so he grabbed her arms, pinning them to her back. At the same time he barked an order to one of the guards, who stepped forward and, grabbing hold of Lisa's cloak by the neck, ripped it from her and thrust it aside.

Lisa gave a cry of dismay as she found herself totally naked. She struggled, but N'dovi's grip was too strong for her. She looked back at Hako, whose eyes were fixed on her breasts and on her bare pubis, where her cunt ring gleamed in the dim light. Even as she watched she saw the swelling in his loin cloth, and he rattled his chains, pulling at them with such violence that she felt sure that they must break.

One of the guards pulled out his whip and struck the mountain man on the thigh, bringing a roar of rage that made the guard laugh aloud. Then N'dovi released Lisa's arms, and the three men moved to the back of the cage.

"See, he desires you, little slave slut," said N'dovi. "Go, remove his cloth and see what he has for you."

Lisa shook her head. "I... I can't," she stammered. "What if he breaks free?"

Whack! N'dovi's whip came down hard across the pale cheeks of her backside, making her cry out in pain and surprise. It was the first time she had been struck since she had been sold, and she realised that she was back amongst the cruelty of which she had experienced so much. Still she hesitated, but when he raised his arm again she took a nervous step forward.

As she came closer to the mountain man he seemed to her even larger than before, his hefty body towering over her slim, petite form. His eyes gleamed as he fixed them on her nudity, and he gave another mighty wrench at his chains, though they held fast.

Lisa was standing only inches from him now, her nipples almost brushing his torso. She could smell the sweat on his dark skin and hear the rasp of his breathing and, for the first time she could sense his maleness and the arousal that the sight of her was engendering in him.

"Remove his cloth," commanded N'dovi. "Let us see the full extent of his feelings."

Lisa reached forward tentatively, her small fingers taking hold of the cloth that surrounded his waist. It was wrapped about him and down under his crotch, so that it contained his genitals. It was fastened with a knot at the front. Her fingers shaking, Lisa began to undo it.

As it finally slipped undone, the cloth fell to the floor, and Lisa was confronted with the largest cock she had ever seen. It was huge, rising stiffly from his groin like a great black truncheon with a capacious ball sac hanging below. As she stared at it, Lisa wondered if she could ever contain such a monster inside her, and the thought of being penetrated by it sent a quiver of excitement through her.

"Touch it. Feel the size and strength of a mountain man."

Lisa looked up into the monster's eyes again. They were filled with lust as he pulled at the chains that held his arms. She dared not think what would happen to her if he broke free. Slowly, nervously, she reached out her hand and closed her fingers about his shaft. At once there came a groan from Hako and she felt it twitch violently. So thick was it that she could barely get her small fingers all the way about it, and she licked her lips as she surveyed its veined length.

"Look at it. Have you ever seen such a magnificent specimen?"

She pulled his foreskin back and surveyed the shiny bulbous tip, bringing another deep groan from him.

"Feel the heat of it. Squeeze it between your breasts."

Lisa glanced back at N'dovi. He was still holding the whip in his hand as he watched her. She turned to the mountain man, who gave a roar, thrusting his groin forward at her. Slowly, timidly she moved forward. Then, crouching down, she pulled Hako's massive penis to her. Taking hold of her breasts in her hands, she pressed them together, trying to enclose his shaft between them. His

165

cock did indeed feel hot on her bare skin and its hardness astounded her. The end pushed up under her chin, and at once she felt him begin to thrust his hips against her.

Lisa held her breasts tight together, her nipples standing out like hard brown knobs as she let Hako tit-fuck her. His bulbous glans rose and fell in front of her face as he grunted with pleasure, shaking her small frame with his violent thrusts. Moments later he came, the tip of his penis spitting great gobs of thick white semen over Lisa's face, neck and breasts. Never, in all her experience, had Lisa seen so violent an orgasm in a man, his bellows ringing about the cell as spurt after spurt of his spunk covered the young white beauty. She kept her breasts pressed about his organ, choking as a great gob of his seed found her mouth, then dribbled from her lips and down her body.

By the time his spurts had reduced to no more than a dribble, Lisa's entire upper body was coated with his spunk. It oozed down between her breasts and dribbled to her crotch, coating her sex and dripping from her cunt ring. She stepped back from him, wiping the warm, viscous liquid from her eyes and licking the drops from her mouth and chin. She turned to face N'dovi and his guards, all of whom were grinning.

"That is good, little white slut," said N'dovi. "I think you will make a good companion for Hako. But his cock is still stiff. Put on a little show for him."

"Sh-show?"

"Certainly. I'm sure you've been taught to entertain men with that exquisite body."

Lisa looked at him, and at the confident expression on his face. Her thoughts went back to the village where she had been held a naked prisoner for so many months and used as prey in the warriors' hunts. They would track her down through the bush, then pin her to the ground and fuck her when they caught her. They had taught her a dance to celebrate the blooding of three new warriors, and she had performed it before the whole tribe, her actions working the men into such a frenzy that all three had taken her together, simultaneously penetrating her cunt, arse and mouth.

N'dovi clapped his hands. "Come on," he said. "First let me see you lick Hako's spunk from your breasts."

Lisa glanced down at herself. Her breasts were covered in semen, the stiff nipples shiny with the substance. Slowly, hesitantly, she lowered her head whilst lifting her right breast up. She protruded her tongue and began to lick the fluid from the soft flesh. Her tongue encircled her teat, making it pucker to hardness again and sending a shiver of arousal through her small frame. She licked it clean of his sperm, swallowing it down with relish, then started on the other one.

By the time she had finished, her nipples were like bullets, shiny with saliva, and she could feel the wetness flowing into her sex as she stimulated herself. Hako's eyes were fixed on her now, his cock twitching once more. She glanced sideways at the other men. They were watching her intently, and her exhibitionist tendencies were suddenly aroused anew. She resumed licking her breasts whilst her other hand slid down between her legs. She slipped a finger into herself, then two. She began slowly to masturbate, moving her fingers back and forth, a slight slopping noise revealing how wet she was down there.

Lisa's fingers began to move faster. As she did so, Hako's spunk continued to trickle down her nude flesh, feeling cold now as it dripped from her hair, coating her breasts anew. She was almost oblivious to the sensation

167

now, though, raising her eyes to Hako's face as she danced her lewd dance before him. The monstrous man was making deep grunting noises as he fixed his eyes on the fingers thrusting into her vagina. He was pressing his hips forward again, his massive cock jumping up and down, and the sight of it spurred Lisa on. Her body was hunched forward now, her knees bent, her fingers shiny with love juice as she pressed them urgently into her.

She came suddenly, her breathing turning to gasps of lust, her breasts bouncing up and down as she brought herself off. As he sensed her climax, Hako gave another roar and shook his chains once more, straining to grasp hold of the naked girl.

Lisa came down slowly, the violence of her thrusting fingers decreasing as she regained her senses. At last she withdrew her hand from her vagina and stood, head bowed, her cheeks glowing as she thought how, once again, she had displayed her lasciviousness to these cruel people.

A grunt from the mountain man made her glance across at him once more. He was straining at his chains again, his cock still projecting stiffly and twitching violently, and the shocked girl realised that he was not yet satisfied and that her own behaviour had aroused him anew. Even as this thought came to her, she felt N'dovi's whip pressing into her back.

"Go on, slave," he ordered. "This time use your mouth."

Once again the young beauty was obliged to approach the fearsome, grunting form of the mountain man. He was thrusting his hips forward at her in a crude gesture, his thick penis jabbing in her direction, a dribble of saliva running down his chin. Lisa wondered how long he had been denied the pleasures of a woman. She eyed his cock nervously. She had been made to suck off many men since

168

her abduction, but never one like this. Hako seemed barely human to her, and the violence with which he pulled at his bonds alarmed her greatly. Then she thought of N'dovi's whip, and she knew she had no choice. Slowly she reached for Hako's cock once more and, bending forward, opened her mouth.

So big was his tool that she could barely get it between her lips, opening her mouth as wide as she was able and lowering her head over it. Hako gave a groan of pleasure as she began to suck at him, licking the spunk from his glans and tasting him properly for the first time. She wrapped a hand about his shaft and began to masturbate him, whilst her other hand felt for his balls, cradling one then the other in her palm, marvelling at their size.

Hako responded to her sucking with enthusiasm, once again ramming his hips against her mouth, so that the petite girl was shaken back and forth, her firm breasts quivering as she sucked hard at him. From the corner of her eye she could see N'dovi and his two henchmen watching, and she knew she made an extraordinary sight, bent forward, her pert behind thrust back, her legs wide, spunk still running down her naked flesh as she fellated this great brute of a man.

Hako's second orgasm was no less violent than his first, short barks of pleasure coming from him as Lisa found her mouth flooded with his sperm. She tried to swallow it down, but so copious was it that she had no chance and it poured from her mouth and down her neck onto her breasts. He seemed to come and come, his hips still jabbing against her face as his seed poured from him. By the time he had finished, Lisa was almost choking and, as he withdrew from her mouth, a final spurt covered her pretty face with his spunk.

Lisa straightened and backed up, aware of the new helping of sticky fluid that was running down from her neck, through the valley between her breasts and on down to her crotch. The girl was exhausted after the rigours of satisfying the mountain man, and she shook slightly as she turned to face the grinning figure of N'dovi. The man ran his eyes up and down her young body, then nodded his approval.

"The master was right to buy you, little slut," he said. "You will prove a great asset in Hako's training."

Chapter 21

Lisa's next two weeks spent as the property of Sulkami were very different from the first two. She was never allowed to return to her cell in the main house. Instead they gave her a barred cage in the area under the arena. She never saw her cloak again either, being forced to remain naked, much to the enjoyment of the male guards who attended her. She had virtually no privacy now, being obliged to eat with the guards, and the arrival of her naked form in the small, scruffy eating area always raised a good deal of mirth. She had to share their ablutions as well, and there was always a group of guards on hand to watch as she washed the spunk and grime from her lovely young body.

Twice a day they took her to Hako. The mountain man would roar frenziedly at the sight of her, his cock rising to hardness almost at once. Sometimes N'dovi would make her suck him, sometimes to take him between her breasts, sometimes to use her hands on him. Whatever the method, it would always result in a violent orgasm, his spunk pouring from him and onto the young slave. She would often be called upon to perform for him too, dancing seductively before him, running her stiff nipples against his hairy torso and sometimes bringing herself off with thick wooden phalluses supplied by N'dovi.

She was never ordered to fuck with him, though. This was a relief to her, as she seriously wondered if she could contain his massive cock in her vagina, though there were times when, such was her arousal at her closeness to this male giant, she felt a burning desire to have a cock inside her. She assumed that the reason N'dovi never made her go the whole way with Hako was because of the need to keep him chained. Or perhaps he too feared that the mountain man was too big for her. It was certainly not due to lack of desire on Hako's part, and she knew instinctively that he wanted her.

As the days past, he became less violent, and she sensed that he was somehow trying to forge a bond with her. Whilst she could never feel affection for this ugly monster of a man, she found that speaking softly to him and stroking his hairy body had a soothing influence on him, though, as soon as he realised she was departing he would become angry again. It was as if he saw her as his own mate, and resented the fact that N'dovi could take her from him.

The two weeks passed quickly, and soon Lisa realised that the big fight was approaching. She saw the men preparing cages for Hako's opponent, and there was much activity in the arena as the big day approached.

On the morning of the fight, Lisa felt strangely apprehensive. The day before she had been taken to Hako three times, but had not been allowed to touch him. Instead N'dovi had paraded her up and down in front of the chained giant whilst he roared his frustration, his stiff cock glistening with his own lubrication as he shouted with rage. Now, as Lisa ate her meal at the long table with the guards, she could sense that something was up. At first she had assumed it was anticipation at the forthcoming fight but, the more time went by, the more she realised that it was her that they were discussing, nudging one another and roaring with laughter.

The day went on. Twice Lisa was taken to Hako, but on neither occasion was she allowed to touch him, despite his obvious rage and frustration. Having been made to parade in front of him, then masturbate to orgasm, she was taken back to be left alone in her cage, listening to the bellows of the frustrated mountain man.

Lisa could already hear the crowds arriving at the arena by the time her guards came for her again. She expected to be led up to a vantage point from which to watch the fight, but instead they seemed to be taking her back down to Hako's cage. This time, though, they led her down an unfamiliar corridor and she found herself in another large cage that was alongside Hako's. She stared at the tethered mountain man through the bars as the sight of her once again sent him into a violent rage.

Lisa turned away, unwilling to watch the frightening man as he strained at his bonds. She looked about at the cage she was in. It was similar in size and structure to Hako's, and on one side was one of the vast doors that led into the arena. There was another large door to the right of this one, that led into a darkened corridor. Already she could hear the chattering of the crowd waiting for the fight to begin. She moved away from the sound, afraid that they might see that she was nude.

All at once the door through which Lisa had entered the cage slammed shut and Lisa swung round in surprise to see that N'dovi and his men stood on the outside looking in at her. More of the guards had gathered about the cage

172

and were watching the youngster. A knot began to form in Lisa's stomach as it occurred to her that something was up, and that she was the centre of attention.

She was startled by another sound behind her, and turned to see that the door that led into the dark passage was opening. As it did so she heard a grunting sound and the shuffling of feet. She backed toward the edge of the cage, her heart beating hard as the door reached the top. Then her hands flew to her mouth to stifle a scream as a figure came into view.

It was another mountain man. He was every bit as big and as ugly as Hako, his body bent forward, his huge biceps flexing. Unlike Hako, though, this monster was untethered and she was trapped inside this cage with him. As she watched, the man pulled himself up to his full, towering height, and looked about him.

For some reason he didn't see Lisa immediately. Hako had emitted an angry bellow on sighting his foe, and this had probably distracted him. He ran to the bars, roaring back at the man who was to be his opponent in the forthcoming fight.

Lisa looked round at the laughing faces of the guards, then across at the door through which the monstrous creature had come. There was no escape, though. It had already clanged shut. She pressed herself back against the bars, wrapping an arm across her bare breasts and covering her crotch with her other hand, staring wide-eyed at the mountain man. As she did so, he turned and his eyes fell on her.

Lisa didn't know how long it was since he had last seen a woman, let alone found one in his cage with him. And this was no ordinary girl. This was a young white girl with an almost perfect figure. And she was stark naked.

173

For a moment he didn't move, simply staring at the beautiful youngster who cowered back against the bars. Then, with a bellow, he leapt forward and grabbed at her.

The mountain man was fast, but his size made his movements cumbersome and Lisa was able to dodge aside at the last minute so that he simply crashed into the bars, making them shake. He lunged for her again, but once more she was able to dodge him, running to the far side and standing with her back to the bars. This time he approached her slowly, his eyes fixed on her body, a small dribble of saliva escaping from his lips as he came closer.

She let him get as near as she dared, then made a dash past him. But this time he was ready for her. He reached out a mighty arm and caught her in the stomach, driving the wind from her body so that she collapsed to the floor. He leapt forward and lifted her with no more effort than an ordinary person would lift a doll, wrapping an arm about her waist and hoisting her up. Then he pushed her against the bars, holding her body with one hand, pressing her against the hard iron like a lovely, helpless butterfly pinned to a board, whilst he surveyed her beauty.

Lisa tried to struggle, but she knew it was useless. He had the power to break her neck with a single blow if he wanted. But she knew that, for the moment at least, he had no intention of doing anything of the kind. It was her body he desired, and he clearly intended to take what he wanted, no matter what she might feel.

He began to paw at her breasts, grabbing and mauling them, pinching her nipples with his great fingers so that she winced with the pain. Then his hand was going lower, forcing her to spread her legs as he explored her sex, thrusting a great, hairy finger deep into her vagina and bringing a cry of surprise from the helpless young beauty.

He continued to run his hands over Lisa's naked body, probing and poking at her soft pale flesh. He turned her, so that she was pressed face forward against the bars, her breasts projecting through them whilst he wormed a finger into her backside. As he fingered her anus, Lisa stared across at Hako. The man was beside himself with rage at the sight of her being manhandled by his opponent, and once again she feared that he might break the chains that held him.

. It was only then that Lisa realised what had been happening during the previous two weeks. The whole thing had been a ploy to make Hako win the fight. They had allowed him to become proprietorial over the young beauty who visited his cage every day and brought him sexual gratification, though he himself had never been allowed to touch her. Then, for the last two days, they had taunted him with the girl, letting him see her and not touch her, working him into a rage of frustration. Now, this was the final part of the process. He was witnessing his girl in a cage with another mountain man. This time, though, the man was free to do what he wanted with Lisa, and she was acquiescing. The whole thing was designed to work him into a terrible rage.

Lisa could scarcely believe the callousness of the plot. The mountain man they had given her to could easily kill her. She knew that her only hope lay in pleasing him. Apparently Hako's winning the fight was more important than her very life, such was her status amongst these people.

All at once the huge man wrenched Lisa away from the bars and flung her to the ground, driving the wind from her body as he did so. As she lay on her back, staring up at him, he reached down and wrenched off his loincloth. Lisa stared in fascination as his cock came into view. It was huge, at least as big as Hako's, and it was stiff and hard. The man stooped over her, his ham-like fist closed about his shaft, working the foreskin back and forth. Then he reached down and, grabbing her by the hair, forced her face down onto his mighty tool.

Lisa opened her mouth and took him inside. His organ had the same taste and scent as Hako's and, despite her fear, she felt a tremor of excitement as she began to suck it. He kept hold of her hair, working her head back and forth on the end of his huge penis. As he did so he looked across at Hako and gave a bellow of triumph. Hako bellowed back, but his shout was of pure rage as he saw how his girl was being used by his opponent, and how she surrendered so easily to his desires.

Suddenly Lisa found herself being lifted once again and pushed up against the bars. She knew what was to come, and she looked down at the man's rampant cock with trepidation, uncertain that she would be able to contain him.

He held her up with a single hand wrapped about her waist. With the other he took hold of his engorged penis and guided it up between her thighs. In response Lisa spread her legs as wide as she was able, shivering as he felt his erection press against her.

He pushed, then pushed again. Lisa gave a cry of pain as his huge knob penetrated her. Then he was pressing it home, and the pain gave way to an extraordinary rush of pleasure as he filled her as she had never been filled before.

It was some weeks since Lisa had felt a cock inside her. Then it had been that of the anonymous guards at the auction. Now the frustration of being deprived of what she desired most drove her to new heights of sexual excitement, and her fear was momentarily forgotten as she cried aloud with sheer lust at the sensation of his mighty erection deep within her.

She couldn't contain his full length. She had known she wouldn't be able to. Still, the sensation was exquisite as she found herself riding his thick shaft, it's black length disappearing into the pink wetness of her vagina. He lifted her bodily from the bars and paraded round the room with her, much to the delight of the watching guards. Lisa wondered at the extraordinary sight they must make, the monstrous, hairy mountain man strutting back and forth with the beautiful and petite white girl impaled on his massive cock, her squirming body and screams of pleasure betraying her total abandonment to the rough fucking she was receiving.

She knew that Hako too could see how completely aroused she was, and his shouts of rage mingled with her own cries of delight as she was manhandled by his opponent, his huge hands wrapped about her waist and working her up and down on his mighty cock, her body arched back, her lovely breasts stretched, her legs spread wide as she revelled in the crude way he fucked her.

She could sense the imminence of his orgasm now, and he carried her back to the bars, slamming her against them and driving the wind from her body once again. She reached up above her, taking hold of the bars, spreadeagling herself in a gesture of total abandonment as he took her, slamming her pretty young body against the hard metal with every thrust of his mighty hips.

As he came, she came too, screaming aloud as she felt his oceans of spunk fill her sopping vagina. As with Hako, his seed was copious, flooding her love-hole and triggering pulse after pulse of delicious pleasure deep within her.

She knew her cunt wouldn't be able to contain his ejaculate and at once she felt it leaking from her and pouring down her thighs. Yet still his hefty penis continued to convulse, pumping yet more of the hot, viscous fluid deep into her until she felt she could take no more.

At last he was spent, and so was Lisa, her body slumped back, her breasts rising and falling as she regained her breath. The man lifted her from his erection, then turned her and forced her face down on the end of his cock, obliging her to lick him clean. Even now his spunk was leaking from him, dribbling down onto her soft breasts as she licked at his shaft, tasting her own arousal as well as his.

Finally he lifted her once more , holding her up against the bars so that Hako could fully see her totally ravished state, bringing new cries of rage from the tethered mountain man. Even as he did so a whirring, clanking sound told Lisa that the gate into the arena was opening, and the cheers of the crowd outside, who had not witnessed her ravishment, met her ears.

The man dropped her to the ground at his feet. Then he picked up his loincloth and wrapped it about himself. He fell onto one knee and ran his hands over her slumped body, crudely fingering her cunt and bringing fresh moans from her. Then he turned away and strode out into the arena, banging his chest in triumph whilst the crowd cheered still louder.

Chapter 22

For a full five minutes Lisa lay sprawled where the mountain man had left her, quite exhausted, his spunk flowing out from her sex and forming a pool of white on the floor between her thighs. She could scarcely believe the way she had reacted to the mountain man's attack. It had been a simple ravishment, with no attempt at all to gain her consent, yet her body itself had given that consent in the way it had reacted to the roughness of his assault, the way she had spread her legs without bidding and, most of all, in the way she had come so violently and deliciously. She wondered whether other girls shared her rapture in being taken so roughly, abandoning herself without question to such a man. All she knew was that the sensation of his rough shagging was irresistible to one with such a lascivious nature, and, as she dragged herself to her feet, the feel of the spunk escaping from her sex sent a new shiver of excitement through her.

Suddenly she heard the crowd roar once again and she remembered the fight. The door into the arena had closed again and she made her way across to it, taking care to keep out of the view of the audience. The man who had screwed her was standing in the centre of the arena, bellowing at the audience who were shouting taunts down to him. Then there came another roar to her left and she turned to see that Hako had been released from his chains. The monstrous man seemed beside himself with rage, pulling at the bars of his cage so that they shook back and forth in the most alarming manner. He was clearly enraged at witnessing what he regarded as his woman giving herself so freely to his opponent.

The great door began to rise, bringing another cheer from those watching. The moment it had risen far enough, the huge man rolled underneath it and sprang to his feet, lunging at his opponent.

This time there was no preamble. The two men launched themselves at each other immediately, each one raining down extraordinarily powerful blows on the other that made the young beauty wince as she watched the fight begin. Lisa was staggered by the sheer rage that Hako was exhibiting. His opponent was the larger and more powerful of the two, yet he seemed to have no answer for the volley of blows that were being hurled at him by his opponent. The crowd screamed their encouragement as Hako beat his adversary back against the side of the arena. The other man's cockiness had given way to panic now as he struggled to stave off Hako's punches, his arms protecting his face as best he could.

It was all over in less than five minutes, with the other man lying unconscious in the dust whilst Hako paraded about the arena, waving his fists in the air in triumph. He seemed to have forgotten Lisa for the moment as the youngster shrank back into the shadows, shaken by the ferocity of what she had witnessed.

All at once she sensed other people in the cage with her. N'dovi and his men were making their way toward the door to the arena. One of the guards held a blowpipe in his hand, and Lisa watched as he raised it to his lips and puffed. The dart flew with unerring accuracy, catching Hako at the back of the neck. He reached a hand up, snatching it out. As he turned to see where it had come from, his eyes fell on Lisa. He gave a sudden roar of recognition and started toward her, nearly reaching the bars before pitching forward into the dust. He tried to raise himself, stretching out a hairy arm in the direction of the girl, then his eyes took on a vacant look and he slumped back down.

At once N'dovi gave a shout and the door into the arena began to rise. He and his men dashed through, carrying chains and shackles to restrain the mountain man. Lisa watched as they pushed Hako's huge body onto its front

180

and reached for his wrists.

What happened next took everyone by surprise. The mountain man gave a sudden roar, and rolled over, shoving the men aside as if they were no more than dolls. At once the guards abandoned the restraints and made a dash back toward the cage where they had come from, clearly terror-stricken. Lisa watched transfixed as the men ran past her, their eyes wide with fear. Hako was on his feet now and lumbering after them. Either the dart had been too short a time embedded in the mountain man's neck, or his sheer rage had overcome the power of the drug. Whichever was the case, he was certainly awake now, and still extremely angry.

Lisa watched horror-stricken as Hako approached, then her heart skipped a beat as she realised that it was not the men that the monstrous creature was pursuing, but her. She barely had time to register what was happening as he came at her, his eyes wide and hungry. She turned to flee but, even as she did so, she felt his mighty hand grab her shoulder and drag her round to face him. He wrapped an arm about her waist and, oblivious to the way she kicked and beat at him, lifted her up under his arm and carried her struggling body back into the arena,

The sight of the stark naked young white girl brought a roar of approval from the crowd, and Lisa suddenly felt overcome by shame as she realised that she was being watched by hundreds of people as he bore her to the middle. He dropped her to the ground and, with one hand, pushed her down onto her back. She lay staring up at him for a moment, her heart racing. At once he began to maul her naked flesh, his hands clutching at her succulent young breasts whilst his other hand forced her thighs apart. Lisa gave a cry of surprise as she felt him suddenly force a fin-

181

ger deep into her vagina. He moved it back and forth, bringing a gasp from the youngster, then withdrew it and examined it.

His finger was coated with a layer of white, glutinous fluid. It was spunk. His enemy's spunk. Lisa realised that he had been seeking confirmation that she had, indeed given herself completely to the other mountain man. Now that he had that confirmation he gave a cry of rage, and Lisa watched him fearfully as he glared down at her. Already he had witnessed her being fucked by his enemy, and had seen her excitement and heard her screams as she had come. Now he could smell the other man's seed inside her, and she knew he was even angrier.

Taking hold of her arm, he dragged her to her feet. He stared down into her face, his small eyes blazing. He shouted some words at her that she didn't understand, and his hand reached for her throat. Fearing that he would snap her neck, Lisa shook her head vigorously.

"You don't understand," she cried. "It wasn't my fault."

At the sound of her words he gave a grunt, and his hand paused, still about her neck.

"I didn't want him," went on the desperate girl. "It was you I wanted."

Whether he understood a word of what she said, Lisa couldn't be sure. All at once, though, his grip about her throat loosened. For a second his eyes narrowed. Then he began to look about him.

Lisa couldn't make out what he was doing at first. He seemed to be searching for something. Then his eyes lighted on a thin, dark object in the sand, and she felt a knot form in her stomach. Amongst the shiny chains and shackles that had been abandoned by the guards, a long, leather whip lay where it had fallen from N'dovi's belt. It was this that

182

the monstrous man was staring at. The hapless girl knew that the whip had been used on his own flesh numerous times when N'dovi had been taunting him. Now, all at once, it had fallen into his possession. Dragging Lisa with him, he crossed to where it lay and picked it up. Another cheer arose from those watching as he held the whip aloft.

Lisa's heart was beating hard as she eyed the instrument. It was clear that, though he didn't wish to kill her, the mountain man intended to punish her for what he saw as her infidelity. She shivered as she thought of the whip on her pale skin, and once again tried to struggle, but he was far too strong for her. Taking her wrists in one hand, he lifted her arms above her body, pulling her up until her feet were clear of the ground. Lisa looked up at the crowd. She wished that he would, at least, take her into the relative privacy of the cage, but it was not to be. Instead he was actually holding her up for the crowd to see, and they roared their approval at the sight of her bare sex, her cunt ring shining in the arena's lights.

He moved to the centre of the arena and, still dangling the naked, helpless beauty by her wrists, raised the whip.

Swish! Whack!

He brought it down across her pale buttocks with tremendous force, bringing a cry of pain from her as it cut into her soft flesh.

Swish! Whack!

Swish! Whack!

Swish! Whack!

The powerful mountain man wielded the whip without mercy, bringing it down hard onto the plump swellings of Lisa's behind, each stroke laying a fresh red stripe across her rear cheeks.

Swish! Whack!

Swish! Whack!

Swish! Whack!

Lisa's small, pale body danced like a marionette as she struggled to escape the fall of the whip, her breasts bouncing in a manner that clearly delighted the crowd. But the mountain man's grip on her wrists was like iron, and there was nothing she could do to escape the stinging force of the whip as it fell time after time across her bottom.

Swish! Whack!

Swish! Whack!

Swish! Whack!

Then, just as she thought she could take no more, he threw the whip aside and let her fall to the dusty floor of the arena. Lisa lay there at his feet, staring up at him, the tears rolling down her cheeks, her legs splayed apart, her thighs still shiny with spunk.

Hako reached for his loincloth, and a shout went up from the crowd as he cast it aside. Lisa found herself faced with his enormous erection. She had seen it before, of course, but then he had been shackled and she had been safe. Now it was she that was the helpless one, and she felt a hollowness at the pit of her stomach as she realised that, not content with whipping her soft, bare flesh, he now intended to publicly fuck her.

He picked her up effortlessly once more and turned her over, forcing her onto her hands and knees. Lisa obeyed, knowing that to resist him would be useless. His great hairy hands forced her to part her thighs, spreading her legs wide and bringing another roar from those watching as she displayed the flaming red of her buttocks.

Giving a grunt of approval, Hako dropped to his knees behind her. Lisa crouched, her body tense, sweat mingling with her tears as she felt him grip her spread thighs. He

184

lifted them clear of the ground so that Lisa was tipped forward, her hands pressed into the dirt floor of the arena, her legs pulled wide apart, her wet sex gaping. Then he began to lower her onto his rampant cock, and she cried aloud as she felt him press against her cunt, pushing insistently. Lisa gritted her teeth as he pushed harder, afraid again that a mountain man's cock would be too much for her. Then another cry escaped her lips as he entered her, his great organ forcing its way deep into her vagina as the crowd about them cheered him on.

Once again Lisa was overwhelmed by the sheer size of the cock that was filling her. He grasped her hips tightly, his hands almost encircling her body as he thrust her down onto his erection, bringing a gasp of pure lust from the lascivious youngster as she felt him press himself all the way home.

He started to fuck her, his huge body thrusting against hers, shaking her small frame as he rammed his stiff erection into her vagina. Lisa dug her hands into the dirt of the arena, pressing her body back at him, all resistance abandoned as she revelled in the delicious sensation of the violent fucking she was receiving. Her breasts shook back and forth with every stroke providing, she knew, an extraordinarily erotic sight to the cheering crowd, who clearly couldn't believe their luck at this addition to their entertainment. The youngster tried not to think of the sight she must be making, her hands supporting her body whilst behind her this monster of a man thrust his enormous cock between her wide-open thighs, to the delight of those watching.

Hako came suddenly, and once again Lisa had the extraordinary sensation of being filled by a copious amount of semen. The spunk simply shot from his erection, immediately triggering an orgasm in her. She screamed aloud at the delicious feeling of spurt after spurt of the mountain man's seed invading her lovely body.

He went on screwing her until the sperm ceased to flow from him, then pulled her from the end of his cock and shoved her into the dirt. He looked about at the crowd, shaking his hands above his head in triumph, whilst the sated girl lay on her back, her legs apart, the sperm still leaking from her throbbing vagina, her lovely breasts rising and falling as she regained her breath.

Hako rose to his feet and picked up the whip, he turned back to the gasping girl and lifting her up effortlessly, flung her over his shoulder. The door to his cage was open, and he carried her in with him, throwing her down onto the pile of hay on which he slept. Then he dragged her legs apart and, to her utter surprise, thrust his still rampant cock into her once again.

Lisa gasped as his huge body drove the breath from her and he began pumping his hips back and forth once more. She glanced across at the bars of the cage, where N'dovi and his men were watching. They were showing no sign of trying to help her, and she guessed that, in the mood the mountain man was in, there was little they could do.

Clearly the young English beauty was destined to be at the mercy of this sex-crazed monster for some time yet.

Chapter 23
It was three days before N'dovi and his men were able to free Lisa from the mountain man. Three days during which he made constant demands on her body, fucking her time

186

after time, making her lie and suck his huge cock for hours on end whilst he relaxed, before pushing her back and entering her yet again. Lisa lost count of the number of orgasms he extracted from her small, exhausted form as he used her for his carnal pleasures. If she showed any reluctance at all she would find herself pinned against the bars once more whilst he set about her with the whip, laying more stripes across her bare behind. He would sleep with her close to him, her mouth filled with his cock, ready, should he wake, to suck him to hardness once more and surrender herself to his desires. When he wasn't fucking her, he would carry her round with him whenever he moved, so that at no time could the guards get a shot at him with their darts.

Lisa's mind was a whirl during her period as Hako's naked and helpless young mate. The way he used her lovely body, penetrating her mouth or sex whenever he wanted and thrashing her if she showed any sign of resistance, left her completely drained. Yet her body still responded to him, even though her mind was disgusted by her behaviour, and the sensation of his spunk spurting into her never failed to trigger an orgasm in the wanton beauty. She was simply overwhelmed by him, her soft, pale flesh covered with his ejaculate and with dirt from the bottom of the cage as she crouched down on the floor, her backside thrust up at him, screaming aloud with passion as he fucked her violently yet again.

Then, on the third day, she got her chance. Hako was asleep and she was curled up against his groin, his cock in her mouth, when she heard a whisper from the guards. She looked up to see the man with the blowpipe waving to her to get out the way. As she rolled off the mountain man, he stirred and sat up. Then came the puff of the guard's blowpipe, and the dart found Hako's neck. He rose to his feet and, for a moment, Lisa thought they had failed, and that she was in for another whipping. Then his legs gave way and he toppled to the ground. At once N'dovi and his men were through the door, placing the restraints on him whilst two others took hold of Lisa's arms and dragged her from the cage.

They almost carried her into the bathroom, where she collapsed to the floor, quite exhausted. One of the men turned on a shower and, pushing at her with his foot, indicated that she was to enter the cubicle. Lisa staggered to her feet and paused momentarily before a mirror.

Her small, naked body was streaked with sperm and dirt. It was on her face, her breasts, her stomach and her thighs, with still more trickling from her cunt. Her hair was knotted and full of wisps of straw. She turned and examined her backside, which was criss-crossed with the marks of the whip. She had never felt such a mess. Wearily she stepped under the shower, gasping at the coldness of the water as it made her nipples harden to large brown bullets. Then she picked up a piece of soap and began to wash the sperm and grime from her.

It took the youngster more than an hour before she was finally satisfied that she had washed the mountain man from her lovely young body. Then she was taken, still nude, from the bathroom, given a meal and led back to her cage, where she fell immediately into a deep sleep.

For the next few days Lisa remained in her cage, untroubled by the guards. Meals were brought to her three times a day, and the only other punctuation to the lonely hours was her visits to the ablutions. One morning she saw the drugged Hako being taken away in a mobile cage, and she learned later that, now that the competition was over for another year, he was being taken to a remote facility to train for the next season.

It soon occurred to Lisa that, without the mountain man, her usefulness to these people was over. That thought gave her little comfort as she lay awake in her cell at night wondering what they would do with her now. Then, one afternoon, she heard footsteps approaching her cage, and was surprised to see Askari standing at the entrance. It was the first time she had seen him since being taken to the Arena. He stood by whilst the cage door was opened, then ordered her out. At once the two guards accompanying him fell in on either side of the girl, then they marched her down the passageway.

They went past Hako's empty cage and on to a part of the building that Lisa hadn't visited before. They came to a halt outside a heavy door, which the guards pushed open. The pair stood aside to allow Askari to enter, then pushed the hapless youngster in behind him.

The room was clearly the guards' rest room. In the middle was a long table strewn with empty cups and bottles, as well as the remains of a meal. A rack at the end held an array of guns, as well as bunches of keys. There were about ten guards inside, including N'dovi, who sat at the head of the table. They all rose to their feet as Askari entered.

Lisa was made to stand at the end of the table, and at once took up her submissive stance, her hands placed behind her head, her legs spread. She glanced nervously about at the guards, all of whom were eyeing her bare breasts and crotch with interest. Since she had stripped for Hako on that fateful first encounter, Lisa had been allowed nothing at all to wear, and now she felt her cheeks redden as she stood there, wishing desperately for some clothes.

Askari gave an order, and a door at the far end of the room opened. Through it came two figures. One was a woman of perhaps fifty, with grey hair. She was very fat, and wore a bright, flowery dress. Her eyes were narrow, her mouth twisted into a frown, and she eyed the lovely youngster with a furrowed brow. Her companion was a youth, not much more than sixteen years old. He was tall, with a broad chest, and was dressed in tatty jeans and an old T-shirt. He grinned at the sight of Lisa, showing an array of gleaming white teeth.

"This is Madam Okicha," said Askari. "Now that the mountain men are no longer here, your use to my master has ceased. You will be sold as soon as a buyer can be found for you."

"Yes Master."

The words sent a chill down Lisa's spine. The thought of being sold yet again was not one she welcomed. It seemed that she would never stay in one place. Whilst the idea of remaining in her cage here under the arena was not one that appealed in any way, the thought of the unknown seemed even worse.

"In the meantime," Askari continued. "You will be placed in Madam Okicha's care. She will ensure that you are kept occupied and that you are properly used until you are sold. You will obey her as you obey me, do you understand?"

"Yes Master."

Lisa looked across at the woman and her companion once more, her eyes seeking some sort of communication. But she was met with blank, friendless stares. The folk here hated white people, a legacy of the cruelty of their colonisation in the early part of the century. To them, Lisa represented the oppressor brought to her just desserts, and she knew she could expect no kindness from them.

"Madam Okicha will have you fetched from here tomorrow," said Askari. "Since you have no belongings, not even clothes, you have no need to prepare."

He nodded to the woman and boy, and the two turned and left the room in silence. Lisa watched them go, wondering why they didn't take her with them now. She looked at Askari, but he too had turned away and, as she watched, the door was opened, then closed behind him.

The room fell silent. Lisa looked about at the array of jet-black faces staring at her, and a knot formed in her stomach as she realised how helpless she was in the power of these strong, cruel men. For a moment nobody moved, then N'dovi crooked a finger, beckoning her toward him.

Slowly, her heart pounding, she made her way down the side of the room, past the guards who watched her with hungry eyes. In front of her, a mirror hung on the wall, and the sight of herself nude amongst all these men, her pert breasts quivering as she walked, made her face redden. She stopped in front of N'dovi, her hands hanging at her side as he his eyes roved up and down her bare form.

"So little slave slut," he said. "No more mountain man. I think this is good. I feared that he would kill you, or that his cock would split you in two. Yet you enjoyed it, didn't you?"

Lisa said nothing, her eyes cast down.

"My men have watched you perform for the mountain men," he continued. "They have never seen a woman give herself so freely. A black woman would be ashamed to act as you do. You seem so innocent, and even now you blush like a demure young lady, yet you spread your legs and fuck like a hyena in heat."

Lisa felt the colour in her cheeks rise. She too was

ashamed by her behaviour. But what choice did she have? She was a slave, wasn't she? It was these men who made her act as she did. Yet deep down she knew that their cruelty and the way they used her had an effect upon her that was difficult to explain. Even now, standing here amongst these rough strangers, she could feel her nipples puckering to hardness and a wetness seep into her crotch as she contemplated her situation.

N'dovi suddenly rose to his feet and took hold of her arm. He pushed open a door behind her and took her through. As he closed the door again, Lisa took in her surroundings. It was an office, with a battered desk standing on a threadbare carpet, a single chair placed behind it. She turned to face N'dovi.

"This is my private office," he said. "We won't be disturbed in here. Sit on the edge of the desk."

Lisa glanced behind her, then took a step backwards and lowered her backside onto the desk. The wood felt hard and cool against her bare behind. She placed her hands down on the surface on either side of her and waited, her heart beating hard.

Askari moved close to her. So close that she could smell his sweat. He reached out a hand and ran it up the smooth, creamy flesh of Lisa's inner thigh. She said nothing, simply gripping the desk harder as she felt his fingers approaching her sex.

Once again, Lisa couldn't reconcile her emotions with her thoughts. Here she was in a dirty little office in a remote African town, with some thug of a guard feeling up her naked body. Yet she was making no move to prevent him. On the contrary, her sex was pulsating as she anticipated his touch there. For a second she thought of Mrs Sadler. What would she make of Lisa's wantonness? She was accustomed to a comfortable bed, with clean sheets and a man she had chosen. Lisa was denied all of these, yet still her body was tingling with arousal.

"Ah!"

Lisa gasped as N'dovi's fingers found her cunt and began to rub the hard bud of her clitoris. At once a gush of wetness was released into her sex, and she bit her lip to prevent another exclamation escaping her as he touched her up with his rough hands.

He took hold of her cunt ring, tugging at it and grinning at her obvious discomfort. Then he touched her slave mark, stroking her smooth, bare pubis. His other hand reached for her breasts, squeezing and kneading them, feeling the hardness of her teats.

"You love to be fucked I think, slave," he murmured. "And you love to have your body touched."

Still Lisa said nothing, but her body was speaking for her. Already her hips were pressing forward against his hand and her breaths were shortening.

"Turn over," he ordered suddenly. "Lean forward over the desk."

Lisa obeyed at once, getting to her feet and turning to face the desk, then prostrating herself over it, the hard wood flattening her breasts as she pressed herself down against it. She gripped the desk top on the far side and spread her legs, then waited.

Once again she could scarcely suppress a cry as his hand closed over her crotch and a finger slipped into her. He delved deep within her, sending shudder after shudder of pleasure through her. Then, just as she thought she must come, he withdrew his finger and, to her surprise, began rubbing her wetness about the tight hole of her anus, spreading the fluid about the orifice, then pressing his finger in-

193

side. He rotated his finger, easing it deeper into her, making her groan with the extraordinary sensation his probing was bringing. Then he withdrew, and she knew that he had been lubricating her for a purpose.

She heard him drop his loincloth to the floor, and braced herself as she felt the tip of his thick cock pressing hard against her nether hole. As before, when she had been buggered, she knew she must relax her sphincter to allow him the access he was intent on, but it wasn't easy, and she gave a small whimper as he penetrated her and drove his cock deep into her rectum, grasping her hips and ramming himself home.

Lisa clung tight to the edge of the desk as he started to fuck her behind, his black belly slapping against the white, soft skin of her backside as he grunted his approval. She had never really come to terms with the ignominy of being buggered by her many captors, yet she couldn't ignore the eroticism of her situation, bent naked and helpless across this hard desk whilst being violated so intimately.

N'dovi drove into her with passion, his long, thick cock stretching the walls of her rectum as he took her without mercy, intent only on his own pleasure. Lisa bit her lip as the force of his onslaught increased, pressing her rear back at him and doing her best to accommodate his insistent thrusts.

He came with a groan, filling her rectum with his thick spunk, more moans of pleasure coming from his lips as he fucked her backside with unabated force, his organ twitching with every jet of semen that escaped from it. Lisa continued to hang on tightly to the edge of the desk, relieved as his thrusts finally began to lose their momentum and his passion slowly ebbed.

When, at last, he had pumped the last of his spunk into

Lisa's rear passage, he began slowly to withdraw, bringing a sigh of relief from the youngster as his cock finally ceased to stretch the muscles of her behind, allowing a trickle of his seed to escape into the crack of her backside.

Lisa remained where she was, not wanting to turn and face the man who had taken her so cruelly. She heard the rustle of clothing as he replaced the cloth about his waist and refastened his belt. Then a hand was placed on her arm and he pulled her round to face him.

"It is lucky that the mountain man did not wish to take you like that," he said.

Lisa shivered at the thought. She knew she could never have accommodated that monster in her backside.

"Now you will go to my men," he went on. "Watching you over the past weeks has been a great temptation to them, and tonight their patience will be rewarded.

Lisa stared at him, then at the door that led back to the guardroom. She was being given to the guards like some trivial plaything , simply for their pleasure. Her farewell to the arena was to consist of a gang-bang by the group of ruffians that had guarded her during the past few weeks. She could scarcely believe this was happening to her, yet she was already resigned to her fate. There were about ten of these strong black men, making them more than a match for a naked, petite English girl such as herself. As N'dovi led her back out into the guardroom she tried to pull back, but he simply grasped her tighter and shoved her through the door, slamming it behind her.

In the guard room the men were lounging round in chairs as they waited for their leader to finish with her. Now they smiled as they surveyed her, standing nervously, her back pressed against the office door, her eyes surveying the grinning men.

195

For a moment nothing happened, then one of the men rose to his feet. He moved closer to the trembling girl, who pushed herself back further, eyeing him apprehensively as he closed on her. He stopped just in front of her. He was a big man, at least six foot four inches tall, with a heavy build and ebony skin. He reached out a hand and placed it over her firm young breast, closing his fingers about it and kneading it with some force. Lisa said nothing, shutting her eyes as she felt the nipple respond to his touch and swell beneath his hand. He slid his other hand down her body, and a rough finger penetrated her sex. Lisa was still wet down there from her previous encounter with N'dovi, and she moaned quietly as he probed her intimately, shoving his finger deep into her and twisting it around whilst still caressing her breast.

Lisa tried to fight down the emotions that his caresses were kindling inside her, but she knew it was a losing battle. As always, her lascivious nature meant that her body soon surrendered to a man's caresses and, as she looked about at the faces watching her, she realised that they sensed her passion and her desires. She opened her legs wider, pressing her pubis down against the guard's finger, suddenly abandoning herself to what she knew was inevitable. As she did so, a smile spread across the guard's face and he turned and said something to his companions.

All at once they were on their feet, closing in about the naked young beauty. Hands reached out and grabbed at Lisa's bare flesh, grasping and tweaking her nipples, probing her sex and her anus, pinching her smooth, pale skin. They were all about her now, their hands all over her body, and Lisa felt her control begin to slip away as her passions overcame her.

She found herself being lifted bodily, then thrown down

196

onto the table with a crash. Plates, bottles and glasses flew everywhere as they dumped her down into the mess of food and beer that covered the table. Hands grabbed her knees, pinning her legs apart whilst others took hold of her wrists, pulling them over her head. She tried to protest at this rough, presumptuous treatment, but her complaints feel on deaf ears. She gazed down through the vale of her firm breasts to see that the man who had originally been groping her was now naked below the waist, his great black cock rising proudly from his groin, the veins standing out on it. Once again she tried to struggle, but it was useless. Then she felt him press his erection against the entrance to her most private place, and drive deep into her.

Despite herself, Lisa came with his first stroke, completely overwhelmed by what was happening to her, her body convulsing as she shouted her passion. Her shouts were cut short, however, as she suddenly felt another cock thrusting into her mouth. She grabbed hold of it at once and began to suck hungrily at it, caressing the man's heavy balls. Then unexpectedly, the man who was screwing her lifted her up from the table, so that the cock she had been sucking slipped from her lips. He raised her up in his powerful arms, still impaled on his thick penis, then he turned her so that he was sitting on the table with her astride him. He lay back, pulling her down on top of him and, almost at once, the cock was jammed back into her mouth.

Then she felt something else. Yet another erect penis was probing at her anus, where N'dovi had taken her such a short time ago. With a jolt, Lisa realised that she was to take on three of them at once. It was something she had done once before, during the initiation of the warriors when she had been enslaved by a bush tribe. Now, once again, she was being driven to her limits, and she winced as she felt the man behind her force his hard cock into her anus.

They started to fuck her hard, the pair in her vagina and rectum thrusting into her simultaneously whilst she sucked hard at the third, her hand flying up and down his shaft as she did so. For Lisa it was the most extraordinary thing, stretched out nude on this hard, dirty table whilst two big, rough men rammed their cocks into her cunt and arse, trying desperately to concentrate on fellating the third thug whose hips were being thrust against her face. They pummelled her with unabated force, bouncing her lovely young body back and forth between them, her breasts slapping down against the chest of the man beneath her.

All three came almost simultaneously, and Lisa bucked and heaved between them as her rectum, vagina and mouth suddenly received a massive dose of thick, hot semen. Her own orgasm was a shattering one, muffled cries coming from her as she struggled to swallow down the spunk that was engulfing her mouth whilst the muscles in her sex and behind pulsated about the spurting cocks inside them.

Barely had the wanton youngster come down from her own climax that she found herself being dragged from the trio and lifted up, her legs pulled apart. One of the other guards was seated in a chair, his cock standing straight up, and they lowered her onto him, impaling her rear hole whilst he reached round and grabbed her breasts. Then another man was kneeling in front of her, thrusting his erection into her sex whilst a third stood on the seat with a foot on either side of her and forced his erection into her mouth. At once they were thrusting once again, triggering yet another orgasm in the now totally aroused girl.

When they had finished there were three more. Then the first ones were back again. All night they used her, making her serve drinks and meals to them whilst they regained their strength, then forcing her to submit to their desires once more as their cocks hardened again.

The sky was beginning to brighten by the time they finally took the exhausted girl back to her cage and left her there, her body still coated with dirt, food and spunk, to fall into a deep sleep on the floor.

Chapter 24

It was late morning when Lisa felt a foot digging into her ribs and opened her eyes to see a tall guard standing over her. She recognised him as one of those that she had sucked off and then been fucked by the night before. Now he stood, grinning down at her with a knowing look on his face that made her cheeks redden.

He gestured for her to get to her feet and she did so, blinking wearily. Her body still felt sore from the night before, and she knew she looked a mess. It was with some gratitude that she found herself being taken from her cage and down toward the bathroom.

She washed herself thoroughly, after which she was made to apply a depilation cream to her pubis and around her sex in order to clear any new growth down there. Afterwards her sex felt smoother than ever, the tattoo that marked her out as a slave looking even more prominent beside the gleaming ring that was a permanent attachment to her sex.

Once clean, she was taken, not back to her cell, but along the same passageway she had seen Hako being taken down the week before. She knew that she was being moved from the arena to yet another phase in her life of servitude, and she pondered on her own total loss of freedom. She had nothing at all to bring with her. Even the most destitute of beggars at least had the clothes on his back, but she didn't even have those. She was alone and naked in this awful country and totally in the power of the cruel people who owned her and despised her for what she was. Yet even this thought brought a quite unexpected spasm of arousal deep inside her. She had yet to come to terms with her masochism, or the perverse way her body became aroused by the cruel and dispassionate treatment she received daily, but she knew that it was a fact, and that few other women could have endured what she did and still retain the burning desires within themselves.

They came to an entrance hall and there, waiting, was the boy who had accompanied Madam Okicha the day before. A look of desire spread across his face as his eyes took in Lisa's bare breasts and sex, making her want to cover them with her hands. But experience had told her that such an action would lead to punishment, so she simply placed her hands behind her head and spread her legs, knowing full well that such a stance left her revealing all and tacitly submitting herself to the whims of her captors.

The boy stepped forward. In his hand he held a dog chain. He raised an eyebrow to the guard beside Lisa, and the man nodded. Then he took hold of Lisa's cunt ring and clipped the lead onto it. As he did so, he ran a finger along the lips of her sex, and Lisa suppressed a gasp at the intimacy of the touch.

One of the guards stepped forward and opened the door. Lisa had been hoping right up until the last minute that they would give her something to wear, but the hope was in vain. Now, as she peered out into the busy streets beyond the door, her heart sank as she realised that she was to walk them totally nude. The boy gave a tug at her lead, and she stepped out into the sunshine.

It was the first time for some weeks that the young beauty had been outdoors, and under any normal circumstances she would have welcomed the fresh air and brightness of the day. But she was completely naked in a street full of people, her soft white breasts and belly in total contrast to the dark-skinned, fully-clothed people around her. Now, as all the people turned to stare at her, she felt her lovely face redden as she was led along between them.

The walk was a long one, and a real ordeal for the young beauty. The dusty streets were full of people. There were cars too, mainly rusting old saloons or battered off-road vehicles, their occupants laughing and sounding their horns as they went by.. Everywhere people stopped and watched as she passed, her firm breasts bouncing, the nipples hard as her latent exhibitionism kindled an odd and unwelcome excitement inside her at the way she was being displayed.

A man jostled against her, and she felt his hand slide between her legs, momentarily touching her up. Another hand ran down the crack of her behind, then pinched the soft flesh. Someone grabbed at her breast as she passed by, laughing as he pinched her nipple. A woman spat at her, the saliva striking her breast and trickling down onto her belly. Others shouted derisive comments, laughing at her obvious discomfort. All the time Lisa kept her eyes staring straight ahead, trying as best she could to ignore those around her.

They turned down a side street strewn with litter and Lisa saw that they were approaching a ramshackle building at the end. It had a concrete facade painted white. There had once been a Coca-Cola advertisement on the wall, but this was now so faded in the sunshine as to be barely readable. Out in front was a veranda on which were placed tables and chairs, of various types and colours. A handwritten sign above the door announced 'Madam Okicha's'. Lisa surveyed the place with some dismay. It looked scruffy and sordid, and not at all the sort of place she would want to be seen even if fully clothed and escorted by a man. As she was, naked and alone, it was a prospect she viewed with a sinking heart.

The boy tugged at her chain, and she stumbled forward. He led her up the steps and through the front door. The whole place had an air of neglect about it and there was a musty smell that seemed to pervade everything. He led her into a room that was furnished with a similar hotchpotch of furniture to that she had seen on the veranda. At the far end was a bar, with dirty glasses and empty bottles all over it. The tables were similarly cluttered, and it was clear that the mess remained from the night before. There was nobody about now though, the bar was obviously closed.

A door opened at the back of the room, startling Lisa. A figure waddled into view. It was Madam Okicha. The stern-faced woman said a few words to the boy, who was obviously in awe of her. He unhitched the lead from Lisa's cunt ring and, going to the corner of the room, pulled out something that rattled noisily. Lisa saw that it was a long chain of a similar thickness to the dog lead he had used to bring her here. Now he crouched down and fastened a metal shackle about her ankle, locking it into place. The other end of the chain was attached to an iron ring embedded into the concrete of the wall. Lisa was now a prisoner here, albeit with plenty of freedom to move about within the confines of the building.

The woman indicated the mess in the room.

"You clean here," she said. "All bottles in crates, glasses and plates washed. Then you clean tables and scrub floors.

202

You clean now."

She turned and walked out of the room, leaving Lisa alone with the boy once more.

"Wh-where are the cleaning things?" she asked timidly.

"Bottle crates out back. Sink behind bar. Buckets and soap in cupboard. You clean."

He grinned and moved back to a table at the side of the room, where he took a seat. Lisa looked about her. There was certainly plenty to do. It was a demeaning task, one the boy could have done easily, but at least it would keep her occupied. With a sigh she picked up a tray from the bar and began collecting the glasses from the tables.

It took nearly two hours to get the tables and bar top clear and wiped, and the glasses and plates all cleaned and dried. Lisa worked hard, carrying the crates out to the yard and stacking them, cleaning everything thoroughly and wiping down the surfaces with vigour, whilst the boy looked on. The ankle chain was awkward, and on more than one occasion she was forced to retrace her steps after getting it tangled about the tables. It rattled loudly with every step she took, and she had to be careful not to trip over it.

Once the clutter was cleared, Lisa set about scrubbing the floor. From the look of it, this was a job that had not been done for some time, and the amount of grime that came off it was considerable. Lisa made her way about the room on her hands and knees, wielding the scrubbing brush with vigour. Every now and again she would catch sight of her reflection in one of the mirrors in the bar and would blush at the sight she made, her bare bottom perfectly displayed, her pretty young breasts dangling beneath her and shaking deliciously as she scrubbed.

By the time she had finished, Lisa was exhausted, her hands, knees and feet brown with grime, more splashes of dirt on her breasts and thighs where it had been kicked up by the brush. She cleaned the brush and bucket carefully and put them away. Then she turned to face the boy, a quizzical look on her face.

He went out and shouted something, and the woman returned. Lisa had taken up her submissive stance by the bar, and she watched anxiously as Madam Okicha entered. The woman looked about her briefly, then went up to the young beauty.

"See the cane?" she said, pointing to a thin bamboo cane that hung above the bar.

"Yes Mistress."

"One stroke for every spot of dirt."

Lisa watched as the woman prowled about the room, closely inspecting every inch of the tables and floor. She had done a good job, but she knew there was no way that the place could be entirely free of dirt. A spot here, a missed corner there, Madam Okicha pointed out each one in a grim tone, whilst the hapless youngster counted with some dismay. By the time she had finished, she had found eleven.

Lisa expected to be thrashed then and there, but instead Madam Okicha simply wrote the number on a blackboard beside the bar, then spoke to the boy, who rose to his feet and took Lisa by the arm. He led her out of the bar and down a short corridor to a tiny room, bare except for a mattress on the floor. A small notch was cut into the door to accommodate Lisa's ankle chain, allowing him to slam and lock the door, leaving her in complete darkness.

Lisa lowered herself onto the mattress and closed her eyes, but sleep eluded her, her mind occupied by the blackboard in the bar, and the number eleven chalked on it.

Chapter 25

Lisa didn't know how long it was before she heard the door being unlocked again. She guessed she must have dozed off, as the previously quiet building was now filled with the sound of chatter. She shielded her eyes from the shaft of light that now flooded into her tiny room. The silhouette in the doorway was that of the boy and, as she rose to her feet, he took hold of her arm and propelled her out into the corridor.

There the sound of chatter was even louder out there, and it was clear to Lisa that the bar was now full of customers. Her stomach churned at the thought of entering the place. She had been in these small African bars before, and she knew that it would be full of drunken men. Men who would mock her nudity and at the same time desire her. Not for the first time, Lisa wondered at the terrible twist of fate that had brought her to this position. She had been snatched away to this cruel land where she was treated as no more than a chattel, and where men could see her, touch her, fuck her on a whim. She glanced down at herself, at her pale, bare skin, at her full, delicious breasts and the shiny ring that drew the eyes down to the prominent slit of her sex. What other woman was made to endure such shame, she wondered as she made her way reluctantly toward the source of the noise.

The boy didn't take her straight into the saloon. Instead he led her round to the back of the bar, where Madam Okicha was waiting for her. She indicated a small bathroom.

"Prepare yourself," she said curtly.

Lisa entered the room. There was a toilet and a sink, with soap and a hairbrush. She stood before the mirror, glancing down at her bare breasts and thinking about the men who would soon see them. Then she picked up the brush and began to run it through her locks.

Five minutes later she was back out, her ankle chain rattling as she walked across to where the woman awaited her. Madam Okicha looked her up and down, then nodded.

"Tonight you work, slave," she said. "Go in bar."

Lisa eyed the entrance to the bar with some trepidation. A curtain was draped across it, and beyond she could hear the chatter and laughter of men's voices. She thought of the time Okama, the rebel leader, had taken her to such a bar shortly after capturing her. It had been a degrading and humiliating ordeal. And then she hadn't been shaved, nor had she worn the brass ring that decorated her cunt, drawing attention to her most private place. She stood for a moment, staring at the curtain, then a shove from the boy told her she could delay no more.

Lisa stepped alone into the noisy, smoky room, blinking at the brightness of the strip lights that lit it. For a moment she stood alone in the doorway. Immediately opposite her was a mirror on the wall, and her eyes took in the slim, pale figure that was reflected in it, her breasts jutting forward, the brown nipples standing proudly, the 'S' that depicted her slave status showing clearly on the bare white patch where once her pubic hair had grown.

For a few seconds nobody noticed her, then a whistle went up and suddenly all eyes were turned in Lisa's direction. She stood, her hands hanging by her sides whilst the room erupted with laughter, shouts and catcalls echoing all around her as the men took in her total nudity. Lisa's cheeks went a bright scarlet and she hung her head in shame as she showed all to the rough crowd of drinkers.

Madam Okicha appeared behind the bar and stood watching whilst the crowd hooted their derision at the young beauty. Then, when the noise had died down, she beckoned to Lisa. The nude white girl walked slowly across to the bar, her ankle chain rattling with every step. When she reached it, Madam Okicha thrust a tin tray into her hands.

"You work," she ordered. "Get glasses."

Lisa looked imploringly at her, but the look was met with cold hostility. She turned and surveyed the room. The patrons were mostly men, dressed in scruffy clothes and swigging down glasses of beer, laughing and nudging one another as their eyes travelled over Lisa's creamy white flesh. There were a few women as well, some of whom scowled at the youngster, whilst others were laughing with the men.

Lisa stepped forward and moved to the nearest table. She started to pick up the empty glasses and place them on her tray. As she reached across to one on the far side, the man sitting there moved it out of her reach. She leant further forward, aware of the way this drew attention to her pretty breasts which hung down in front of her. Still he moved the glass away, a broad grin on his face as he watched Lisa's discomfort at being forced to bend over as she was. A hand grasped her buttocks and squeezed them, a finger brushing over her anus. For a moment she felt trapped, as the man beside her continued to feel her bare flesh, then she grabbed at the glass and straightened up, her face bright scarlet. As she raised the tray, more hands felt for her breasts, and she noticed with dismay that her nipples were now bullet-hard as her body responded to the treatment it was receiving.

Lisa carried the tray to the bar, where the woman was waiting with an array of beer bottles. She indicated a table on the far side of the room, and the girl set off for it, trying her best to dodge the hands that reached out to caress her bare flesh. She weaved a tortured path through the tables, wincing as her bottom was pinched, then gasping as a hand closed over her vagina and a rough finger rubbed briefly at her swollen clitoris. She had nearly got there when a tug at her ankle told her she had reached the limit of her chain, and she was forced to retrace her footsteps, enduring more groping, probing and pinching before she was finally able to unload her tray onto the table whilst its occupants felt her up.

For the next three hours the ordeal continued without respite. Lisa tried her best to shut her mind to what was happening to her, this beautiful young English rose forced to work stark naked amongst these jeering, drunken men in the seediest of bars. Yet even here she couldn't escape the perversity of her own desires as the men's caresses began, slowly but surely, to sexually arouse her. She couldn't explain why or how, but every touch on her bare body sent an unwanted shiver of excitement through her, making her nipples stand erect and causing a thin sheen of wetness to seep onto her bare sex lips. None of this was lost on the customers, who groped at her still more, laughing at the gasps of arousal they brought from her when they touched her most intimate places.

It was about midnight when Lisa finally succumbed to her desires. Up until then she had been fighting down the urges within her. Then, whilst leaning across a table for the umpteenth time that evening, the two men opposite her had grasped her wrists whilst their other hands closed over the softness of her exposed breasts. Almost at once a large, black hand slipped up between her legs and two fingers were thrust deep into her vagina. Lisa tried to free herself, but the men were too strong for her, and the man behind her began to frig her. She struggled for a moment longer, then gave a sudden moan as the man's thumb rubbed against her clitoris. Suddenly the nudity, the humiliation and the rough treatment took their effect on the lascivious young masochist and she found herself grinding her crotch down against the man's fingers, moaning aloud at the delicious sensation of having his fingers probe her so intimately. The room went suddenly quiet and she looked about her to see that all eyes were upon her. She glanced across at the mirror, and bit her lip as she saw the scene reflected there, the young white beauty prostrated across the beer-stained table top, her breasts being mauled by big rough hands, her legs spread, her pert behind jabbing down against the fingers that slid in and out of her wet sex.

She came with a cry, her backside continuing to thrust down against the man's fingers as she took her pleasure from them. All around she knew she was being watched as she rode out her shameful pleasure, red-faced and naked in this sleazy dive of a bar.

The man kept his fingers embedded in her until, at last, her cries died to moans, then to silence, and her body relaxed. Her wrists were released and the fingers slid from inside her. She lay for a moment face-down across the table, then slowly straightened. Her face glowing she moved across to the bar. She picked up a damp dishcloth and used it to wipe away the beer stains from her breasts and belly. Then she lifted her tray again and, amid the laughter and shouts, resumed her work.

A further fifteen minutes passed, during which Lisa's treatment was worse than ever. She could detect an air of expectancy amongst the customers now, and she knew that something was about to happen, though she couldn't be certain what. Then she returned to the bar with a tray full of bottles to discover something lying across it.

It was the cane.

All at once the memory came back to her of Madam Okicha's threat that afternoon. She had found eleven spots of dirt, and had chalked up the number eleven on the board. Lisa felt a cold sensation as she read the number once again. Her eyes dropped to the cane, then she looked about at the bar's customers. All were staring expectantly at her, and she knew at once that they had been told about the punishment.

The curtain parted and Madam Okicha strode in. She paused by Lisa, looking her up and down, then walked across the room. She came to a halt beside the man who had brought the youngster off with his fingers and spoke to him. He laughed and nodded, then the woman turned and beckoned to Lisa. The naked girl took a step toward them, but Madam Okicha held up a hand and pointed to the bar. Lisa stared at her uncomprehendingly for a moment, then realised what she wanted. Slowly she turned and picked up the cane. It felt cool and hard between her fingers and she shivered as she felt how thin and supple it was. She glanced at her mistress again, who nodded her head. Then she walked toward her, her heart hammering against her chest.

The room was silent now, apart from the sound of chairs scraping back as the customers positioned themselves to watch what was happening. Lisa kept her eyes cast down as she carried the object of her punishment across the room to where Madam Okicha and the man were standing. Most of the customers were on their feet now, craning to get a view as she came to a halt in front of them and held out the cane.

210

Madam Okicha took it from her.

"You bend over the table," she ordered.

Lisa turned to face the table over which she had been sprawled earlier. It was still swimming with spilt beer and cigarette ash. She moved closer until she could feel the cool formica edge against her bare pubis. Then she leaned forward over it, pressing her breasts down into the cold liquid and reaching out to grasp the far edge of the surface. Her ankles were kicked, making her spread her legs apart, so that she knew that the wetness inside her sex was on open view to those watching.

She glanced behind her. Madam Okicha had passed the cane to the man and he was flexing it in his hands, all the time gazing down at the pale mounds of Lisa's bare behind. He held out the weapon and traced a line down the crack of her bottom, pausing to probe at her anus so that, for a second, she feared that he would penetrate her with it. Then he moved it lower, and the young beauty could barely suppress a gasp as he slid it down her moist sex lips and poked at her clitoris.

Madam Okicha spoke again, and Lisa heard a murmur from the crowd that told her that her punishment was about to begin. She gripped the table with white knuckles as the man drew back his arm.

Swish! Whack!

The thin cane came down with terrific force, cutting into the pale, tender flesh of Lisa's bottom and bringing a cry of pain from her lips as she felt the terrible sting of the blow.

Swish! Whack!

Barely had the unfortunate girl had time to absorb the first stroke than the cane fell again, slicing another agonising stripe onto her naked behind. Lisa could hear

211

the crowd cheer as she was struck and she gritted her teeth to try to stop herself from screaming too loud.

Swish! Whack!

Swish! Whack!

The blows fell relentlessly, with no mercy being shown for the petite English girl whose backside was now aflame with the force of the punishment.

Swish! Whack!

Swish! Whack!

Swish! Whack!

Tears were streaming down her cheeks now, blurring her sight , though she was unable to blot from her mind the vision she knew she must make, her pale, naked body stretched across a dirty table, her pert behind criss-crossed with stripe after stripe as the beating continued, her bare sex leaking her love juices onto her thighs as her masochism came to the fore once again.

Swish! Whack!

Swish! Whack!

Swish! Whack!

Lisa was barely able to keep count as the dreadful stinging of the cane drove all other thoughts from her mind. Her entire body was covered in a thin sheen of sweat that gleamed under the harsh fluorescent lights of the bar. She tensed her muscles as the man lifted the cane for the eleventh and final time.

Swish! Whack!

Down came the cane again, laying a final scarlet weal across Lisa's burning backside. As the man lowered the cane and handed it back to Madam Okicha, the only sound to be heard was that of the sobs that wracked the youngster's body as she remained, prostrated over the table.

For a few minutes nothing happened. The customers

returned to their seats and the chatter in the bar slowly resumed. Lisa lay where she was, unwilling to get up and face the people who had witnessed her humiliation. Then she felt a hand on her arm and she looked up to see the face of Madam Okicha.

"You go now," said the woman. "Too many men want fuck you. Maybe fight. You go."

Slowly, painfully, Lisa rose to her feet, her backside still on fire with pain. The boy was standing beside her, and he took her arm, propelling her toward the door. By the mirror he paused so that she could look at herself. Lisa gazed at the sorry figure before her, her breasts and belly stained with beer and streaked with cigarette ash, her cheeks red with her tears, her pretty backside a mass of red stripes. Then she was pushed out through the door and back toward her cell, the shouts of the customers still ringing in her ears.

Chapter 26

For the next few weeks Lisa's life was dominated by Madam Okicha. Every day she would wake up to the mess in the bar from the night before, and would spend the morning clearing up, washing glasses and scrubbing the bar and veranda under the watchful eye of the boy. In the afternoons she would be found other menial tasks to do about the house. Occasionally she would be sent out to market with the boy, following behind him, a dog lead attached to her cunt ring. This was what she hated most, as wherever she went she was the object of derision, her pale, naked body the target of the other shoppers' laughter and jeering.

213

The women would spit on her as she passed, whilst the men would try to feel her up in the crowded market. Once she had burdened herself with a heavy basket in each hand there was little she could do to protect herself from their groping and, occasionally, she would suffer the humiliation of experiencing an orgasm right in the middle of the market as her sensuous body responded to the fingers that probed her so intimately.

About once a week Madam Okicha would inspect her work. Lisa never knew when it would happen, so that she was obliged to be scrupulous in her cleaning. Such were the woman's standards, though, that she never escaped a thrashing, although she never received as many strokes as on that first night. The beatings were always carried out in the bar, sometimes by Madam Okicha herself, but more often by one of the customers.

Occasionally she had to whore for the old woman. A man would appear, sometimes one of the customers, sometimes just someone who turned up at the house, money would change hands and they would be shown to Lisa's cell. There she would give herself to them, sometimes sucking them off, sometimes being fucked, sometimes offering her rear hole for their enjoyment. She never quite fathomed how the arrangement worked. After all, Madam Okicha could have made a fortune selling her to whoever she wished. Lisa suspected that someone else, possibly even Omar Sulkami himself, was involved in choosing the men who took her.

She had learned, through snippets of conversation, that Madam Okicha was somehow greatly favoured by Sulkami, hence the fact that she had the use of his young white slave. Occasionally one of his guards would visit the house with some kind of message or gift for the old woman. Always

214

Lisa would be required to give herself to the visitor, stretching out in her cell and allowing him to fuck her. She never saw any money change hands on these occasions, and guessed that giving the naked, nubile young white girl to the guard represented some kind of gratuity for the guard's services. It pained her to think that she should be obliged to perform the most intimate act a woman was capable of with a complete stranger simply as a tip for some trivial service rendered. But she had long since resigned herself to the fact that, as a slave, her services were cheap and no longer within her own power to bestow.

Then Lisa began to notice a gradual change in the bar. As the days passed, fewer and fewer patrons came, and the atmosphere became more subdued. Madam Okicha started introducing new attractions to improve attendances. One night the woman had her dancing naked on the bar to loud music whilst the customers gathered round. They were encouraged to show their appreciation by slipping folded banknotes into her vagina, until the sensation of all the notes brought Lisa to a shuddering climax in front of them. Some nights a raffle would be held, and Lisa herself would be made to draw out the winner. The prize was, of course, the young slave herself, and Lisa would be led away to be fucked amid much cheering from the other customers.

Still, though, fewer and fewer came, and the atmosphere in the bar changed palpably. On her visits to the market, too, Lisa noticed that the crowds were much thinner than before, and occasionally she would see cars laden with luggage heading out of town.

The first inkling of what was happening came one afternoon in her cell. A guard from the big house had brought a message for Madam Okicha and, as usual, the services of Lisa had been offered to him. He had fucked the young-

215

ster with vigour, bringing her to three separate orgasms before pumping his own seed deep inside her. Now, as she knelt naked by his side, dutifully licking clean his long, black cock, he began to speak to her.

"Bad time coming," he said. "This town not safe."

The youngster ceased to lick at the coating of love juice and sperm on his penis and looked up at him.

"What do you mean, Sir?"

"Kombians coming. Government say we are winning war. Not true. Kombians advancing fast."

"You mean they're actually invading Negorvia?"

"Many rebels help them. Rebels everywhere. I tell Askari, time to move. But Omar Sulkami proud man. Not move away."

"So that's why the place is so empty?"

"Not safe," he said, then narrowed his eyes. "You not talk. You slave."

Lisa looked at him for a moment longer, then lowered her head and began licking his cock once again, her pretty breasts dangling as she bent over his crotch.

After he had left, she pondered his words. She knew that a border war between Negorvia and the neighbouring state of Kombu had been raging for some time, but little progress had been made by either side during the fighting. Now, though, it would seem that things were hotting up. All the other slaves she had encountered had been Kombians taken prisoners of war during the conflict. Her own situation was, however, somewhat different. She guessed that the Kombians had no more love of their previous white rulers than had the Negorvians. Whatever happened, it seemed that she was caught in the middle of the conflict, a prospect that didn't appeal to the youngster at all.

Another week passed, during which the clientele at the bar continued to dwindle. In the evenings distant gunfire could be heard, and there was a general air of nervousness pervading everyone who was left. Then, one evening, Madame Okicha announced that they would be moving into Sulkami's house the following day, as it was a safer place.

That night the gunfire was louder than ever, and only a few customers showed up, all of whom left early. Lisa lay on the mattress of her cell, listening to the guns and wondering what would become of her. When she eventually dropped off to sleep, it was a troubled one, beset with dreams.

She was wakened by the sound of shouting, and she sat up in alarm. She could hear men's voices raised in anger, accompanied by that of Madam Okicha. The woman's voice had lost all its confidence and authority, and she sounded strained and afraid as she answered the questions that were being barked at her. More gunfire sounded, this time very close indeed, and Lisa realised with a shock that the rebel insurgents must already have reached the town, and that the men questioning Madam Okicha were, almost certainly, Kombians. She shrank to the back of the cell, suddenly very apprehensive indeed. If the men were already in the house, how long would it be before they discovered her hiding place?

In fact, as it turned out, the men never had to search for her. Madam Okicha it was who pulled open the door of her cell and dragged her out into the light. Lisa found herself facing four heavily armed men who stood, open mouthed, staring at the naked young beauty as Madam Okicha thrust her toward them.. It was clear that the woman was using her as a bargaining card to try to save her own

217

skin, and the grins on the men's faces as they looked her up and down told Lisa that they were pleased with their end of the bargain.

"Get them drinks, slave," ordered the woman. "Hurry up, before they shoot us."

Lisa hastened into the bar, her cheeks glowing as the men laughed at the mass of stripes that still covered her bare backside. She grabbed two bottles and some glasses and set them out on a table. The men swaggered in, cradling their sub-machine guns, kicking back the chairs and settling down. Outside, Lisa could still hear the rattle of guns, but they seemed oblivious to it.

She poured each one a drink, then went to move back to the bar, but one of them grabbed her arm.

"You got no clothes, white girl?" he asked.

Lisa lowered her eyes. "No Sir."

"What, none at all?"

"No Sir, none at all."

"You go round like that all the time?"

"Yes Sir. I'm a slave, as you see. Like the other Kombians." she added, hopefully.

"You no Kombian," he said.

"She good girl for fuck," put in Madam Okicha. "She work as whore here. White whore," she added unnecessarily.

The man pulled Lisa round to face him, reaching up and grasping her breast.

"That true? You whore?"

Lisa's colour deepened. "I have to do as I'm told, Sir," she mumbled.

"Including fuck?"

"Including that, Sir."

He sat down on one of the chairs. "Pour drinks."

218

Lisa turned to the table and began pouring more whisky into the glasses. As she did so she felt a hand slide up her thigh from behind and run along the soft lips of her sex, making her shiver. It was all she could do to keep a steady hand as she passed the glasses back to the other three men.

When she turned to the leader once again, her eyes widened in surprise. He had undone his fly and his cock was standing proud from it, thick and black. He was masturbating himself gently as he stared up into her eyes.

"You like black man's cock, little white whore?" he asked.

"I..."

"Come here."

She hesitated for a moment, staring round at the faces in front of her. Even Madam Okicha hadn't made her fuck her customers here, in the bar. These men, it seemed, had other ideas. A shiver of excitement suddenly ran through her as she realised she was about to be taken.

The man grabbed her hips and pulled her close to him, forcing her to straddle his knees. He slid a finger into her open vagina, and she knew he could feel the heat and moisture inside her. Then he began to drag her down, positioning his cock at the entrance to her sex.

Lisa gave a stifled moan as he penetrated her, pressing her downwards onto his rigid organ, so that it drove deep inside her.

"You see," said the old woman. "Good whore for you. Give you good fuck."

One of the other men shouted something at the woman and she fell silent, whilst all eyes turned back to Lisa. Such was the suddenness of the man's assault that she was taken completely by surprise, but the sensation of a hard cock being driven into her was already having an effect on the

219

wanton youngster, and almost instinctively she began moving her body up and down, allowing his rod to slide in and out of her wet vagina.

Across the room, Lisa could see the mirror once again, and he sight it reflected back to her was a very odd one. Here she sat, quite naked, her legs astride the lap of this large and heavily armed man, her body moving up and down as she fucked him hard, her breasts bouncing with every stroke. She turned to look at his companions. They were clearly delighted at the sight of this young white beauty who gave herself so easily, riding out her passion on the erect cock of their leader, her face a picture of lust. She glanced down at the bulge in their trousers, and even as she did so one of them pulled out his cock and showed it to her, making it clear that they all expected the same service as their leader was receiving.

The man who was screwing her grabbed hold of her thighs, forcing her to move faster, pressing her down into his lap so that she cried aloud with the exquisite feeling of his cock penetrating her all the way. She squeezed the muscles of her sex together, caressing his cock with her cunt, suddenly overcome by carnal desires. He responded by thrusting even harder as his body grew more and more tense.

He came with a groan, his hard organ throbbing as he pumped his seed into her. Lisa responded at once with an orgasm of her own, throwing back her head and shouting aloud as she was overcome by carnal pleasure. Then, almost before his cock had ceased to spurt into her, she was being dragged off him and bent forward over the table whilst another cock was rammed into her from behind, bringing new cries of desire from her as she surrendered herself once again.

All four of the men took her, as she knew they would, and all four triggered loud and long orgasms in her as they spurted their seed into her vagina. Then they made her bring them fresh drinks before each fucking her again in different positions, laughing at her obvious passion as more orgasms coursed through her..

It was more than an hour before they finally rose to their feet. Lisa had taken the opportunity to slip into the bathroom, where she had been able to wash some of the men's spunk from her. Now, as she re-entered the room, the leader turned to Madam Okicha and raised his gun.

The woman shrank back with a cry of terror, but he didn't pull the trigger. Instead he spoke a few words, and she scurried off, returning a few minutes later with a small key. To Lisa's surprise she dropped to one knee beside her and, with a click, undid the shackle on her ankle. Then she placed it about her own leg, and closed it once again, handing the key to the man.

He gave another order, and Lisa found herself being grabbed and forced forward over the table. For a second she thought they planned to take her again, but instead they produced a length of rope and began to bind her wrists together. They tied them tight, then set about doing the same to her elbows. By the time they had finished, Lisa was quite helpless, her firm breasts thrust forward by the awkward position of her arms, her naked body defenceless.

Madam Okicha was taken to Lisa's cell and locked inside, protesting vigorously. Then the leader raised his gun and pointed it at Lisa.

"Out," he ordered.

Lisa looked nervously at him for a moment, then round at her surroundings. The bar had been her home for some time now and, after the cruelty of Madam Okicha and the casual way in which she had been used by her, she had no regrets at all about turning her back on the place. But any relief she might feel about leaving the place was completely overshadowed by her fear of these men, who had fucked her without any thought for her consent on finding her, and who had made no concession to her feminine modesty before tying her and taking her with them.

She stumbled down the steps with the cold muzzle of the machine gun digging into the bare flesh of her back. Outside was parked a battered old jeep, and she was made to climb into the back seat, between two of the Kombians. The leader climbed in beside the fourth man, who was driving. Then the engine came to life, and the vehicle swung out into the road.

Chapter 27

As they drove through the town, Lisa looked about her, seeing for the first time the effects of the invasion. The streets were full of uniformed men, though there was no longer any sign of fighting. Here and there they passed groups of prisoners being rounded up. In the big house the lights were on, but the men who stood at the gates were not Askari's troops, so she guessed that the place had fallen to the rebels.

They drove out of the town in a direction that she estimated was taking them toward the border. The road was in bad disrepair, and the vehicle bumped along, occasionally passing military vehicles going the other way. Lisa was extremely uncomfortable with her arms tied behind her, and quite helpless to prevent the rough pair on either side of her feeling her up, their hands roving over her soft, pale flesh, bringing her sensuous young body to new levels of arousal, despite her situation.

It was nearly an hour later when the vehicle pulled off the road and headed up a wide track. Ahead Lisa could see lights blazing, and before long they had pulled into the middle of a large army camp. The vehicle stopped and Lisa was pulled from it. Then, with the gun still in her back, she was marched into a low building and up to a counter, behind which stood another soldier. The leader of Lisa's guards went forward, saluting the man as he approached.

There was a short conversation, then he returned and barked an order to his men. At once Lisa felt her arms grabbed as they dragged her through a door to one side. She found herself in a brightly-lit room that was filled with all kinds of strange equipment. At first she wondered if it was a gymnasium, but a second look at the equipment revealed it to be much more sinister. The benches and frames were all equipped with shiny chains and manacles. All about the walls were more chains, as well as a variety of whips and canes. Other cabinets were hung with objects, the use of which Lisa was unable even to guess at.

Inside were about four soldiers, dressed in black uniforms with long leather boots and shiny peaked caps. They strode across to Lisa's captors who let go of her and shrank back, clearly in awe of these men

One of the black-clad men barked an order, and the four guards retreated, leaving Lisa alone with this new and frightening group. At once they grabbed the naked girl and dragged her across to where a thick wooden post stood. The men undid the bonds on her arms but, before she could loosen her aching muscles they grabbed her and thrust her, face forward, against the post. The wood felt rough and

223

hard, and it chafed against Lisa's bare nipples as they dragged her arms about the circumference. They tied one wrist, then threaded the rope through a ring at the top of the post and tied the other, so that her hands were pulled up around the girth of the structure, forcing her to hug it close to her naked flesh. Then her legs were pulled apart and tied to rings set in the floor. The post didn't stand straight, so that the hapless girl found herself having to lean forward against it.

Once the bonds were secure, she saw one of the officers hand something to her captors. It was a whip, and Lisa knew then that she was to be beaten, though she knew not why. She clung to the wood, only too aware of what a perfect target her bare behind would make for the man as he sauntered over, making a few practice strokes as he did so.

One of the men moved close beside her so that he was staring down into her face.

"The Captain says you are a spy, and that you need whipping to discover what your orders are," he said.

"But I'm not a spy. Look at me. Look at my mark. They made me a slave, just like your own people."

"You are a white woman. You cannot, therefore, be a slave. You worked for that bastard Mbogu, isn't that true?"

"No I..."

"Thrash her."

Swish! Whack!

The man with the whip moved suddenly, quite taking her by surprise as the cruel weapon came down hard onto her naked flesh.

"Are you saying you didn't know Mbogu?"

"I met him once. He made me..." her voice trailed off.

Swish! Whack!

224

The second blow fell as rapidly as the first, cutting into Lisa's backside and bringing a cry of pain from her.

"He made you what?"

"He-he made me suck him."

"So you were his lover?"

"No"

Swish! Whack!

"Tell the truth!"

"I... He was making some kind of deal with Mr Bulcher. I didn't understand what it was about."

"So, you knew Bulcher? And you knew he was selling arms to Mbogu to defeat us Kombians?"

"No!"

Swish! Whack!

Swish! Whack!

Swish! Whack!

The strokes came down hard, laying stripes across Lisa's behind, then working down to the tops of her legs and lower still.

"Tell us where Bulcher is."

"I don't know!"

Swish! Whack!

Swish! Whack!

Swish! Whack!

The man was working so fast that one stroke had barely time to sting her before another was falling. Quite suddenly the man switched his target and the blows began to rain down across her shoulders and back.

"Tell us!"

"I think he left the country!"

"Where did he go?"

"I don't know!"

"Thrash her harder."

Lisa could scarcely believe that she could be beaten any harder. But the whip was now laid across her trembling flesh with a force that left her breathless. Thighs, buttocks and back all came under the searing lash, jerking her forward against the stake at each impact. But deep under the inferno of pain which engulfed her, she felt the treacherous moistening of her sex as her vulnerability fed the masochistic side of her nature.

Swish! Whack!

Swish! Whack!

Swish! Whack!

Swish! Whack!

The beating and the questioning went on and on for nearly half an hour, with the men taking it in turns to thrash her and to question her. By the time they finally stopped, Lisa's whole back was aflame with pain, and tears were coursing down her cheeks. At last, though, they seemed to have heard enough, and the man with the whip was told to stand down. Then the leader gave an order to another of the men, who saluted smartly, then marched away.

"We'll see what the General has to say about your evidence," he said.

They waited for nearly fifteen minutes, the men conversing quietly with one another whilst Lisa hung, still sobbing, in her bondage. Then the door behind her opened and she heard footsteps approaching.

Suddenly there came a barked order from behind them. The guards sprang to attention as the footsteps came up behind Lisa. The new arrival said a few more words to them, then Lisa felt something hard trace the length of her spine, making her shiver. It came round and ran over the softness of her breast. Glancing down she saw that it was a swagger stick, of the kind carried by a senior army officer.

"So, slut, you are still using that pretty body to entertain men."

Lisa froze. There was something strangely familiar about the cold tones of the man's voice. He had been standing behind her up until now, but as he spoke he moved round beside her, where she could see his face clearly. She took in the ebony features, the piercing eyes and the scar, in the shape of a snake, that ran down his cheek, then gave a gasp of recognition.

Okama!

Okama, the rebel leader who had captured her within days of her abduction from London. Who had whipped her and used her as a whore for his men, and who had finally sold her on to the remote tribe who had branded her, placed the ring in her cunt and used her as a quarry for their huntsmen.

No wonder he had had her whipped. Okama hated the white man, and had used the young beauty as a scapegoat for his prejudices. And now she had fallen into his hands again, and he had already resumed his cruel treatment of her.

"You see I have been promoted, slut," he said. "I am now General Okama. And you see too how powerful my men are. We will drive the Negorvian filth from our lands and make them free again. And you will help us."

"M-me?" she stammered.

"Certainly. We know you lived with Bulcher, the bastard who supplied guns to our enemies. That is true isn't it?"

"I had no choice. He was my master."

Whack! The swagger stick came down hard on her already stinging buttocks.

227

"Do not make excuses. You spoke too with Mbogu, didn't you?"

"I didn't speak with him. I..." her voice trailed away.

"Well?"

"I... I sucked him once."

"Whack!" The stick struck her again.

"We will see. This torture chamber is suitable to extract the truth from you. A few hours on the rack should see to it. We have a man who is an expert with clamps and needles."

Lisa shivered at these words. She was no stranger to torture, indeed her masochistic nature meant that she knew that she would almost certainly be aroused by what they did to her. In fact, that was her main fear. She could take the pain. Her months in naked servitude had hardened her to that. It was the humiliation that she hated. The way in which her beautiful young body responded to the cruel treatment it so often received. Even now she could still feel the wetness inside her that the beating had brought on.

"Soon you will experience our techniques at getting the truth," Okama continued. "Then, we will kill you."

Lisa gasped as he spoke the words. He smiled grimly, and gestured for her to look at the far end of the room. A tall, thin black man with the darkest eyes Lisa had ever seen stood by one of the sinister benches. On it he had opened a sort of small suitcase and inside, laid out on green baize, Lisa could see dozens of wickedly gleaming needles and an assortment of spring loaded, and screw clamps.

Lisa whimpered. What was coming would be worse than anything she had endured to date. But worst of all was the knowledge that her arousal would scale new heights at this fresh twist to her torment.

"Or........" Okama continued, "if we are pleased with

228

what you tell us, maybe you can go back to your duties as whore. My men will need a diversion after the fight, and fucking a young white woman will fulfil that need."

Lisa said nothing, but a shiver ran through her as she contemplated her fate. She didn't know how many men Okama commanded, but it was clear that, should he decide to spare her, her duties under Okama would be much worse than in Madam Okicha's bar.

Okama traced the shape of her flank with his stick, making her shudder at the feel of the hard wood, then he turned to the guards, who were still staring at the naked girl.

"She will be have to be a good whore to satisfy our gallant men," he said. "Perhaps you would like to sample her and give your opinions."

With that he turned and walked away.

Lisa looked at the man. For a moment he did nothing, simply staring at her. Then he glanced round at the other men present.

"You will all have your turn," he said. "Tonight, though, she is mine."

He smiled at Lisa, gesturing to the contents of his case.

"If you satisfy me, I shall use these sparingly. Otherwise you'll wish you'd never been born. Either way, I'm looking forward to using your filthy white body."

He undid his fly, and Lisa saw his long, stiff cock projecting from his pants. He moved round behind her and, reaching down between her open legs, prised apart the lips of her sex.

As he slid his cock into her hot vagina, Lisa cried aloud, and a powerful orgasm immediately shook her young body as he fucked her hard against the whipping post.

The beautiful, naked Bush Slave realised, with a shock,

that she was now working for the enemy.

Where would her torment end, she wondered, despairingly.

THE END

And here is the opening of next months release "Racheal in Servitude" by J.L. Jones

The morning sun shining through the tall windows of the library illuminated the work on Master Stephen Hawthorne's desk. His posture was stiff as he methodically signed the documents before him.

One of the man's young chambermaids, a girl by the name of Heather, was seated, if such was the term, in the center of a maroon couch, the couch being on the other side of the room. Since she was awaiting punishment, the girl's splendid body was entirely naked, two of Stephen's assistants having divested her of all clothing earlier, and she was severely bound in leather straps, both hand and foot, her delicate wrists behind her back, ankles cinched snugly together, only the toes of her bare feet touching the rich Persian carpeting.

Two more straps rendered the girl even more immobile, one cinching her legs together just below the knees, the other just above. In addition, they'd gagged and blindfolded her with strips of black velvet.

In the stringent bonds of leather, Heather made for a beautifully erotic picture. Her strawberry-tinted hair fell over her shoulders and breasts, the straps accentuating the contours of her slender figure.

Finished with his paper work, Stephen rose from behind the desk and walked slowly across the room, his footsteps causing the blindfolded girl to become anxious. She'd never been subjected to one of Master Hawthorne's punishment sessions, and she had no idea of what might happen to her. And when Stephen sat down, running a hand over her bare flesh, Heather let out a surprised gasp that was muffled by the gag of velvet.

Stephen's hand sought out the strained breasts, massaging them gently, almost lovingly at first, but then squeezing them in a manner that made the nude girl squirm in her fastenings. Then he took the nipple of the left tit between his thumb and forefinger and applied pressure to the swollen bud until it became stiff and red. With a thin smile on his lips, he twisted it, sending darts of fire through the breast-flesh, making Heather struggle and chafe herself on her bindings. The girl was trying to protest, but her words were stifled by the gag.

"In a few minutes, Mistresses Katherine and Eunice will be here to punish you for the impertinence you displayed last night," Stephen was saying as he removed his fingers from the nipple and began undoing the mouth gag, taking it off and giving Heather the freedom to speak. In truth, the girl had done nothing wrong. She'd been in service to Master Hawthorne for two weeks, and during that time, her behavior had been exemplary.

Heather had begun to tremble inside, knowing full well that Master Hawthorne could do whatever he chose to with her, and her bare skin began going through both hot and cold flushes of fear. She felt so shamed to be naked and bound, helpless while this man toyed with her.

Stephen was removing the leg and ankle restraints with a few practiced flicks of his wrists, then spreading the girl's thighs and running his fingers between them in a teasing, tickling motion until they reached the slit of Heather's vulva.

"So nice and smooth you are, my dear," he said. "And who gave you your first shave?" He was a fanatic on cleanliness, insisting that all of his servant girls observe Spartan-like habits of shaving and bathing.

"Mistress Eunice. I do it myself now."

"I see. Do you enjoy the freedom of having your pubis so fresh and clean?"

"I'm not sure, Master Hawthorne. This is all so new to me."

A flash of anger crossed Stephen's face. He told Heather to spread her legs still further, and when the girl obeyed, he gave the shaven mound several, sharp, spanking slaps.

"You will learn to live clean, you ungrateful little wretch," he said in a growl. "I will not tolerate filthy habits in my home or in my hotel. Do I make myself clear?" Heather was biting her lower lip, afraid to speak. "You'd better answer me unless you want to be returned to your father's farm."

Just the thought of being taken back to her parents, disappointing them by not fulfilling their obligation to Master Hawthorne sent cold fright through the bound girl.

"No, Master," she blurted out. "Anything but that. I understand."

Stephen smiled triumphantly. Heather had gone into indentured service to him to pay off a debt owed by her parents. He had this naked thing right where he wanted her.

The door was opening as Stephen removed the girl's blindfold, and Heather's eyes grew wide with fear when she saw Katherine and Eunice. The two middle-aged women looked quite imposing in their starched, black uniforms, opaque stockings, and heavy, utilitarian shoes. And their appearance made her even more aware of her nudity.

Eunice was carrying a long, black case, the kind used for billiard cues.

They stared at her, their eyes glowing, for both of them relished the opportunity to have a naked girl at their mercy.

233

"Thank you for coming," Stephen was saying. "Sorry to bother you so early in the morning, but this young lady is in dire need of a sound thrashing, and the sooner she receives one, the sooner she'll feel better about herself."

Katherine and Eunice had performed this routine many times, and they worked together with a practiced sureness. They helped Heather to her feet and marched her into the center of the spacious room, then further helped her to lie on the floor, face down, feet together.

Heather, with her head turned to the side, could see Mistress Eunice opening the black case and taking out two well-oiled birch rods. The woman was grinning as she snapped one of them in the air and handed the other to Katherine. Suddenly, the girl knew her fate. They were going to give her a switching!

"I see you've guessed that you're about to taste the birch," Mistress Katherine said when she saw the expression in Heather's eyes. "I'd advise you to remain still for it. If you give us any trouble, you'll be taken to the chambers."

Heather clenched her buttocks tightly together, determined to follow Mistress Katherine's advice. She didn't know exactly what went on down in the chambers, but she'd heard the other chambermaids whispering of it, and she knew that she didn't want to be taken there.

The two uniformed women took up a stance on either side of her, waiting, knowing that Stephen liked to say a few words to his girls just before they were put through corporal chastisement.

"This is going to do you a lot of good, Heather," he said, his tone flat. "In your case, it might do you well if I put you on a program of regular discipline." He paused for a few moments, looking into the girl's pleading eyes. Then

234

he gave the order for the flogging to begin.

Hearing the two switches whistling through the air, Heather braced herself for the worst. And then the birch rods were blazing across her unprotected backside, the sound of the wooden whips on bare flesh filling the room.

The girl let out a shriek, her wrists yanking at the leather fastenings, the nude feet tightening and stretching. "Please!" she yelled as the women began thrashing her with a regular, clocklike momentum, "my bottom can't stand it!"

All three of the fully-clothed adults were grinning at Heather's pleas. They shared the love of having a naked girl at their mercy, and her cries only added to that enjoyment.

Peering up at Master Hawthorne, Heather could see the man staring at her with a fierce gleam in his eyes, and it gave the girl a sense of being wanted, perhaps in the most perverse sense of the word, but wanted nonetheless, and it sent an odd tingling throughout her pubic mound. She'd begun twisting about on the carpeting as the switches found their marks, and she wondered what kind of picture she presented to her tormentors.

As the cruel punishment continued, she began moaning each time the birch crossed her exposed flesh. Her eyes became glazed as her hair fell across her field of vision, and her bare feet rubbed frantically at each other. Her breasts were swollen, the nipples painfully erect as they ground themselves into the carpet.

"I've had enough," the girl whined. "I've learned my lesson. Please let me go!"

"We'll decide when you've learned your lesson," Katherine said, laughing at Heather's impudence and giving the bare buttocks an especially smart lick.

After Heather's flesh had turned to a bright crimson

235

color, Stephen had the two women stop for a minute. He wanted to check on something. Rising from the couch, he walked over and spread the girl's thighs with his fingertips and then reached in to feel her pubic mound, smiling when he found it moist, knowing that it was going to be easy to train the girl into willing slavery.

He nodded to Katherine and Eunice and then told them to resume the beating. "I want her thoroughly thrashed," he said. "All of her. Her entire body."

Heather's wrists were freed and then refastened with her hands stretched far out in front of her, to bare her back. And then the two women started in on her again, snapping the switches at the girl's back, thighs, calves, and feet, scorching her up and down.

"I have to go down to the hotel now," Stephen was saying as he strode toward the door. "Use the birch on her for as long as you she think she needs it, and if you feel she requires still more corrective treatment, do as you choose with her. If she balks at any order you give her, please let me know so I can have her sent to the chambers."

When the door closed, Heather became even more frightened, not knowing what the two mistresses might do to her. The girl was naive about such matters, but it was easy for her to tell that both of them were deriving some dark pleasure from inflicting pain on her.

Eunice was undoing the girl's fastenings while Katherine spoke to her. "Get up, Heather, and kneel," she said once the leather had been removed. "Put your insolent rump between the heels of your naked feet"

Knowing what was good for her, Heather was quick to comply, and as she did, Mistress Eunice drew a hassock up in front of her and sat down, a thin smile on her lips. At the same time, Mistress Katherine was putting the blindfold back over Heather's eyes, standing behind the girl, her thick-soled shoes in odd contrast to Heather's bare feet.

"Raise your hands up straight and high into the air," Eunice said to her, "and spread your legs so we can have a better look at your pubis."

Again, Heather obeyed, but now she was visibly trembling from both apprehension and the shame of having to display herself in such a flagrant manner. Nervously, she licked her lips, wondering what they were going to do with her.

When her hands were raised high, the blindfold in place, she suddenly felt Eunice's hands touching her with a lover's caress, massaging her shoulders and then softly fondling her aching breasts, kneading them intimately.

"So very tender is your flesh, my dear," the woman said, cooing to the girl. "Do you like what I'm doing to you?"

Heather, not quite sure of what to say, nodded a yes, and in a way, she was sincere. Being felt was a far cry better than being beaten.

"Of course it does," Eunice said, "and I want you to feel good. We only thrashed you for your own good. You understand that, don't you?"

The bare girl nodded yes again, and just as she did, Mistress Katherine brought a switch down on her sore behind, but she didn't do it hard. Instead, she flicked it gently, letting it kiss the flesh with love.

Eunice moved one of her hands to the flesh-mound between Heather's legs, feeling it, stimulating the sex, and causing Heather to emit a soft moan of contentment.

"You see, my dear," Katherine was saying, still switching the girl's buttocks, "being punished doesn't have to be all suffering. It can be quite enjoyable if done right."

Eunice's finger had penetrated Heather's shaven pubis,

237

and it was manipulating her clitoris. The girl began to rotate her buttocks in a tight circle, her moans growing louder as she was overwhelmed by what they were doing to her.

Then the pangs of orgasm began to build deep within her, getting ready to explode in full flower, and the two women looking down at her saw what was about to happen. They'd taken many a potential slave through this same process.

"We know what you're undergoing," the girl heard Katherine saying. "Now you can ask me to switch your pretty little rumpus good and hard while you climax for us."

Heather was losing control of herself. Somehow, she wanted nothing more than to obey, and it didn't matter to her if she was debasing herself in front of these two women. She truly didn't want the punishing switch to come down any harder on her already-punished flesh, but she felt a compulsion to ask for it nonetheless.

"Yes, that's what I want, Mistress," she gasped. "Beat me hard and long!"

Then the switch burned into her, searing the tender flesh, and orgasms in profusion began erupting through her loins, causing Heather to cry out in both pain and rapture.

What the girl didn't know was that she'd taken the first step in becoming a genuine subservient. Stephen Hawthorne's family had been in the international slave trade for generations, plucking destitute girls from the hungry jaws of poverty, training them to full obedience, and then selling them to those who desired to own a slavegirl.

TITLES IN PRINT

Silver Moon
ISBN 1-897809-16-6   Rorigs Dawn *Ray Arneson*
ISBN 1-897809-17-4   Bikers Girl on the Run *Lia Anderssen*
ISBN 1-897809-23-9   Slave to the System *Rosetta Stone*
ISBN 1-897809-25-5   Barbary Revenge *Allan Aldiss*
ISBN 1-897809-27-1   White Slavers *Jack Norman*
ISBN 1-897809-31-X   Slave to the State *Rosetta Stone*
ISBN 1-897809-36-0   Island of Slavegirls *Mark Slade*
ISBN 1-897809-37-9   Bush Slave *Lia Anderssen*
ISBN 1-897809-38-7   Desert Discipline *Mark Stewart*
ISBN 1-897809-40-9   Voyage of Shame *Nicole Dere*
ISBN 1-897809-41-7   Plantation Punishment *Rick Adams*
ISBN 1-897809-42-5   Naked Plunder *J.T. Pearce*
ISBN 1-897809-43-3   Selling Stephanie *Rosetta Stone*
ISBN 1-897809-44-1   SM Double value (Olivia/Lucy) *Graham/Slade**
ISBN 1-897809-46-8   Eliska *von Metchingen*
ISBN 1-897809-47-6   Hacienda, *Allan Aldiss*
ISBN 1-897809-48-4   Angel of Lust, *Lia Anderssen**
ISBN 1-897809-50-6   Naked Truth, *Nicole Dere**
ISBN 1-897809-51-4   I Confess!, *Dr Gerald Rochelle**
ISBN 1-897809-52-2   Barbary Slavedriver, *Allan Aldiss**
ISBN 1-897809-53-0   A Toy for Jay, *J.T. Pearce**
ISBN 1-897809-54-9   The Confessions of Amy Mansfield, *R. Hurst**
ISBN 1-897809-55-7   Gentleman's Club, *John Angus**
ISBN 1-897809-57-3   Sinfinder General *Johnathan Tate**
ISBN 1-897809-59-X   Slaves for the Sheik *Allan Aldiss**
ISBN 1-897809-60-3   Church of Chains *Sean O'Kane**
ISBN 1-897809-62-X   Slavegirl from Suburbia *Mark Slade**
ISBN 1-897809-64-6   Submission of a Clan Girl *Mark Stewart**
ISBN 1-897809-65-4   Taming the Brat *Sean O'Kane**
ISBN 1-897809-66-2   Slave for Sale *J.T. Pearce**

Silver Mink
ISBN 1-897809-22-0   The Captive *Amber Jameson*
ISBN 1-897809-24-7   Dear Master *Terry Smith*
ISBN 1-897809-26-3   Sisters in Servitude *Nicole Dere*
ISBN 1-897809-28-X   Cradle of Pain *Krys Antarakis*
ISBN 1-897809-32-8   The Contract *Sarah Fisher*
ISBN 1-897809-33-6   Virgin for Sale *Nicole Dere*
ISBN 1-897809-39-5   Training Jenny *Rosetta Stone*
ISBN 1-897898-45-X   Dominating Obsession *Terry Smith*
ISBN 1-897809-49-2   The Penitent *Charles Arnold**
ISBN 1-897809-56-5   Please Save Me! *Dr. Gerald Rochelle**
ISBN 1-897809-58-1   Private Tuition *Jay Merson**
ISBN 1-897809-61-1   Little One *Rachel Hurst**
ISBN 1-897809-63-8   Naked Truth II *Nicole Dere**
ISBN 1-897809-67-0   Tales from the Lodge *Bridges/O'Kane**

*UK £4.99 except *£5.99 --USA $8.95 except *$9.95*